Protection of The Pack

The Other Wolf Series, Book 1

Heather G. Harris

Chapter 1

Death was the best thing that ever happened to me. Okay, so I didn't actually *die*, but it was a damned near thing. I planned my funeral, I quit my job, I was in a freaking hospice. The end was nigh, the light at the end of the tunnel was shining down on me. It was ... terrifying. Turns out I wasn't ready to die.

I got lucky. My best friend, Jess, was my salvation. She broke some rules, busted me out of the hospice – and the rest, as they say, is history. Sure, I'm a werewolf now, but I wouldn't have it any other way. Even so, it was hard to feel anything warm and fuzzy as I looked at the man who had caused my near-death experience. James hadn't known that Jess would save me. He had slept with me and condemned me to death, all the while making me fall a little in love with him. Bloody succubus.

And here he was, on the floor in front of me, looking up at me with angry eyes. Everything in his defiant body language said a clear 'fuck you'. I glared back. Of the two of us, I had far more right to feel hard done by. He'd nearly *killed* me, for God's sake, and I'd loved him. Or I thought I had. Now all I felt was bitter and disillusioned. I hadn't been his first victim – but I would be his last.

James had left a trail of broken hearts and dead bodies in his wake. I'd managed to account for nineteen women who'd had organ failure after dating him. Nineteen. And those were just the ones I'd found out about. Consequently, I didn't feel any remorse about the karma that was about to kick his ass. Karma's name is Esme; she's my wolf, and she loves killing things.

It turns out being a werewolf isn't at all like *Underworld* or *Van Helsing*. I should know; after I got turned into one, I binge-watched a bunch of movies to see if any of them are accurate. None of them are, not a one.

Vampires are real, except they're called vampyrs. Werewolves are real, too, except it's just like having your own personal wolf inside your head. When you shift, there's no walking on hind legs or having jaws like a crocodile, you just become a huge wolf with extra strength, speed and a side of super-fast healing.

Esme and I have a deal: I drive when we're on two legs, and she drives when we're on four. It works for us. She has a ruthlessness that I'll never match because my human morality gets in the way, but Esme sees things in black and white. She never hesitates. Which is good because, as much as I hated James for what he'd done to me and all the other girls before me, *I* couldn't deal with him. But Esme? She'd make mincemeat out of him, and I'd hold her handbag for her while she did it.

This was, of course, another test set by my pack. Since I'd become alpha, the weeks had been filled with test after test after test. My second, Manners, had dealt with as many of them as he could, but now the pack needed to see Esme and me in action.

I turned my thoughts inward. *Ready for some violence?* I asked Esme lightly.

I felt her delight rise up. **Always,** she responded eagerly.

It's time to show them that we're not all mouth and no trousers.

All mouth and no trousers? she repeated dubiously, sending me an image of myself butt-naked with a Joker-esque grin on my face.

I managed not to snort with laughter. *It means we need to show them that we mean business. We're not just braggarts – we can back up what we say with action.*

So, violence? Her excitement thrummed through us.

Yeah, in this case violence. But don't give me nightmares, I half-commanded, half-pleaded. I love Esme. She's tough and honest, and never beats around the bush. She's also incredibly violent and has a very skewed moral compass. But being a wolf, it's not like she's had the chance to read Aristotle.

Lord Samuel had told me that most werewolves struggle, the human side battling the wolf side that is always raging for dominance and control. Esme and I have none of that; she's my sister from another mister, and I trust her completely. How could I not? We share one body and one heart, but two very different minds. We have no secrets from each other. She is more than my wolf; she's literally the other half of me that I didn't know was missing.

Who says you need a man to complete you? Not me. It turns out I just need a wolf.

Esme's eagerness had me rising from my chair – it was time to get our hands dirty. As I started undoing the buttons of my shirt, I felt the excitement in the room ratchet up. It wasn't because of my striptease but because they knew what it meant. Finally the members of my pack were going to see me change. They'd been trying to force me into a change for the last few weeks because they wanted to know how quickly I could shift, but I'd resisted their juvenile attempts to provoke me.

The fact is that Esme and I are different to other were-wolves. For starters, we can communicate not just in flashes of images or feelings, but with actual clear-as-day words. It gives us a huge advantage. Whether it's that, or that I was made Other by a magical artifact rather than by another wolf, we can also change in seconds. The strongest werewolves take a minute or two, and five minutes for a shift is perfectly normal, but Esme and I transform in a heartbeat. I'd pored over every text I could find in Lord Samuel's library and everything I read suggested that our change was the fastest seen in centuries.

For good or ill, Esme and I are different – and my pack was about to learn a little more about their new alpha. I calmly finished undressing. I've never been body conscious because I'm the girl you love to hate. Willowy and model-like, I am blessed with modest curves and a toned tummy.

My gaze fixed on James. He'd seen it all before lots of times when he'd been my boyfriend and I'd naïvely thought he might be *the one*.

I didn't know how the pack had found out about him, but they had. The Other is a tough-ass magical realm and it demands justice. I could have turned him over to the Connection and had him arrested and tried. The Connection is judge, jury and, all too often, executioner; it is the political power, the law maker and the police all in one very scary organisation. But if I turned James over to the proper authorities, I'd lose *my* authority – what little I had.

Manners was standing with his broad arms folded, slate-grey eyes glaring. Everything about his body language screamed belligerence. He is my protector, he's constantly ready for a fight, and the pack knows it. But now it was my turn to show them all, including Manners, that Esme and I didn't need a protector.

Let it rip, I murmured, and I felt pleasure roll over us as we embraced our Other form. Suddenly we were standing on four legs and looking around. Esme took front and centre and I relaxed into the passenger seat for the ride.

The colours around us were dull and muted, like everything was painted with a watery palette. We didn't need our heightened hearing to catch the gasps from the pack; amazement and sudden anxiety pervaded the room like a scent. Esme laughed darkly in the confines of our mind. She likes to shock, and I'm growing to like it too.

She prowled forward menacingly, head low, teeth bared. James was still sprawled on the floor. His hands were bound behind him but that hardly seemed sporting. He was scum, but my morality demanded that we level the playing field a little – it wouldn't do for him to be perceived as a victim when he was anything but. James was a dangerous predator, but we could handle him.

Esme doesn't understand my need to be fair but she does respect it. With a dexterous move that was both human and wolf, we swiped through his bindings and freed his limbs. He scrambled to his feet as though the extra height would protect him.

We could hear his wrathful heart hammering away, its beat loud and rapid. Esme filtered through the extraneous noises and muted the ones we didn't need as we focused on James. He had nearly killed me. You'd think death by sex would be a great way to go, but he'd drained the life from me gradually, leaving me confused and panicking, feeling unending lethargy and not knowing why. My death had been the scariest time of my life, but I'd come out the other side a little harder, a lot faster and even more determined than ever.

When Emory, Prime Elite and King of the Dragons, had found out about my succubus boyfriend James, he'd dug deeper and discovered a string of corpses. James may have been charming, but he was also a serial killer. He'd broken the rules of the Other realm by dating us, shagging us, making us believe he loved us and then killing us.

Now, even though I'd once fancied myself in love with him, I didn't feel any sympathy. I was all out of fucks to give and, more importantly, so was Esme. She hadn't been with me then, but she could feel the echoes of my remembered fear and it made her rage.

Esme prowled around James and let out a fierce growl. He took an involuntary step back. I wondered what I'd ever seen in him. He didn't look so sexy now; he was sullen faced and his hard eyes showed no remorse.

He looked around the room, turned and tried to flee. The gathered werewolves wouldn't let that happen, nor would Esme. With another growl, she bounded two steps and landed on his back. He let out an 'oof' as he fell, the breath knocked out of him.

Esme grabbed his arm in her jaws and flipped him onto his back. For the first time, I saw panic flare in his eyes, and a dark part of me took pleasure in that. It turns out we can all engage in a little *schadenfreude* now and again.

But James's panic wasn't wholly justified. After all, we weren't going to kill him.

Esme paused. **We're not?**

No, I confirmed. *Just some maiming.*

She sighed, but I didn't need to explain again to her about my moral compass. We'd discussed it at length and, although she hadn't really grasped it, she understood some lines in the sand were important to me. She wanted me to be happy, so she agreed to observe them. She's good like that.

James was still staring at us, his chestnut eyes filled with defiance and an edge of fear. He'd had a moment of panic but he still didn't think I'd do anything to him. He'd dated me, *known* me, and a few months ago I couldn't kill a spider. He was scared but he thought he was safe. Perhaps he was safe from me – but he wasn't safe from Esme.

Pathetic. Esme slunk around him as he lay immobile, as if playing dead. We didn't buy his act. She prowled for a good minute or two. When he started to relax and think we weren't going to hurt him – that was when she struck.

She ripped into the crotch of his trousers, tearing away the fabric and burying into his soft flesh. That was when he started to scream. Esme kept tearing, ripping his family jewels away from his body. Hot blood filled our mouth and we liked the taste.

James sobbed hopelessly, but all I felt was Esme's satisfaction mirroring my own. He would never kill another innocent again. He was a succubus, cursed now to live a half-life. He would get his energy through stolen kisses, but never again could he take a life force. I suspected he might have preferred death.

When Esme had finished shredding James's manhood, she padded back to our clothes. **Over to you,** she murmured and relinquished her hold on us.

The transformation rolled over us and we barely bit back a moan of pleasure. Changing was *good*. The blood that had been coating our muzzle was gone; I was naked, but clean.

I dressed unhurriedly and turned to the pack members who were still standing in the living room, hunched together in a confusion of limbs. 'Staunch the bleeding and keep him alive for the next fifteen minutes,' I said in my bossiest voice, as if orders came naturally. They didn't, but I was working on it. Then I pulled my phone out of my pocket and called Amber DeLea.

My favourite witch answered on the second ring. 'Lucy, what do you want?' she bit out. She is so warm and fuzzy.

'You remember how a succubus nearly killed me?'

'I recall the story, yes.'

'Well, I've maimed him a little. Can you come and heal him so he doesn't die? I want him to live a long and unhappy life.'

'Remind me not to piss you off,' Amber commented drily. 'You're in luck, I'm just driving back from Rosie's

and I was on my way to see you. I'll be with you in five.'
She rang off.

Amber is abrupt, blunt and pushy; when I grow up, I
want to be just like her. I wondered why she was coming
to see me; we weren't quite friends, so it wasn't like she was
coming to plait my hair. I pushed it from my mind; I had
more pressing concerns.

I pocketed the phone and picked a comforting face out
of the crowd. 'I'm sorry, Mrs Dawes,' I said to our resident
housekeeper. 'I've made a bit of a mess of the lounge carpet.'

The lounge is our name for the gargantuan room that
frequently hosts the pack members. It has numerous sofas,
TVs and beanbags strewn around. There is a corner with
kids' toys and books for when the pack's pups come to
play, and there's a corner with game consoles for when the
pack's grown-up pups come to play.

Mrs Dawes gave me a warm smile. 'Never mind, dear. I
have an excellent carpet cleaner. If I treat it fresh, it will
come right out.' The carpet in the lounge is a dark floral
monstrosity, which I hate, but at least the pattern helped
hide the stains that had amassed over the years. This pool
of blood was much like the other marks the carpet bore
witness to.

Nothing fazes Mrs Dawes. Like me she came late to the supernatural game, and like me she was turned by the former alpha, Lord Samuel. He'd saved her life too, just like he had saved mine. I tried not to think about how I'd ended his.

Two werewolves had stepped out of the crowd to obey me: Manners, my second, was no surprise, but Archie, who was twelfth in the pack, was quite a shock. Archie was Lord Samuel's son, and he hadn't managed much in the way of friendliness so far. I didn't blame him; even knowing the circumstances, I still blamed myself for his father's death. Evidently, so did he.

Manners took control of the situation and gruffly ordered Archie to help compress the grisly wound to staunch the blood. The rest of the room was silent, watching. I stared right back. You craved this, I wanted to growl. You wanted to see me – well, see me. I won't blink first and I'm not giving up my throne for anyone. Abdication isn't an option in werewolf culture and, as I've said already, I'm not ready to die.

I held their gazes one by one until they looked away. One point to Lucy.

Chapter 2

Amber bustled in with her customary black skirt swishing around her ankles. Today it was paired with a sky-blue top that made her scarlet hair pop. Her black tote bag swung by her side. She barely spared the room and its occupants a glance before she turned her attention to my murdering ex.

James had stopped screaming and was quietly whimpering instead. To be honest, I was slightly impressed that he hadn't fainted. Amber motioned Archie and Manners away with a jerk of her head, and they scrambled back. She would make a fine alpha, I thought somewhat jealously. This commanding business came easily to her. She ran her own coven and was touted to become the next Symposium member following the unfortunate demise of the last witch who'd had the role. The Symposium is the ruling body of the almighty Connection. Witches take the appointment seriously; it would be weeks before a successor would be chosen, but I'd bet money on Amber's success.

I studied her surreptitiously. She looked tired, which was rare for her, and her eyes showed strain. I wondered if it was the pressure of the battle to become the next Symposium member or if she was still battling grief. Her lover Jake had been killed – assassinated – only a few weeks earlier.

Amber donned sterile gloves and pulled various potions out of her bag. She took a paintbrush and was about to start painting a rune when she paused. She turned to me. 'I'm guessing you want his de-manning to be permanent?'

'Yes please.' I smiled pleasantly, like we weren't discussing mutilating someone.

She nodded, turned back to James and painted the runes on his ruined crotch. She's a witch with real honest-to-goodness magic, so I guess growing back his cock was actually an option. This realm keeps surprising me.

What was left of James's manhood would be operational for the purposes of having a pee, but I doubted he'd ever be able to bring himself joy or shag his victims to death. It seemed a fitting punishment.

Once Amber was done 'healing' him, I turned to the huddle of werewolves. As always, my gaze met Mark's first. Mark was officially third in the pack; he'd been Lord Samuel's second and had been supremely pissed off to be demoted to number three. But Manners had beaten him fairly in combat, and pack rules are simple.

Greg Manners was brethren before he was turned into a werewolf. He'd lived alongside the dragons and protected their family and human offspring. He'd grown up with a weapon in his hand, and had been bundled off to the military at sixteen. He'd undertaken rigorous training and become the type of operative who'd have to kill you if he told you what he'd done.

Mark was a bruiser, always fixing for a fight, but he was no match for Manners' raw strength and skill. It had been a shock to Mark to discover he wasn't the toughest mother in town anymore, and his new position as third hadn't settled well.

He was my most vocal opponent, never going so far as to actually insult me or to call me out but constantly undermining me. I went to a school which had far more girls than boys, so I recognise bitch guerrilla warfare when I see it and, unluckily for him, I know it like the back of my hand. I was popular at school, which made me supremely unpopular with a section of the not-so-popular girls. I did my best to rise above it all. It wasn't my fault that I was athletic, clever, beautiful and could sing, and I wasn't dumbing down to make anyone else feel better. I never made fun of others, but neither did I demean myself. My mum taught me to take pride in my successes, just like I was a man.

I held Mark's challenging gaze and smiled at him. 'Well volunteered, Mark,' I said calmly. 'You can dump James back where you found him.'

He opened his mouth to argue then closed it with an audible clack. He wouldn't disobey me – yet.

He motioned to Liam to help him and the pack's fifth stepped up to the plate. Liam was young, but I thought he'd have potential if I could get him out from under Mark's claws. He seemed intelligent and sharp; despite him treating me with undisguised dislike, I thought he could be an asset one day.

The two of them lifted James by his armpits and carried him effortlessly out of the room. Werewolf strength is a huge advantage, though I'd broken any number of lip-sticks before I'd learnt to moderate my grasp. First-world werewolf problems, hey?

I looked at the rest of the group. We didn't have a full house today, not by a long shot. The majority of the local wolves have normal jobs that keep them busy and, though they belong to the pack, they don't live in the mansion.

The few that were there were my housemates, albeit in a house that is a massive Edwardian building in pristine condition with rolling, landscaped gardens that cost a pretty penny to maintain. I should know: as a qualified accountant, I'd reviewed the books and winced at the monumental expense. Not to mention the cost of looking after freeloading pack members.

I contemplated trying to make a point to the gathered wolves, but I felt that Esme had already done that quite eloquently: we weren't weak, and we weren't afraid to get bloody.

Nobody's face shone with respect, but something had changed. Tristan was glaring, as usual, but Marissa looked contemplative. Seren's face was blank. They might not like me, but now they understood that I was capable of violence, capable of protecting myself – and them, too.

'Don't mind me,' Mrs Dawes said. 'I'll just get that carpet cleaner.' She left the room and returned a moment later wearing gloves and carrying a jar of gloop. She opened the lid and carefully painted thick green liquid onto the bloodstains. It glowed for a moment before fading entirely, leaving behind an unblemished carpet.

'Nice potion work,' Amber commented. 'Who did it for you?'

'Shauna,' Mrs Dawes replied. 'She's such a dear. She gave me a discount for bulk buying.'

Amber nodded. 'I'll congratulate her. That worked expeditiously.'

'She's always good at producing a quick result.'

'Indeed,' Amber said drily. 'And you never know who's going to come calling.' Her tone had greater meaning in it than the words conveyed.

'Thank you, Mrs Dawes,' I said. She nodded her neatly bobbed head and backed out of the room, shutting the heavy door behind her.

'Manners, Amber, come with me,' I ordered. Amber raised an eyebrow at my tone but followed me down the corridor to my private lounge. The large yellow room was empty, but with the fire burning it had a much cosier feel than the big room.

'Good to see you,' Manners said to Amber when the door was shut.

Amber nodded in acknowledgement. 'I come with a message from Maxwell. He's heard on the down-low that you're about to get a visit.'

'From whom?' I asked.

'The werewolf council.'

Well, shit.

'Does Maxwell have an ETA on the council's arrival?'

She shook her head. 'Soon, was all he's heard.'

'Great. How am I supposed to host an entire freaking council without any notice?' I grumped.

Amber rolled her eyes. 'Not the whole council, Lucy, just a representative.'

'Sent to investigate Lord Samuel's death, I presume?'

'That, and your turning. I understand that it was … irregular. It's a rubber-stamping exercise – they should be out of your hair in a day or two. Without Lord Samuel here to testify about your turning there are no other witnesses, are there?'

'No,' I lied. My turning had been irregular. Werewolves are largely born, and turning someone into a werewolf is generally a big no-no. Turned werewolves often have difficulties in adapting to a new way of life, and they don't often survive. The exception is that you're allowed to *try* to turn someone who is dying of natural causes.

I was dying of magical causes because of James, so I hadn't qualified for a turn. My best friend Jess had stabbed me; at that point, blood loss became the overriding cause of my imminent death and Lord Samuel was able to turn me. It was pure sophistry, but technically no rules were broken – except he hadn't had time to ask the council's permission. So maybe there was a little rule-breaking, but it's better to ask for forgiveness rather than permission, right? Jess was there when I was turned, but it was better for everyone if we kept her out of it.

'Irregular is one way of putting it,' I agreed. I liked Amber, but even she didn't need to know that Jess had used the magical artefact known as Glimmer in my turning. I suspect it was the dagger's involvement that has made me a different breed of wolf. For one thing, I have the ability to pipe – to talk to animals. Think Dr Doolittle but with fewer songs. It is because of my piping that I can speak to Esme. I'm not sure why I can turn super-fast, but suffice to say I'm different.

I changed the subject. 'How much do I owe you for healing my ex?'

'I'll send an invoice,' Amber said brusquely. I hoped she'd give me mate's rates. She stood, gave Manners and me a nod and swept out of the room. I guessed the chit-chat was done.

As she left, Mrs Dawes popped in with a massive plate of barbeque ribs and fries. 'You'll need to eat after that change,' she said in her usual calm fashion. She deposited the laden plate on the table and left.

Manners and I were left alone. I dug into the ribs and gestured for him to help himself. He grabbed a couple but left me most of the food. He hadn't changed, so he wasn't combatting the ravenous hunger that was sweeping through me.

Greg Manners had become indispensable to me during these last few weeks. He was also a newly turned wolf and, like me, he'd been stabbed by Glimmer. I wondered if his change was as fast as mine. He'd been a strong human before the turn and so far, even when he'd needed to resort to brute strength, he'd just used his human form. He was tall, bulky and muscle bound, with cropped blond hair. He always had an air about him that suggested he was ready for action.

After he'd left the military, Manners had re-joined the mysterious brethren and taken up a position as part of the Prime Elite's personal security team. The brethren are the dragon-shifters' human counterparts who help look after the immortal beings and keep them grounded in modern life. From what Manners had told me, dragons are largely resistant to accepting new technology – with the notable exception of Emory, the Prime Elite.

I liked Emory; he was dating Jess and making her deliriously happy, so what was not to like? Being a good friend, I was ninety-five percent happy for her and only five percent jealous that she seemed to have found the love of her life at the age of twenty-five. I'd only managed to find the killer of mine. Still, the whole mess had led me here. I was grateful for that, and for having Manners. I trusted him with my life.

He's a good pack mate, Esme agreed. Now that she had wrought violence, I could see that she was content. In our mind's eye she turned three times, settled down comfortably and started to groom our fur, which was sticky with blood. The change had removed the blood from my body but not, it seemed, from our fur. I wondered whether it was representative of my feelings of guilt. However, I calmed as Esme settled down to the task of cleaning and soothing us.

I sighed and slumped back into one of the sofas. 'Just what we need,' I muttered. 'A visit from the council when half of my wolves hate me.'

'More than half,' Manners interjected helpfully.

I glared at him. 'Yes, thank you for that. I'll win them over. Mrs Dawes likes me.'

'She does, and I think Archie does too, despite himself.'

I ran my hands through my long blonde hair and sighed again. Poor Archie. I didn't blame him for his antagonism – he was barely eighteen and I'd killed his father. Regardless of pack law, I would have struggled with that too.

But Mark and Tristan actively hated me, and Liam still followed whatever Mark did. Brian seemed hostile, but with an edge of indifference. That was probably as good as it would get, and I could work with it.

Seren glared at me constantly, sending me dark gazes from her eyelinered eyes. She dressed as a goth and her attitude matched her dark clothes; she loathed me and she wanted me to know it. I'd seen her and Mark cosied up together in the lounge and I suspected a romance was in the works, despite their sizeable age gap.

Marissa was more subtle in her hatred. She smiled and simpered then she burnt my toast and made me cups of tea with curdled milk. She was passive-aggressive, queen of constant small rebellions that she could claim were accidents or mistakes, eyes wide with a breathless apology. I'd suffered worse. People loved me, and the pack were going to love me; they just didn't know it yet.

'Any bright ideas on how to win them over?' I asked Manners.

He thought about it carefully, then said, 'I don't know. The pack dynamic is very different to how the brethren operates. The brethren members are born and raised together, but it is made up of small family units. The pack is one big group. Yes, there are factions, but so far it seems to be very much them versus us. Mark and Tristan are your most vocal detractors. From what scuttle I heard before they noticed me, they're trying to push Archie into a bid to become alpha.'

I bit my lip. I liked Archie, and I hoped he didn't find himself aligning against me. If he wanted to be alpha he'd have to kill me. He was only eighteen, but he was ranked twelfth in the whole pack; that meant he was a strong fighter, strong enough to form part of the illustrious thirteen.

Not that long ago, Esme and I had battled together with Lord Samuel against a rival pack. The numbers against us had been overwhelming, but Esme got stuck in without flinching. We'd killed and maimed other wolves with relative ease – we just seemed a little faster, a little stronger, and a helluva lot more determined. I wasn't sure where we'd rank within this pack if a tourney was held, but I knew we could hold our own. I didn't want to kill Archie, but I would if I had to in order to survive. I hoped it wouldn't come to that.

Manners read the distaste on my face. 'It might happen,' he warned softly.

'I know.' I bit my thumb. 'We'd better go to Rosie's tonight. I'll see if Maxwell will let us stay over, then we can both get a full re-charge before the council arrives.'

'Good idea.'

I hauled out my phone and dialled Maxwell, who guards the local portal that allows us to travel from the Other realm to the Common one. Werewolves need to re-charge their batteries by staying in the Common realm now and again – it is one of our vulnerabilities. Maxwell takes his role as guardian seriously – and he likes me.

He answered on the second ring. 'Lucy! My favourite alpha! What can I do for you?'

'Can I do a stay-and-play?' I asked.

His tone lost its joviality and suddenly he was all business. 'How long do you want to stay for?'

'The night, if possible.'

'How many of you?'

'Just me and Manners.' Perhaps a stronger alpha, more secure in her position, would have taken some more of her wolves, but at that moment I didn't trust them not to slit my throat whilst I was sleeping.

'Okay. Roscoe is in Liverpool, so I'll call in a couple more elementals for back up. I'll be ready to receive you in thirty.'

'Noted. Thanks, Maxwell.' I rang off and turned to Manners. 'Pack an overnight bag and let's move.'

'Yes ma'am,' he responded. His military efficiency is one of the things I really appreciate about him, that and the fact that he never balks at an order. Of course, my orders so far hadn't been especially controversial, but I had a feeling that might change soon. With the council arriving, we were about to dive into turbulent waters.

Chapter 3

The car journey was silent. I'm not sure what Manners was thinking about, but I was still plotting how to win over the pack.

You worry too much. We will win them over. Esme's tone was assured.

How?

She huffed, **Just by being.**

I admired her confidence in us, but I wasn't sure a 'just keep swimming' attitude *would* win over the pack. I was equally sure that cookies and cake weren't going to cut it, even though I'd seriously considered them as an option. I like baking and the pack likes eating – a lot. But when they gathered in the huge mansion kitchen, they always fell silent when I walked in. It was enough to make a girl paranoid.

We drew up outside Rosie's. Darkness had already fallen, and the trendy café was lit with fairy lights and candles. It looked warm and inviting, more welcoming than the mansion, that was for sure.

A few patrons were in. Three fire elementals sat nursing a brew, their heads dancing with flames. If you saw them in the Common realm you'd see three normal guys, but here in the Other – flames. It still made me smile. The Other realm is magic; not a day goes by that I'm not genuinely thrilled at the thought of living in a place where magic is everything. The elementals gave us cursory nods and I guessed they were Maxwell's back up.

Two green-skinned dryads were eating cake and having a giggle. Apart from them, the place was empty.

I headed to the back room, which is the portal to the Other realm. You'd think it would be filled with shimmery lights or something, but no. You walk into it and back out again. When you walk out, you're in the opposite realm to the one where you started. Simple.

Esme was turning around and stretching out in our head. She settled down for a rest and I tried not to feel anxious at the thought of losing her from my mind.

I'll be back soon, she reassured me. **Relax. Sleep. In the morning we'll be reunited.**

As always her calm soothed me. *Thanks. Have a good rest.*

And you. Run in your dreams. She sent me an affectionate lick across my hair, the equivalent of a kiss goodnight. She may be a kick-ass killer wolf, but she's *my* kick-ass killer wolf. And maybe one day she'll understand that casual killing is frowned on. Maybe I could read Aristotle to her.

As I stepped into the back room, Esme was ripped away from me. It was a separation so total and complete that it took my breath away. Tears rose in my eyes and I took a moment to catch my breath. I couldn't let anyone see how much I suffered from her loss.

When I was steady, I stepped back out into the Common realm. I felt a skitter of anxiety at being unable to change. Sure, I was still faster and tougher than most people – but I had no wolf.

To distract myself, I looked around. The dryads were still laughing, but now their skin was pale pink. Gone were the elementals' flames; instead, waves of curly hair cascaded down their brows. I couldn't see the triangle of the Other, which I knew was on their foreheads.

They just looked ordinary – but they weren't. I was in the Common realm but they had remained in the Other; they could broil me where I stood, if they wanted to. My brain still kept trying to see them with flames dancing on their heads but, try as I might, all I could see was their hair. The Other protects itself from being revealed in myriad ways that I have yet to fully understand.

Manners had followed me into the portal and, for now, we were ordinary and vulnerable, so we headed up to the flat that Maxwell keeps above the café. It is like Fort Knox, and I relaxed a little more as we went through each heavy door secured by thick metal bolts.

Calling it a flat is ungenerous: it's a huge, open-plan space. A fire was roaring – no surprise there – and Maxwell had the TV on. He rose from the leather sofa to greet us. 'Lucy, Greg. Great to see you both. Are you tired? Or do you want to hang?'

It was late but I was too edgy to relax. 'Let's chill for a bit,' I suggested. I like Maxwell; there's something about his easy joviality that always puts me at ease. In him I have found a kindred spirit.

Manners bolted the door behind us and chucked our two duffel bags on the floor. I kicked off my shoes and he followed suit. My mum is always a stickler for removing your shoes as you enter other people's homes.

Maxwell headed to the fridge. 'Beer?' he called.

Manners slid his eyes to me. 'Go ahead,' I said. We were away from the mansion and we had four fire elementals protecting us. Even Manners needed to relax now and again. 'I'm okay, though,' I said to Maxwell. I'm not much of a beer drinker; I'm more of cocktail girl.

Maxwell handed a beer to Manners and we sat on the sofas. He chucked me a blanket, which I snuggled into. I watched the flames dance in the grate and the stress of the portal gradually drained away. Fires always calm me; I guess it's something primordial in every human, a leftover from our caveman days.

'How's Jinx?' Maxwell asked.

I smiled. Jinx is Jess's nickname. 'She's good. She's smitten.'

Maxwell grinned. 'Yeah, Roscoe said. Emory seems like a good guy.'

'I think so.'

'I *know* so,' Manners interrupted. Before he'd changed into a werewolf, Emory was his boss. Despite the power divide between them, they always seemed pretty close, and Manners is fiercely protective of him.

'Let's hope you're both right. Trouble seems to be brewing between the creatures and the human side. I hope Emory can calm it down before it explodes,' Maxwell said.

31

I sighed. 'No politics, please. I'm too tired for politics.'

Maxwell flashed me a grin with his perfectly white teeth. 'No problem. Let's watch something light and easy.' He flicked on *Sex and The City* and winked at me.

Manners resisted giving an audible groan, and I tried to swallow my smile. 'Perfect,' I said.

We settled down into Sarah Jessica Parker's inner monologue. It was a fairly feisty episode, with Kim Cattrall giving her boyfriend a blowjob. I felt my cheeks warm and focused on the screen so hard that it hurt. I did *not* want to catch Manners' eye just now. Maxwell watched me squirm with barely concealed amusement.

As the episode finished, I took my duffel and beat a hasty retreat into one of the many bedrooms. I followed my nightly routine: I removed my makeup, cleansed, toned and moisturised. You've got to moisturise – you can skip the rest, as long as you moisturise. My mum uses her creams religiously and looks so much younger than her sixty years. As she's not my biological mum I have no idea how I'll look when I age, but moisturising certainly isn't going to hurt me. With my skin taken care of, I washed and slipped into a pink silk pyjama set.

I missed Esme. I was so rarely in the Common realm that I'd grown used to her constant presence. She isn't a chatterbox like me but her solid presence is reassuring, like having someone constantly hugging you. I tried to remind myself that she would be back soon, but it was a hollow consolation. I wondered if she felt as bereft as me, wherever she was.

I nestled into the clean bedsheets and felt entirely too lonely. 'Night, Esme,' I whispered. There was no response. Exhaustion clawed at me. Lonely or not, sleep soon took me.

I was woken from a deep sleep by the blaring of my phone. Even though I was still half asleep, the abrupt noise set my heart racing and I felt panicky. I took a moment to calm myself before I answered.

The call was from the mansion. I'd never been called by the pack before. It was only 6.10 am and dread curled in my belly. It wasn't going to be good news; no one wakes you at 6.10 am to tell you that you've won a thousand pounds.

'Lucy speaking.'

There was a long pause while my caller debated what to say. I tried to swallow my impatience. Finally someone spoke and I recognised his voice. It was Liam. 'You should be here. The others don't want me to call you, but you should be here. Mark is dead.' He hung up.

What the hell? Doziness was swept from my brain as alarm surged in. How could Mark be dead? He was an obnoxious asshole, but he was a werewolf. We are incredibly strong and incredibly fast, and we don't die easily. Mark had been the third in the pack; whatever had killed him was a threat not just to me, but to the pack as a whole.

I grabbed my duffel bag, yanked out some clothes and sighed. I hadn't anticipated death when I'd packed, and all I could find were pale, washed-out jeans and a pink satin shirt with flamingos on it. Hardly appropriate. Still, I couldn't go back in yesterday's clothes; not only would that be unhygienic, but the smell would be offensive to anyone who was currently in wolf form.

As I dressed, I fervently hoped that Mark had had an allergy to something I didn't know about. Accidental death by peanut. Fingers crossed.

I shoved everything else back in the duffel and went into the lounge where the guys were talking at the breakfast bar over coffee and croissants.

'You're up early, ma'am,' Manners greeted me.

I'd never delivered news like this before, so I went with the 'ripping-off-a-plaster' technique: quick and hard. 'I got a call from the mansion. Mark is dead.'

Manners stilled. 'This is bad.'

'No shit.'

'Not Mark dying but us being away when it happened. He made no bones about not considering you fit to lead, and it was only a question of time before he challenged you. The fact that he's died before that challenge will make people more suspicious of you.'

'You said I didn't need to worry about him and he'd come around!'

'I lied. I figured we'd have time to get you trained in combat before the challenge came. Mark wasn't a hasty man. He was still assessing you, trying to find your weaknesses. We had time.'

I glared at him and snagged a croissant off his plate. I bit into it and tried to make the buttery flavour distract me from the fact that Manners had lied to me. For some reason, I hadn't expected that.

Jess has always been so anti-liar; I'd recently discovered that's because she is a truth-seeker who knows every time you fib to her. I'm a people pleaser, and a little white lie now and again is necessary in my book. I expect Manners felt his lie was in the same category, so why did it make me feel a bit sick?

When my mouth was empty – my mum didn't raise me to be rude – I looked him in the eyes. 'Don't lie to me again. I need to know that I can trust you and your advice. Don't sugar coat things, just give them to me straight.' It came out a little more forcefully than I'd intended, but I meant every word. I needed him to be honest; I didn't want a yes-man, I wanted an ally.

Manners nodded slowly. 'Alright,' he said. It wasn't an oath, but I'd always felt that he was a man of his word. And it would have to do for now because I had more important things to worry about.

'I can – and will – alibi you both,' Maxwell stated. 'The premises have video surveillance, so it will be easy to prove that you both spent the night here.'

Manners scrubbed his hand through his hair. 'There's a slight problem with that.'

'What?'

'I went out at around 1am. An old friend called, asking for help. I got back in about 3am.'

I sat down heavily at the breakfast bar. 'Fuck. They're going to say you killed Mark for me.'

'We don't know that,' Manners replied levelly. 'Did they say how he'd died? Maybe he just tripped and fell.'

I stared at him, stone-faced.

He gave a one-shouldered shrug. 'It could happen,' he muttered.

'This complicates things,' Maxwell said. 'Did one of my guys go with you when you left the premises?'

Manners shook his head. 'They offered but I turned them down. My whole life I've been brethren – human with a side of dragon. Whether I'm in Common or not, I'm still dangerous. I don't need protection.'

I snorted. 'What bullshit! A fire elemental could barbecue you before you could say Guy Fawkes.'

'Barbecuing people is very much frowned on,' Maxwell interjected. 'Despite what you think, most fire elementals work as firemen. We use our innate skills to put out fires, not start them. We don't use our flames to harm others.'

'Unless you're Benedict,' I pointed out.

Maxwell flinched. 'Benedict was an aberration. He came to power in an uncertain time, and he seemed strong and charismatic. We didn't realise how unhinged he was until he started to throw his little flare parties.'

'In which he set his enemies alight,' I pointed out.

'As I said, he was an aberration. Roscoe has worked hard to stamp out any hint of us using our element to hurt people.' There was pride in Maxwell's voice as he spoke of his lover. Roscoe had stepped up to the plate when Benedict died; now he was the fire elemental member for the Symposium and head of all of the fire elementals in the UK.

'We're getting off topic,' I pointed out. 'Who did you go and help, and why?' I asked Manners.

'A fellow brethren member. She was drunk and needed a lift home. No big deal.'

'And she called you rather than a taxi?' Suspicion laced my tone.

'She's been ... lonely since she was posted here. There's not a big Other presence, not like Liverpool. She just wanted to see a friendly face.'

I wanted to ask how friendly – after all, it had been a two-hour round trip. I suspected the dark feeling I was trying to ignore was jealousy. I had thought it was Manners and me against the world, but when a woman had called him for a lift he'd left me vulnerable without a thought. Okay, I was being melodramatic: he'd left me with four fire elementals, and if they couldn't protect me nothing could. But still, he'd left me and he'd lied to me about Mark being a threat to me.

I needed to get my head screwed on straight. Manners might be my second in command, but perhaps I was relying on him too much. At the end of the day, the only one I could rely on was myself – and Esme.

Chapter 4

I strode into the portal and felt the world right itself. Esme reappeared in my mind, a solid presence in my body and my brain that I could rely on. *We've got a problem. Mark is dead.*

We will find who killed Mark and deal with him, Esme promised fiercely. Her anger surprised me because she had no reason to love Mark anymore than I did.

Maybe he died accidentally, I replied hopefully.

She snorted. **He is wolf. We do not die accidentally.**

I wanted to argue but I couldn't. An accident didn't seem likely, not with a panicked call from Liam at 6.10am. Maybe I could hope for a car accident or a raging allergy.

You need to eat. We will need our energy. We will be changing before the day is out. Esme's logic was sound.

Changing doesn't seem to take much magical energy from us – we've yet to be expelled into the Common realm from accidental overuse of magic – but something in the shift makes us ravenously hungry. Usually we hunt whilst we're in our wolf form and that helps take the edge off, but she was right: if Mark's death was suspicious, we'd need to shift to see what we could find out.

I moseyed up to the café's counter. The place was still closed but the smells from the kitchen were making my tummy rumble. They were already baking and prepping for the 7am rush.

I dinged the little service bell and Maxwell popped up from behind the counter, like he really was just a café owner. 'Can I grab a cappuccino and sausage sandwich to go?'

'Sure, I'll pop it on the overnight invoice.' Maxwell called the food order back to the kitchen. He poured some milk into a metal jug, held the jug for a minute, then briefly frothed the milk. Huh. I guess fire elemental powers are handy to heat things in a jiffy. Moments later he passed me my drink and a hot sandwich wrapped in a to-go packet.

Manners grabbed both of our duffels and we headed out into the heavy rain. He stowed our bags and slid into the driver's seat. I sat in the passenger side, unwrapped my sandwich and dug in. Esme was right: we would need our energy. Besides, uncouth as it was to stuff my face, I was hungry.

Manners started the engine. 'Are we okay?' he asked finally.

No. 'Sure.' I sent him a bright smile and kept on eating. The rest of the drive was silent.

When we pulled up outside the mansion, our car wasn't the only one on the drive; a police vehicle was already there. My hopes for an accidental death for Mark dwindled and died. I took one last pull of my cappuccino and put the empty cup in the cupholder. It didn't seem right to stroll in casually sipping coffee like everything was normal. My flamingo shirt was bad enough.

I turned to Manners and handed him my unlocked phone. 'I'll need a name, address and a telephone number for this brethren lady you visited.'

Manners tapped in the details and passed it back to me. *Mindy – Brethren.* Mindy? What kind of a name was Mindy? Fucking Mindy.

I bet she is a terrible hunter, Esme murmured.

That made me smile. She was trying to make me feel better, her equivalent of telling me that Mindy's boobs were probably fake.

Thanks. I sent her a mental hug, which she returned. It steadied me. I had Esme, and we'd sort out whatever had been done to Mark.

I slid out of the car, rang the doorbell and waited, thankful for the covered porch that protected me from the rain. Mrs Dawes opened the door but today her ever-present smile was missing. She'd clearly been crying; her eyes were red and her face was puffy.

As I stepped inside, I pulled her into a hug. She cried on my shoulder for a few moments before pulling herself together and dabbing her eyes with her handkerchief. 'I'm sorry,' she murmured. 'It's still so raw.'

'Of course. The police are here?'

'Yes. Someone called them – I'm sorry, I'm not sure who. I know you might have preferred to investigate without the authorities being involved.'

I kept my face blank. I'm not an investigator, and I wouldn't know the first thing about getting to the bottom of this. Hell, I didn't even know what *this* was. I'm an accountant for Christ's sake. I know numbers, and the answer is always right or wrong. There is no grey line in maths; maths is comforting in that way. This was so far out of my comfort zone, I didn't know where to begin. But I guessed whatever was going on fell under the remit of the alpha, and the presence of the police was a good thing. Right?

Once I knew what was going on, I'd ring Jess for advice. She's a private investigator – she'd know what to do.

'How did Mark die?' I asked Mrs Dawes.

Her eyes filled with tears again. 'Horribly,' she whispered. 'So horribly. Tortured – you'll have to see.'

Ugh, I didn't want to see a tortured body. I didn't want to see *any* kind of body. I'd seen far more than my fair share of corpses lately. I said nothing and followed her through the mansion to the pack wing where Mark had lived. When Mrs Dawes led me through into the communal living room, it fell silent apart from Marissa's weeping.

Tristan's face flushed with anger. 'What are you doing here?' he spat. 'You can't help us. He was killed under your roof, your protection. His death is on you. Get out and start running, and maybe you'll get some life before I kill you.'

Manners crossed the space between them with a few angry strides and punched Tristan in the face. He knew how to punch; Tristan flew through the room and crashed against the oak bookshelf.

'Threaten the alpha again and I'll kill you,' Manners growled. His eyes flashed with yellow and I didn't doubt that he'd do it.

Someone cleared their throat. 'I'll pretend I didn't hear that,' said a voice drily.

I knew that voice. I turned toward Steve Marley. I'd gone to school with him and he'd dated one of my school friends. He had two triangles on his forehead: the first triangle was the mark of the Other, and the second was the mark of the Connection. Because both triangles were visible, I knew he was in the Other realm with full access to his magic. He was working for the big guys. When he's in the Common realm his triangles disappear, and with them his magic. Most of the human species spend as much time as possible in the Other, but we all have to re-charge our magical batteries now and again with a stint in the Common.

When Steve and I were growing up together, I'd had no idea he was Other. I'd known fuck all about the dangerous, co-existent magical realm. I couldn't say that ignorance was bliss, but life was certainly simpler.

Steve's eyes flashed a warning. 'Alpha,' he greeted me coolly, as if we didn't know each other. 'I've no doubt you wish to examine the scene. I've secured it, but you can see it before I call in the forensic team.'

I nodded and followed him, gesturing for Manners to stay behind. Yes, I was leaving him with my hostile pack, but he could handle himself. I absolutely wasn't punishing him for lying to me. Not in the slightest.

Steve paused outside a door. 'It's horrific,' he warned. He passed me a pair of booties to slip on over my shoes and gloves to snap on. 'Don't touch anything,' he instructed.

I nodded calmly, even though I was feeling faintly sick. I didn't want to see this.

Steve opened the door, we stepped in and I sneezed violently. How embarrassing.

Vile, Esme hissed. **This cannot stand. We will find out who did this and rip out their throat.** I didn't disagree.

Mark was naked, chained to a chair. His bed was unmade, as if he'd been dragged from it in his sleep. His body was covered in deep cuts, gashes, and a whole lot of dried blood. The wounds were tinged with green. His mouth was gagged and his eyes had been gouged out. The stench of death and human faeces assaulted my nose. He'd been dead for more than an hour or two.

I struggled with the urge to vomit. 'Any idea on time of death?' I asked when I was confident my breakfast would stay down.

'It's not a precise science like they portray in the movies. The body is still slightly warm to the touch, but rigor mortis has set in. I'd say he was killed less than six hours ago.'

I was impressed. Steve sounded like he knew what he was doing. 'That, and the fact that Marissa said goodnight to him at midnight,' he added.

Okay, slightly less impressed now. 'Why are his wounds tinged green? A potion?'

'Nothing so complex.' He studied me. 'You must be new to the Other?'

'Recently turned werewolf at your service.'

'And an alpha already? You always were ambitious.'

'It was an accident. I was in the right place at the wrong time.'

'I'm sorry. I admired Lord Samuel – he was eccentric but he always seemed to rule fairly. He didn't trust the Connection, but I liked him on a personal level.'

I battled with my feelings of guilt. I'd killed Lord Samuel at his behest because he'd already been mortally wounded, poisoned by another werewolf alpha called Jimmy Rain. Lord Samuel hadn't wanted his pack to fall into Rain's sadistic claws. I'd been the only wolf there at the time, so I'd killed him and taken his place as alpha, snatching victory from Rain. And here I was, stuck with a role ceded only in death or old age. Lucky me.

'Lord Samuel was poisoned – by someone else,' I hastened to add. 'I killed him before he died so that the pack wasn't passed to his poisoner.' I gestured to Mark's body, 'But if this wasn't poison, then why are the wounds green? We're not in the age of gangrene anymore.'

'Not gangrene, not poison. These wounds were made using a silver blade.'

'Silver? Is that really a thing?'

'You didn't know that silver and werewolves don't mix?'

'Well, sure. I mean, I grew up with the idea that silver was bad for werewolves, but back then I didn't believe that werewolves were real either. I've learnt that whatever the Common knows about the Other is always a bit twisted. Take vampires – here they're called vampyrs, they come out in the daytime, they have a reflection and they don't sleep in coffins.'

'No, but they do need permission to enter a residence and they do drink blood. Some of the stuff you hear about Other creatures is true. With werewolves, the full moon gives you extra strength – and silver is a no-no.'

'Great. So now I need to chuck out all my silver jewellery.'

'That would probably be sensible, though unless you cut yourself with it or ingest it the worst that will happen is that you'll get a rash. But you don't want someone grabbing your pretty silver necklace, ramming it down your throat and killing you by making you eat it.' He seemed to be speaking from experience. He looked down at the ruined corpse. 'I'm not sure if Mark Oates died from silver poisoning or blood loss. The pathologist will know.'

I wasn't sure it mattered a whole lot. Mark was dead. Whether the cause was a silver weapon or the deep cuts that littered his body, his assailant's intentions were clear.

I studied the body as clinically as I could. 'Someone went a bit nuts. The eye-gouging thing makes it look personal.'

'Yeah, it's a violent way to go. Perhaps passion was involved, though the eye removal could have been symbolic. Maybe Mark saw something he shouldn't have. The Other realm is a violent place,' Steve pointed out.

I sighed. 'Yeah. I'm beginning to realise that.' It worried me; I'm not well-equipped for violence.

I am, Esme confirmed. Her words shouldn't have reassured me, but they did.

'As alpha, I'm supposed to take care of this shit, right?'

Steve slid me a sidelong glance. 'Obviously, as an officer of the Connection I need to tell you that this is my investigation and you should stay away from it. But as your friend? If you want to survive as alpha, yeah, you need to take care of this shit. Get to the bottom of it, either with or without me. Find out who killed your wolf and do something about it. Either I can arrest them, or you can take them down.'

'How is it that you don't seem even slightly fazed by vigilante justice?'

He shrugged. 'If you hadn't noticed by now, the Other realm is a different kettle of fish.'

I haven't noticed many fish, Esme commented, bemused. **Why would you put them in a kettle? I know you like tea...**

Trying not to giggle out loud, I briefly explained the idiom to her.

Steve was still talking. 'With so many species co-existing with different moral frameworks, violence is to be expected. It's reduced a lot since the Connection came into existence eighty-odd years ago, but it's a dog-eat-dog realm and the strong survive. The Connection can't stop that, even if it wanted to. Vigilante justice is par for the course.'

'Great. I've stumbled into a world where Superman and Batman are A-okay with the authorities.'

'It's not Superman and Batman you need to worry about, it's Lex Luthor and the Joker. Everything here is extreme. Life is under the magnifying glass – and everything here is larger than in Common life.'

Chapter 5

I paced the floor impatiently. 'So how do I go about investigating murder? I'm an accountant. If you came to me with embezzlement, I'd be your girl – but murder? I don't know where to start.'

'You always start with the victim,' Steve advised. 'But honestly? I don't want to use a cliché, but most murders are carried out by loved ones. The gouging out of the eyes thing could indicate passion – or just your regular torture. Either Mark Oates was into some dark stuff or his ex-wife got pissed off.'

'Does Mark have an ex-wife?'

'Luckily for you, Mark was a person of interest not too long ago so I've got a jump- start on this case. Mark has an ex-everything. Of all of your people, he's going to be the toughest one to investigate. He had fingers in lots of pies and some of those pies weren't all that savoury.'

'Apple and cinnamon pie?' I asked, tongue in cheek.

He slid me an amused glance. 'Nothing so sweet, I'm afraid.'

'So, unsavoury pies. What are we talking about? Sex, drugs, rock and roll?'

'Drugs, yes.'

'Crack cocaine, weed, steroids?' Steroids I could believe; Mark had been a total beefcake and I wasn't sure how much of it was natural and how much of it was werewolf. My body has undoubtedly strengthened since I turned, but I'm not exactly covered in rippling muscles.

'By all accounts, Mark experimented with the drug named Boost. He was documented buying it a couple of months ago when we were investigating the drug cartel that was producing and selling it. Did you hear about Boost?'

Hear about it? Jess had been in the middle of the investigation and take down. Boost was a drug that temporarily boosted your Other powers and made you faster, stronger. It was the first drug that was designed specifically for the Others. The problem, besides the fact that it was illegal and highly addictive, was that it was also Russian roulette as to whether you got high or you died.

'What was Mark doing with Boost?' I asked. 'Was he taking it or selling it?'

'As far as we could tell, he was only a customer. We were investigating the drugs cartel and drug sales in the area when Jinx managed to get the whole organisation shut down.'

Most people in the Other know Jess by her nickname, but for me she'll always be snot-nosed little Jessica Sharp who played unicorns with me in the playground.

Steve continued. 'Mark was seen buying it, but not in big enough quantities to distribute it. By the time we got round to a sting operation, Boost had been taken off the market so we just kept an eye on him and a few of the other customers. Boost was expensive, though – crazy expensive. The question is, where was Mark getting the money to buy it on a park ranger's salary?'

'A little recreational drug use is hardly the smoking gun we need.'

'No, but drug users can be unpredictable and Mark was mixing with them.'

'So I need to question the pack about drug use?'

'That's probably not a bad place to start. See if any of the others were enjoying the highs and lows of the pink powder.'

'What else?'

'Well, I'm sorry to ask, but where were you?'

'Me?' I replied incredulously.

'It's well-known that Mark was eyeing the alpha role, then in swept an unknown – you,' Steve commented. 'Honestly, if it was you that killed him, the Connection would just close down the investigation and pass it to the werewolf council. Pack politics are something else.'

'I'm not going round killing my packmates.' Mutilating sociopath exes is different, right?

'It will be easier if I investigate and clear you, then leak it to the pack "accidentally" so they know you're not involved. Where were you?'

'At Rosie's with Maxwell. All night.'

Steve nodded. 'Great. That's easily verified.'

'There's a fly in the ointment,' I admitted. 'Manners slipped out to meet an ... old friend.'

'What time?'

'Between 1am and 3am.'

Steve sighed. 'That's right in the window.'

'I know,' I grumped. 'This is who he went to meet.' I pulled up Mindy's details and Steve jotted them down.

'I'll contact Mindy and Maxwell and get you two alibied asap,' he said.

'How are you going to let it slip to the pack?' I asked curiously.

'I'll tell Marissa. We're friendly and she's ... loquacious.'

Loquacious was fancy talk for a gossip. 'Are you now?' I queried with interest. Marissa was a total two-faced bitch to me: she smiled and then spat in my coffee. I changed the topic. 'Tell me about Mark's ex. What is she like?'

He snorted. 'Bat-shit crazy. She wanted kids but she and Mark never managed to have them. They tried but she had a lot of miscarriages. It's much harder for werewolves to conceive successfully.'

'She's a werewolf too?'

'Yeah, she's in your pack. Cassie Oates. She's kept her married name, even though they're divorced.'

Great. I hadn't even known that Mark had an ex-wife within the pack. What kind of shitty-ass alpha was I? 'All those miscarriages would be hard on anyone, but that hardly makes her crazy.' I glared at Steve. The feminist in me hated the label that was applied to women all too often: guys were berserk, women were crazy.

'No,' he agreed. 'After all the heartbreak, Mark tried to persuade her to adopt but she wanted a child of her own. She didn't think an adopted child would count as really theirs. '

That comment stung because, even after all this time, it struck a chord. My mum and dad adopted me when I was three. They already had a biological son, Ben, who was five at the time, but I'm as much a part of the family as he is.

There were times when I'd thought about my birth parents, but for most of my life I've carefully shut them out. I'm happy with my family; they are amazing, and they are everything I need. I don't need my birth parents to be part of my life. I don't feel less for being adopted because my mum and dad love me as much as they love my brother.

Of course, I've had wobbles occasionally, especially when I was a teenager. It bothers me now and again that my birth parents saw fit to put me up for adoption. That's such an innocuous phrase – 'abandon me' feels more accurate. But I try not to be bitter because I was adopted by a wonderful family. Who knows what my circumstances would have been otherwise? My parents might have been druggies and I could have been raised in a crack den. Perhaps giving me up for adoption was the best thing that could have happened to me. Perhaps, perhaps, perhaps.

It's the not knowing that sometimes kills me. When I thought I was dying from a mysterious illness, I cursed the fact that I'd buried my head in the sand about who my birth parents were. I didn't know my medical history, if the illness were hereditary and could have been prevented, treated or cured. Then it had felt like my ignorance was killing me. If I was going to don an investigator's hat, maybe I needed to look into that too.

Step one: find out who killed Mark. Step two: rain some vigilante justice on their heads. Step three: stay alive to accomplish steps one and two. Step four: discover the identity of my biological parents. I didn't even admit to myself that there might be a step five: meet them.

I pulled myself back to the present. Wallowing wasn't helping Mark, and no matter how much of an asshole he'd been, he was *my* asshole. I was responsible for him and I'd failed him. Woefully. 'So his ex-wife didn't want to adopt. That hardly makes her crazy.'

'No,' Steve agreed. 'It was more the stalking, shouting and drinking that gave that impression. There were a lot of drunk-and-disorderly incidents. At first Mark didn't file charges, but then she refused to accept the divorce. She still saw Mark as the love of her life and being married to him elevated her in the pack. Even though she was only thirty-something in the ranks, she was the mate of the number two. By divorcing him, she was losing more than her husband and she struggled to cope. Eventually Mark got a restraining order against her, which is why you won't have seen her at the mansion. Rumour was that he took up with a much younger model, someone else in the pack, though I don't know who yet. Marissa was surprisingly close-mouthed about that. The point is, Mark had moved on and Cassie hadn't.'

My money was on doe-eyed Seren being the new love interest; she was the only one I'd seen smiling at Mark. He may have been number two but, despite the apparent outpouring of grief, he hadn't been popular.

I think most of the pack were scared about who'd been capable of murdering him in such a horrific manner. And whether they were finished...

'Gouging out the love of your life's eyes is quite a leap from shouting and stalking,' I said.

'Cassie might not be the main suspect but she's in the mix. I agree, though. The gouging and slashes seems a little more organised crime than spurned wife.'

'Who do we know locally that's so ruthless?'

'There's a number of shadowy organisations in these parts, but not as many as you'd get if we were up in Liverpool. There we'd have a plethora of suspects. Down here, we're nothing but small fry, and the sharks in the pond are correspondingly small.'

'Baby sharks.' I hummed the tune.

Steve shook his head at me. I was being irreverent again. Oops.

'I'll tackle the organised crime element,' he suggested. 'That's going to be beyond you. But there's no reason why you can't investigate the pack, the drugs and the ex. At least then the pack will think you're doing something.'

'Why are you helping me? Why aren't you forbidding me to investigate this crime and telling me to keep out of your way? That's what happens on all the crime shows.'

'I'm only one man, and I'm the only cross-over detective in the area. Unless they can call someone else in... Well, I can only do so much.'

'Cross-over?' I asked dumbly, hating my ignorance.

'I work the same job in both realms – I'm a police detective in the Common *and* in the Connection. I have resources in both worlds but, to be honest, I'm spread thin at the best of times. Plus, you need to investigate to solidify your position as alpha and save your life. It seems like it's win-win for us to help each other. And I don't doubt that Greg Manners will be helping you out.'

'What's Manners got to do with anything?'

'He's a force to be reckoned with. What do you know about him?' Steve asked.

I shrugged. 'He's on my side and he used to be brethren.'

'He still is brethren,' Steve warned. 'He'll always be brethren. It's as ingrained in him as breathing. Manners and Smith are the Prime Elite's right-hand men, and the Prime is not to be messed with. His reputation is formidable, and Manners and Smith always stand behind him.

They should be seen as less because they're brethren – a Prime should have dragons behind him – but he always chooses Smith and Manners. They were born and raised by dragon shifters, but they are only human.

He explained some more. 'Instead of being discarded, the brethren are trained from a young age to help and protect their dragon family. They are supposedly in a sub-servient role, but without them the dragons' whole ecosystem would collapse. The brethren force across the United Kingdom answers to Smith and Manners. So yeah ... Manners isn't a man to mess with. Rumour is there's not a weapon he can't use. He was deadly before he was a werewolf, and with werewolf strength, speed and rejuvenation...'

He trailed off and gave me a warning look. 'He has a military background – special forces. He's used to giving orders. He'd make a helluva alpha.'

I swallowed hard. Manners had been my right-hand man since he'd been changed, and he'd never given me a moment's impression that he wanted to do anything other than help me. Of course Emory, the Prime Elite, was dating Jess and it would create all sorts of mess if Manners killed me to take over my alpha role. Emory had ordered him to protect me, but I hadn't appreciated that he was still under Emory's rule rather than mine.

Steve went on. 'By all accounts, Manners was born to a dragon high up in the Prime Elite's court. He was born to privilege, but he's still brethren and that will always make him a second-class citizen in the dragons' eyes. Perhaps even in his mother's. It's given him a need to prove himself time and time again. He's got a reputation – his name may be Manners, but he's not polite and he won't hesitate to get his hands dirty. If he's sworn to help you, I'm confident he'll support you through this. The brethren down here fall under his command, rather than Smith's. He'll keep you safe.'

I glared indignantly. I didn't need to be kept safe. I was a modern woman, I kept myself safe. I'd taken self-defence classes and I had a rape whistle. More importantly, I had Esme.

Damn right, she murmured.

I sent her a mental hug and she basked in it.

However, the truth was that I didn't have the best track record for keeping myself safe. I'd almost been killed by a succubus, and then I'd killed an alpha werewolf and elevated myself to one hell of a tricky position. But I was done being a damsel in distress; from here on, Esme and I would be self-reliant.

Chapter 6

I wanted to move the subject away from Manners because it made me uncomfortable to realise how naïve I'd been about his allegiances. 'Anything else I need to know? About this room?'

I looked around the modest space. It had an en-suite bathroom, a small balcony, a double bed and a bookcase filled with DVDs and video games. The balcony door was slightly ajar. That was the site of ingress or exit. Or it was a red herring to make it look like it was an outside job. Next to the bookcase of DVDs there was a large flat-screen TV mounted on the wall with a games console attached. The DVDs had been pulled off the shelf, the cases opened and the discs flung around the room.

Steve shook his head. 'Not really. It's been tossed, but I don't know if they found what they were looking for. The state of Mark's body suggests not.'

'So what *were* they looking for?'

He shrugged. 'That's the million-dollar question. Find out that, and we'll probably find out who killed Mr Oates.'

'Surely the room being trashed like this rules out the ex?'

'Not really. She could have been looking for his wedding ring, or some frozen sperm, or evidence he was shagging a new lady. The room could have been trashed as a red herring to make it look like it was something other than a personal grudge. I agree that it makes it less likely to have been the ex, but you have to keep an open mind and follow the evidence.'

Huh. He seemed to be keen to pin it on Cassie, and that didn't seem especially open minded to me.

Steve interpreted my look. 'I'm not saying it's definitely the ex, I'm just saying it's more common than you think. It's a cliché for a reason. It's a good place to start, and it's also a good way for you to make it clear to the pack that you're investigating.'

'Did you find anything illicit in the room?'

'Not really. I found a packet with some traces of Boost in it. Apart from that, just your usual porno mags and sex toys.'

I snorted. 'Who uses porno mags in this day and age? That's what the internet is for.'

Steve looked amused. 'Some people just prefer a more ... hands-on experience.'

I turned my attention back to him. He was tall and willowy. His dark hair was prematurely scattered with grey but it made him look distinguished rather than old. He looked good in uniform and it helped remind me that *his* allegiance wasn't to me, but to the Connection. 'So, we're what – going to information share?'

'Exactly that,' he agreed.

'You're going to tell me classified information?' I tried to keep the disbelief out of my voice.

'I'm going to share what I can when I can. I'll give you what hints, tips and leads I can, I'll bend the rules – but I won't break them. Ultimately, we're both working towards the same goal of finding and stopping Mr Oates' killer.'

Before he strikes again. The unspoken words hung heavily between us. I wasn't one to ignore the elephant in the room. 'Do you think he'll attack someone else?'

'I think it's a possibility, particularly if the killer thinks the pack is weak.'

'The pack isn't weak,' I glared.

'The pack is fragmented and everyone knows it. Half the pack wanted Mark as the leader and the other half wants Archie.'

'And no one wants me,' I muttered.

'Not yet,' he agreed. 'But you were Miss Popular in high school. If you can win over bitchy teens, you can win over lunar lunatics. But until you do, it's a dangerous time for you all. You can't have them bitching about you at the usual watering holes. If you don't consolidate your position and earn their respect, the pack will be perceived as weak.'

Earning the pack's respect was already high on my to-do list. I even had a handy spreadsheet with ideas on how to do it. Now I had a new direction: I needed to find Mark's killer and punish him. Hopefully that would go some way to reassuring the pack that I was here for the long haul and capable of protecting them. And hopefully our little demonstration with my ex had highlighted that I wasn't squeamish.

I needed to address the immediate issue. Someone had walked right into our mansion – our stronghold – and killed our third without anyone batting an eyelid. That made an inside job seem even more likely, but I needed the pack to focus outwards for now. I also needed to examine our security and assess what improvements could be made. I had no doubt Manners could help me with that.

I felt better, even though I was standing in a room with a dead body. I had a plan of action; I always work better when I have a clear objective.

Although the body stank even to my human nose, I figured I'd better shift into my wolf form and see if our heightened senses could pick out anything that Steve might have missed. 'I'm going to shift,' I warned him.

He nodded like he had expected nothing less. He turned his back to give me some privacy and I appreciated the gesture, though I'd only recently stripped off in a room full of my werewolves. Modesty isn't something I have a lot of.

I removed the plastic gloves, the booties and the shoes they covered. Then I unbuttoned my flamingo shirt and slid out of my jeans. My underwear followed, and I piled everything neatly on the floor next to me.

Let's go, I said to Esme, and the change rippled over us, warm and pleasant. They say that a sneeze is an eighth of the pleasure of an orgasm; if that's the case, then a shift is at least half. Shifting is *good*. Pleasure rolled over me as Esme and I assumed four paws again.

The room grew as we shrank to wolf height. The colours dulled and muted and the smells intensified, momentarily overwhelming us with their stench. People often defecate during their death throes and Mark had been no exception. The room reeked of his urine and faeces. I could smell his panicked sweat that had dried hours before; it was stale and heavy.

I heard the steady thrum of Steve's heart but no sounds emanated from Mark. It was chilling. Death steals everything from us.

Underneath the putrid smell of death was another tantalising scent – vanilla? Cinnamon and sandalwood? Something else – lavender, maybe? Something spicy? It clung to the air rather than Mark's body. I scented around the room and my delicate olfactory sense led me to a candle that had not long been extinguished. There was a hint of smoke in the air. I dismissed it. Perhaps Mark liked wanking with his paper magazines in some flattering candlelight. Shadows make everything look bigger.

We scented around the room a bit more. The bed smelled of stale sex, but we couldn't distinguish individual scents on the floor. After Mark's death, half the pack had been coming and going like it was Grand Central Station. I grimaced. For all our explorations, we had found next to nothing. Mark liked candles and sex. Hurrah, I've solved the case.

Patience, Esme chided gently. **We will find the killer. I am an excellent hunter.**

I let her certainty reassure me, even though hunting rabbits and murderers is somewhat different. I nudged her and she willingly gave the reins to me. Disgruntled with our findings, I changed back to human form and dressed quickly.

'Anything?' Steve asked.

I shook my head. 'Nothing that helps. Way too many people have been in and out of this room. The bed smells of sex.'

'Well, that's something. Find out who he's shagging. A lot of investigating a crime is about investigating the victim.'

Great. I had a feeling I was about to get to know Mark more intimately than I'd ever wanted to. I straightened my shoulders. He was my pack, my responsibility, and I'd find out who killed him – even if it killed me.

Chapter 7

I left. The forensic types were lingering in the hall, waiting for us to finish. They didn't seem to find it odd that I was in the crime scene with Steve, so either they were Other or they'd worked with him often enough not to call him out on his eccentricities.

I took advantage of the empty corridor and speed-dialled Jess for some advice. She answered on the second ring, her voice jubilant. 'Lucy! How are you getting on?'

'I'm up shit creek without a paddle. The paddle didn't even make it into the boat. In fact, there *is* no boat and I'm swimming in shit.'

'That doesn't sound very hygienic.'

'I'm *covered* in shit.'

'Literally or figuratively? Because if it's the former, hang up and grab a shower.'

That made me smile. 'Figuratively. One of my pack mates is dead.'

'And you didn't kill him?' Jess's voice held no censure. Her morality had undergone quite a shift since her introduction to the Other.

'No. It would probably be better if he'd challenged me to mortal combat or something. Instead he's been circling me like an insidious snake, waiting for his chance to strike. And now he's dead.'

'And you're upset about it?'

'I'm not pleased. Someone marched into the mansion and killed him in his room.'

'Crap. The pack is not going to like that.'

'No shit.'

'How is Archie?' Jess asked. 'Is he helping you?'

'He's not actively obstructing me, which I'm counting as a win. After all, I did kill his father.'

'After his father started to die! At worst, it was euthanasia. And Wilf asked you to kill him so the pack wouldn't fall into Rain's paws.'

'Yeah,' I muttered. 'So why do I feel like the bad guy?'

'You're not the bad guy, you're the kick-ass heroine. You just need to realise it.'

Her faith made me smile and steadied something in me that had been in danger of breaking. I hadn't admitted to myself how fragile I was feeling. It wasn't like me – but neither was having a wolf in my head.

'Okay. Dead guy. What do I do?'

'Call the police?'

I snorted. 'Done. Steve Marley is here doing his thing. You remember Steve?'

'Sure, he's good people. We've worked together a fair bit over the years. He's a straight arrow.' She sounded relieved.

'You were worried about someone pinning it on me?'

There was a beat of silence. 'It occurred to me that someone could have been setting you up.'

'I was at Rosie's with Maxwell, having a recharge.'

'Great. He'll alibi you.'

'Yeah, but Manners sneaked out right around time of death.'

'Really?' Jess sounded surprised. 'Did he say where he went?'

'To help a brethren mate.' I paused. 'How much do you trust him?'

'Completely,' she replied without reservation. 'Manners is a pain in the ass but he's trustworthy.'

'He's not been a pain in the ass for me.'

'He doesn't call you Toots?'

'Nope. He's all respectful,' I sighed.

'And that's a bad thing?'

'I don't know. He's always … glaring at people.'

'Intimidating the local yokels?' she suggested.

'Definitely. He's giving the pack members pause. If I didn't have him, I bet I'd already be dead.'

'That's good, right?'

'Sure, but I need to stand on my own two feet.'

'Or four,' she countered.

I rolled my eyes. 'You think you're so funny.'

'Hilarious. Do you need me to come?'

'No. You're supposed to be meeting Emory's dragon court this week, aren't you?'

'Finally,' she grouched.

'So you're busy.'

'Never too busy for you. Dragons are immortal – they can wait.'

'I'm good. I have Esme and Manners.'

'And a dead body.'

'Yeah. Any advice on that?'

'Find out who killed him.'

'Cheers,' I said drily.

Jess laughed. 'Dig into who your man was. Most deaths are carried out by people known to the victims. If the killer got into the mansion and into Mark's room without being questioned, chances are that he or she is a member of the pack.'

'Yeah, that thought had occurred to me.'

All joviality was gone from her tone. 'Watch your back, Luce.'

'I will,' I promised. 'Love you.'

'Love you too. Keep me in the loop.' We rang off.

It's handy having a private investigator for a best friend because she won't bat an eyelid when you tell her you have a dead body to investigate. Jess invented cucumber cool and I wish I had half of her attitude. She is queen of no fucks to give. I want people to like me too much, but people pleasing wasn't going to win me this pack.

My chat with Jess relaxed me a little. Steve had rattled me about Manners and his allegiances, but Jess has a gut instinct second to none. If she trusted Manners, I trusted Manners. Now I just needed to work out who, out of the sixty-odd pack members, I shouldn't trust. Easy.

I slid my phone into my pocket and cursed the fashion for women to have obscenely small pockets and obscenely large phones, then I walked into the living room. It immediately fell silent.

Liam was comforting Marissa. Tristan had left. Manners was sitting on the sofa, his stony face giving nothing away.

PROTECTION OF THE PACK

I decided there was no time like the present to get cracking and tried to channel my inner Inspector Morse.

'I'm going to ask you a few questions,' I said to Liam and Marissa. 'And you're going to answer them.' Rule 101: don't ask, order. See? I could totally do this. 'Mark and his ex-wife had an acrimonious split. He was seeing someone new. Who?'

Marissa looked down and away, but Liam met my gaze neutrally. 'He and Seren had been dating, but I don't know if it was serious. She's taken a sedative and gone to bed.' He hesitated. 'She's very upset.'

I'd seen Seren and Mark cuddling together. She didn't strike me as mature; she flounced around the mansion with her earphones in, dressed all in black and with a perma-glare like a teenager in the middle of a rebellion. Who she was rebelling against I didn't know, but she felt – young. It squicked me a bit to think that she was shagging Mark; there was an age gap of fifteen years between them. It wasn't the number of years that was the issue, but she seemed so youthful that it felt a little like Mark had taken advantage of her.

Liam's neutrality when providing the information was refreshing. Before I'd de-manned my ex, he'd displayed barely concealed dislike bordering on rudeness, so it was an improvement. Dead body or not, the day was looking up.

'You were friends with Mark,' I started.

He snorted. 'No one was friends with Mark. He was number two – three, after you arrived. He took competitive edge to a whole new level, and he was always ready to come down hard if there were any pack infractions. I toed the line so we didn't have any issues.' He trailed off and I sensed the 'but'.

'Who did have issues with him?'

'Cassie, for one. She's a spitfire. She believed in marriage for life. Mark disagreed.'

'He initiated the split?'

'That's the way he portrayed it.'

'Who else had a beef with Mark?'

'Easier to ask who didn't,' Liam muttered. 'Noah and Mark had a few issues.' He looked at me reluctantly. 'And Elena,' he admitted finally.

I'd seen Liam, Elena and Archie hanging out. They were friends, and it felt like a big deal that Liam was willing to admit that they'd had a problem with Mark.

'And David.' Marissa joined the conversation, though she stared determinedly past my shoulder.

Liam nodded. 'Yeah, I guess David too. Though it's hard to see him doing anything about it.'

'What about drugs?'

They met each other's eyes and looked away again. Neither of them looked at me. Okay then.

Then the living room door burst open, and Manners was on his feet with a gun drawn before I could blink.

Chapter 8

Manners' gun was raised and pointing at the intruder. Where had he been hiding it? His T-shirt was painted on and I hadn't notice any weird bulges. Some not-so-weird bulges, maybe…

'It's not true!' the woman shouted as she marched in. 'I don't believe it.' She ignored Manners and me. 'Liam, it's not true, is it?'

He started towards her. 'I'm so sorry, Cassie. I saw his body myself.'

'Me too,' Marissa muttered, looking green.

Cassie drew shaking hands up to her lips. 'No,' she moaned through her fingers.

'I'm sorry,' Liam repeated softly, his eyes sympathetic. He may not have liked Mark but he obviously had some affection for Cassie.

'Let me see him! I need to see him!' She started for the door to the corridor but Liam pulled her back and into his arms. 'You don't want to see, Cass.'

'You really don't,' agreed Marissa, swallowing hard.

I studied Mark's ex-wife carefully. She had mousy-brown hair streaked with the odd wiry grey; her skin was well-cared for but showed her age – I'd have put her in her mid-thirties, the same as Mark. She was athletic in build and she was dressed in workout clothes. She looked to be in great shape.

'I need to see his body. I won't believe it's true, not until I see his body. It can't be true. Not Mark!'

I stepped forward. 'You don't want to see him just now. He doesn't look like the Mark you know. Let the coroner and undertaker do their thing, then pay your respects. You can't unsee death like that. Remember Mark as he was – strong and vibrant.' And a total asshole. 'That's what he would have wanted.'

She gave me a look full of scorn. 'And what do you know about death?'

I gave her a warning look; grieving or not, she still needed to show me the respect that the alpha title deserved. 'I saw a great deal of death when Lord Samuel and I fought with the Rain pack, just us two to their fifty.' Of course I'd had other allies, but she didn't need to know that right now. 'Suffice to say, there was plenty of death dealt that day.'

Cassie glared. 'Including Lord Samuel's,' she said stridently. Finally, someone had voiced the words that the whole pack had been thinking for weeks.

I nodded solemnly. 'Yes. And if I had to do it all over again, I would. I might be a new werewolf, but Jimmy Rain was something else. If he were alpha, things here would be very different.'

'If he were alpha, Mark would still be alive!' she accused.

I shook my head. 'No, Jimmy Rain would have killed Mark straight away.' Everything I knew about Rain suggested he would have got rid of anyone he deemed a threat. If Mark had been sniffing around the alpha role, Rain would have killed him. Simple.

Silence fell; no one disagreed with my assessment. It was the first time that I'd spoken openly about what had happened. I saw Liam exchange meaningful glances with Marissa.

I turned the topic back to Mark. I needed to question Cassie because she was Steve's number-one suspect and I didn't know when I'd get the chance to speak to her again.

This was the first time I'd seen her at the mansion, courtesy of that restraining order, I guess.

I gestured for her to sit and she obeyed reluctantly. Liam and Marissa sat next to her and I sat on the sofa opposite with Manners. Dammit: once again it was us versus them.

'I need to ask you some questions. I'm sorry about that, but no one else knew Mark as well as you did,' I said, slathering on the flattery.

Cassie nodded. 'Of course,' she replied in a more reasonable tone of voice. 'I want to see his killer brought to justice.' As she stumbled over the word killer, Liam reached out and linked his fingers through hers. It was an effort to stop my eyebrows from meeting my hairline.

'Do you know anyone who had a grudge against Mark?' I asked.

She snorted, 'Don't be ridiculous. Everyone loved Mark. He was number two in the pack.' She sat straighter. 'Of course he had to enforce Lord Samuel's rule, but he was always firm but fair. People respected him.'

Marissa gave a small eyeroll which Cassie caught. 'They did,' she insisted. 'A few people might not have liked his methods, and there were a few naysayers. You'd know about that, if you'd been here more than five minutes,' she sniped at me.

Esme growled and in my mind I saw her bare her teeth. I ignored Cassie's comment and silently told my wolf to settle down. She growled more loudly.

'Tell me about the naysayers.'

'That's Mark's business,' she retorted.

'Mark's business became my business when he died under my roof.'

'You leave him and his reputation alone,' she snarled.

It was interesting that she'd become so defensive. There was obviously dirt to find. 'I won't fling mud at his reputation. He's dead, so it serves no purpose,' I reassured her. 'But I do intend to find his killer and bring them to justice.'

Cassie eyed me scornfully. 'You? You couldn't mete out justice. You're a tiny waif of a thing.'

I'm not, Esme growled.

She hasn't seen you, I pointed out. Cassie wasn't there during our showdown with James. I'd earned some circumspection from those who were, but apparently the news hadn't spread as far as Cassie.

I smiled, not in a friendly way but more of a queen-bitch smile. 'I'm built like an athlete and so is my wolf. She'd be more than happy to show you the justice she can mete out...' I let the threat hang in the air.

Cassie held my gaze for a long moment before she looked down and away. It was a submissive sign and Esme crowed in triumph.

'Tell me about Mark's drug habit,' I continued.

Cassie shook her head. 'Drugs? He didn't take drugs. He used steroids a few years ago, but that's all. He was strong even by wolf standards, so he stopped the steds years ago. Nowadays the strongest thing he takes is paracetamol.'

Marissa smirked, but this time Cassie didn't catch it. I did. Marissa knew something about the little pink bags of Boost; I'd question her later about that, one on one.

'Tell me about his naysayers,' I repeated.

She glared. 'Mark was Lord Samuel's enforcer – and Lord Samuel didn't like getting his hands dirty.' Her tone was a tad bitter. 'Mark got his hands and his soul dirty for him.'

I thought of Manners because I was guilty of doing exactly the same thing. Maybe it was the alpha way to give orders whilst sitting pretty up on high? 'So who had Mark told off recently?'

'There was the issue with the pups and the dryads, the spat with those vampyrs, and the usual problems with the pipers.' She reeled the incidents off effortlessly, one after the other.

I didn't know about *any* of those things. I hate admitting ignorance and I'd worked hard to increase my knowledge since I'd been turned, spending most evenings in the Samuel library reading up on all things Other. I wasn't sure all of it was true – gargoyles singing and causing madness in humans, and griffins driven mad by their bloodlust if it were not sated – it all seemed a little far-fetched to me. However, I wouldn't have been surprised by anything in this crazy realm I'd found myself in.

I knew a little about dryads. They are literally green fingered, green bodied and green faced, varying in shade from eau de nil to dark jade. They have an affinity with plants and trees – hell, they can even *sink* into a tree and become one.

Dryads are classified as 'creatures', which means they don't have triangles on their foreheads like us wolves and they don't need to go to the Common for a recharge. From what I'd read, they go to a tree to fill up their magical batteries. A lot of dryads work in garden centres, nurseries or as park rangers. Mark was a park ranger; maybe there was something to dig into there, though as far as I knew the werewolves and dryads tended to get along fine.

'Tell me about the dryad thing,' I ordered.

Cassie's look was patronising, her body language suggesting that I should know about it already. Esme growled. I narrowed my eyes a little and the ex started talking.

'The dryads are based in Black Park.' Black Park is the pack's main stomping ground, where we go to run and let off steam in our wolf forms. The mansion has plenty of grounds but they are largely manicured and limited; wolves need miles to roam and there isn't enough space here for free running. The woods around the mansion are sparse.

'There have been a few incidents,' Cassie continued. 'The dryads requested a meet with Lord Samuel, but he sent Mark instead. Apparently they were accusing some of our younger wolves of straying into dryad territory.'

'And were they?' I asked.

She smirked. 'You'll have to ask the younger werewolves.'

I couldn't imagine Mark being particularly diplomatic or tactful, and I wondered why Lord Samuel had sent him. He would surely have poured petrol on any flame .

'Archie?' I asked.

'Amongst others.'

That made more sense; it would be hard for Lord Samuel to appear impartial if the accused was his own son. I doubted he'd have wanted to chastise Archie when they finally appeared to be getting on. From what Jess had told me, Archie had been a drug-taking, indolent lout. He'd only recently stepped up to the plate and been blooded. He ranked twelfth, and he'd steadied once he'd taken his place in the pack.

'And the issue with the vampyrs?'

'The Wokeshire clan. Nothing unusual in us having beef with the local vamps.' Cassie gave me a flat look, like I was an idiot.

'Sure,' I said easily. 'But according to the Connection, we're all supposed to be playing nicely and getting along like one happy, fuzzy family. So what's the current issue that sent Mark a-knocking?'

'One of ours was set upon by five vampyrs. They were only playing or they'd have killed him, but Amber had to be called.' 'Playing' seemed like a poor word for assault, especially if it was bad enough to call a healer rather than relying on a wolf's natural restorative powers.

'Which wolf was attacked?'

'Noah.'

'And the names of the vampyrs?'

She snorted. 'They didn't exchange names and telephone numbers. It was an *attack*.' Her lack of respect was grating on Esme, and I was working hard to stop us from lunging across and slamming Cassie's snarky little head onto the coffee table.

She's grieving, I calmed Esme. *Cut her some slack.*

I have. She's not bleeding.

Yet.

Cassie must have caught some of the wolf lurking in my eyes because she looked down and away again, put her hands in her lap and hunched down, making herself smaller.

I cleared my throat and made sure my tone was even. 'And the pipers?'

'Same issue as always.' Her voice was softer now and she was still looking down. Esme gave a little sound of contentment; finally, Cassie was taking us seriously.

'The upstart little piper shits used us in a prank, a rite of adulthood for the younger ones. "See if you can pipe a wolf, I bet you can't",' she said in a sing-song voice. 'There's been a spate of attempted pipings on our more vulnerable pups. Mark had words with the local pipers – in his human form,' she hastened to add.

'Words?' Manners asked.

She smirked. 'Lord Samuel always insisted on coming down quite hard on that kind of thing. Mark will have told them that if the piping didn't stop, he'd rip the little pipers to shreds when they were next in Common. Mark didn't need his claws in order to be lethal.'

I had a fair amount of experience when it came to pipers. I'd been dog-sitting Gato, Jess's hellhound, when a local piper had lured him away. It turned out that Gato had deliberately allowed himself to be lured, but the initial distrust of pipers had triggered something in my mind. It was unfortunate that I was now a piper – a closely guarded secret that I wouldn't be spilling any time soon – because it made me nervous about talking to them. What if they could tell somehow that I was one of them?

Like most things Other, I still didn't know my ass from my elbow. In piper terms, I barely had my training wheels off. I hadn't refined my skills; at the moment I needed to be physically touching an animal I wanted to speak to.

Lisette, Emory's ex-girlfriend, had grudgingly shown me the basics. I'd used my skills a time or two, notably once on a giant ouroboros, but apart from that my ability to talk to animals was something I hid away. Sooner or later, being both a piper and a werewolf would put me on a headlong collision course with conflict. I hoped it would be later.

Chapter 9

Questioning Cassie ended abruptly as the scene of crime officers wheeled out Mark's body in a black body bag. I glared at them. They could have checked the way was clear before rolling the corpse through the house.

Cassie dissolved into sobs. Liam looked away. Was he uncomfortable – or guilty? I met Marissa's eyes and nodded towards Cassie. Marissa's mouth twisted in a moue of distaste, but she obligingly shuffled closer and embraced her. There seemed to be no great affection between the two, and for some reason that comforted me. Mine wasn't the only rift in the pack.

Mrs Dawes bustled in, a frown lining her face. She went into the hallway and moments later we heard her giving

Steve and the remainder of the SOCO team a dressing down. She used the word 'decorum' a lot.

She marched back in, and her eyes softened as she took in Cassie. 'Come on, love,' she murmured. 'Let's get you some cake.'

Marissa happily relinquished her hold on the grieving widow but also followed Mrs Dawes out to the kitchen. I guess she needed cake, too. I didn't blame her: I was craving some sugar. Maybe I could snaffle some ice cream later.

Liam rose and went out to the dormitory corridor, presumably to his bedroom. I let him go for now. The living room was comfortable, but it wasn't one of 'my' areas.

I stood up and gestured for Manners to follow me. We wound our way through the mansion to what was Lord Samuel's old office. It is mine now. It's still decidedly masculine, all leather and beiges, but I've put in some brightly coloured cushions and plants and I feel like I've put my stamp on the room. It would probably be crass to roll out the paint just yet; I should wait a few more weeks before painting it a calming sage or a nice duck-egg blue. Interior design is important to me, and I'm itching to do some renovations on the mansion. All in good time.

I sat behind the expansive mahogany desk. Manners lifted the heavy chair opposite and turned it so he was sitting at an angle and could see me, the windows and the door.

He was never off duty. He studied me carefully. 'Are you okay?' he asked.

Was he concerned about me? That was nice – surprising, but nice. 'Right as rain,' I responded flippantly.

What is right about rain? Esme complained. **It makes you wet and cold and smell bad. No one likes rain.**

Farmers like rain, I countered.

Esme snorted. **They plant things in mud.** Her tone suggested they were deranged.

Yes, food. It's helpful.

Food should be hunted, she said firmly.

I was at a loss how to respond, so I didn't. Manners was watching me curiously. I'd been silent for too long. That made me blurt out something that had been playing on my mind. 'If I gave you an order and Emory countermanded it, whose order would you follow?'

There was a very long pause. Shit.

Manners shook his head. 'I don't know,' he admitted finally. 'But I promise you this – I will never follow an order from Emory that would put you or the pack in danger. You don't know Emory, but he would never order me to do something that would put me in a shitty position like that. He hasn't given me an order since I've been here. You and I don't know each other properly yet, but I've given you my oath and my loyalty. I promise you, you won't need anything else.'

I felt a visceral thrill at that. I believed him. In my head, Esme purred loudly. Having command of a man like Manners was the stuff of dreams.

I searched around for a topic that would distract me from how breathless I suddenly felt. 'How come you don't call me Toots?' I asked.

He blinked, but that was all the surprise he showed. Note to self: do not play poker with Manners.

'Ah ... you're my boss?' he said finally.

'You called Jess "Toots".'

'I was trying to provoke a reaction, see what she was made of. She'll face a lot more adversity than a little name calling for dating the Prime Elite. Calling my boss names is disrespectful.'

I sighed. 'I kind of need you to be a bit disrespectful to your boss now and again. You're the only one I can trust, and I need a friend more than I need an obedient automaton. In front of the pack, you can ma'am me all you like, but behind closed doors call me names. Tell me the truth. I don't need a yes-man.'

He watched me for a long moment before nodding, leaned back until he was slumped in the chair and crossed one leg over his other knee. It was only then that I realised he'd been sitting to attention. 'Alright. We've got a dead packmate. What do we intend to do about it?' he asked.

'We're going to find the fucker that killed him and bring him to justice.'

'And justice means ... what?'

I thought about it. I didn't trust the Connection, not after everything Jess and Emory had told me about them. I trusted Steve as an individual, but that wasn't enough, not when the corruption Jess had warned me about seemed to be endemic. 'We bring him to justice,' I repeated. 'Pack justice.'

'So we're going to get our hands dirty.' He looked pointedly at my manicured nails. 'Are you good with that?'

'I have to be, or I'm not going to survive as alpha for more than a New York minute. I'm a werewolf, an alpha. I'm not an accountant, not anymore.' I could mourn my career later, not now. 'If I'm going to make it, I'm going to need to toughen up.'

'You're tougher than you give yourself credit for, Toots.'

You are, Esme agreed. **And I definitely am.**

I rolled my eyes. 'Don't call me Toots.'

'You just told me to call you Toots.'

'No, I said knock off the ma'ams and be my friend. Toots is your thing with Jess. We need a new thing. An "us" thing. Be original.'

He smirked. 'Noted, sweetheart.'

'Ugh. Too patronising.'

He laughed. 'You're difficult to please.' It was the first time I'd noticed him laughing. It was nice.

'I have standards.' I sniffed and pretended to poke my nose in the air, but secretly I was pleased. Our little chat seemed to have broken the formality between us and I needed that desperately. Jess was two hundred miles away and she had her own crap to contend with. I needed a pal in this strange and violent realm I'd stumbled into. I didn't know the rules and regulations; I barely knew how to be a werewolf. I had Esme, thank goodness, but I needed more than an amusing inner monologue to keep me sane. Manners was it.

'I guess I should start thinking of you as Greg.'

'That works, given that it's my name.'

I shot him a mock glare. 'Funny guy.'

He grinned. 'I am. You're going to love my sense of humour.'

I smiled in genuine response. Here was the guy I'd glimpsed at Jess's house: relaxed, joking and jovial. Maybe he needed this as much as me. 'You're a laugh a minute,' I agreed.

He winked.

There was a knock on the door. Manners was instantly upright in his chair, almost vibrating with contained energy. His gun had appeared again; this time I saw him remove it from his ankle holster. 'Come,' I called.

Mrs Dawes entered. 'The council's here, dear.'

Fantastic timing. 'How many?'

'Two delegates, but only one of them is the council member.' She took pity on my blank expression. 'The council member is Adam Frost. Everyone calls him "Ace". He's part of the Devon pack where his brother, Beckett, is the alpha. Ace is his second. Ace has been part of the council for the last three years. Rumour has it that Beckett pulled some strings to get his brother out of his hair before Ace was tempted to challenge him.'

She gave a little shrug. 'Like most council members, Ace has got his own support team. Only a fool would wander into another wolf pack without backup. He introduced today's backup as Lauren Gallagher. She also works for the council. I haven't heard of her, but presumably he trusts her.'

'She's sixth in the Devon pack, and both she and Ace have diplomatic immunity,' Manners warned. 'They have to be able to carry out their investigations without fear of reprisals. If you have a problem with either of them, you report it to the council and they investigate internally.'

'So I have two rival top dogs coming into my house, and if they piss me off I can't do anything about it?'

'That's about the size of it,' Manners agreed.

'Fuck's sake,' I muttered. 'Just what I need.'

'I'm sure they'll be in and out of our hair before we know it,' said Mrs Dawes.

Somehow I didn't share her optimism, especially with the complication of Mark's unfortunate demise.

We can kill them and hide the bodies, Esme said confidently.

I smiled. She always had a solution – mostly killing someone – and I liked her upbeat attitude.

'Alright, let's face the music.' I pushed away from the desk. 'Have you shown them to my living room?'

Mrs Dawes nodded. I was grateful she'd had the forethought to take them there rather than to the lounge, which probably still smelled of James's blood.

Manners and I marched down the hall. Liam was loitering outside the living room; I raised an eyebrow, questioning his presence. 'I'll come in with you,' he offered uncomfortably. 'Then you'll have three to their two.'

I resisted the urge to beam at him or pull him into a giant hug, both of which he would probably have scorned, but it was so damn refreshing to be treated with anything other than derision.

'Appreciate it,' I said laconically. 'Let's go greet our guests.'

And here's hoping that they weren't here to stir up trouble.

Chapter 10

My living room is bright, airy and painted a warm yellow. It has a fireplace and floor-to-ceiling bookshelves which I find incredibly useful. The focal point of the room is the three sofas around the fireplace.

My guests had seated themselves so they had full view of the door and the windows. That put us on the back foot, even though we were on home turf.

I appraised them. Lauren had dyed her hair a black-purple colour and, with her pale skin, it made her look a little gothic. Maybe she and Seren could do some bonding.

Ace was muscle-bound and dressed in jeans and a shirt – the casual werewolf. It was no exaggeration to say that he was ridiculously handsome: he had a square jawline, tanned skin, ginger hair and green eyes. If I hadn't known he was a werewolf, I'd have thought he was a vampyr because he was so perfect.

He smiled warmly and stood up. Lauren followed suit, reluctance in every line of her body. I guess they'd agreed on a good cop, bad cop routine.

'Lucy,' Ace greeted me familiarly. He touched his right hand to his heart and gave a shallow bow. 'You may call me Ace. It is my honour to meet you,' he intoned. He ignored Manners and Liam, which said something right away. Smiley as he was, he thought the others were beneath him even though Manners was a second, too.

I copied his gesture and gave him a similar-level bow. 'My honour to meet you,' I responded with a cool smile. I didn't acknowledge his underling either: two could play at that game. 'Please be seated.' I sat on the sofa opposite the one they'd taken, Manners to my left and Liam to my right.

Christ, was I supposed to do small talk? That hadn't been covered in the wolf handbook.

Be silent, Esme urged. **Let him yip first. He is in _our_ den.**

I didn't know if she was right or not, but she hadn't led me astray yet so I fixed a warm smile on my face and waited. The silence dragged out, long and uncomfortable, but I let it ride. Manners sat statue-still next to me.

Finally, Ace let out a soft laugh. 'And you said she wouldn't know our ways,' he murmured to Lauren, his lips barely moving. For whatever reason, he didn't expect me to hear it.

He raised his voice. 'Well met, alpha. The council greets you and welcomes you in your new role. We have been sent here as a mere formality, to review the conditions of your turning and the passing of Lord Wilfred Samuel. Are there any other issues we should discuss?'

His tone was too knowing; he already knew about Mark. I didn't know how, but I was certain he did. This was a test. What was it with werewolves and their bloody tests?

Matters of pack importance should be discussed after a hunt, Esme said firmly. **Whilst we rip into the carcass of the hunted.**

Over dinner?

That's what I said, she huffed impatiently. **Let's run with them, then eat with them, then we will yap about pack matters.**

'There is much to discuss,' I acknowledged coolly. 'Tonight we will run and hunt together, then we will talk.' I stood. 'Meanwhile, rest and explore the grounds. You are welcome in our mansion. Our housekeeper will show you to your rooms.'

Ace stood and bowed his head in acknowledgement. Manners and Liam followed me out. We walked down the corridor into my office, shutting the heavy door firmly behind us. I sat behind the mahogany desk. Manners positioned himself so he could see all exits and entrances, and Liam took the other seat.

Liam was looking at me with open surprise. 'How did you know to hold silent? You haven't met any other packs yet.'

'I'm full of surprises,' I said drily.

'And inviting them on the hunt?' he continued, bemused.

I didn't deign to respond. I couldn't tell him that I was a piper and I had my very own wolf guide helping me to navigate the murky pack waters. And it was interesting that Liam had been willing to sit with me but hadn't warned me about the protocol. He might not hate me anymore, but he still wasn't completely on Team Lucy. I'd wear him down.

He cleared his throat and stood up. 'I'll ready the pack for a full hunt and alert the dryads to our presence tonight in Black Park.'

I nodded, like I had expected him to take such action, and he gave a small bow before he exited, carefully shutting the door behind him. That was a significant improvement in his behaviour, and I dared to feel a glimmer of hope.

Manners lounged back into his seat. 'How did you know about the silence thing? I didn't know that, and I've been in the Other my whole life.'

I studied him for a long moment. I'd asked him to be my friend and my ally; keeping secrets isn't the healthiest thing in a true friendship...

'I'm a piper,' I explained, 'so I can talk directly to my wolf. She told me what to do.'

He froze. 'You can converse with her?' There was wonder in his voice.

I nodded.

'All I get from my wolf is emotions – distrust, happiness, anger,' he said slowly. 'Nothing more, just flashes that can guide me. When I'm in the Other I can feel my wolf all the time, like a heavy coat wrapped around me. Being in the Common is almost a relief to feel that weight lift.'

His gaze was assessing. 'It's a huge advantage to be able to talk to your wolf. When I turn, we have to wrestle for supremacy. Each time we seem to manage a compromise. When we're on four legs, he guides our body but I still control our mind – just about. But every single time I turn, I have to fight him. I can feel him wanting to take over.'

'There's no battle between Esme and me.'

'Esme?' He smirked. 'Your wolf is called Esme? Not Fang or Claw, or something dramatic?'

'My name is Lucy, and she wanted a name that was nice like mine. Anyway, her name is just for us. When we turn, she has full control.'

'What?' He was genuinely surprised.

'I sit back and let her have the reins. Why not? I have the reins when we're on two legs, she has them when we're on four. We're equal partners. I trust her and she trusts me.'

'That might be part of the reason why your change is so quick,' Manners mused. 'You're not fighting it from the minute it starts. You wholly embrace it – and your wolf.'

'Maybe you should try giving your wolf the reins.'

He shook his head. 'No. He's bloodthirsty. He just wants to run and hunt.'

'So does Esme,' I confirmed. 'We hunt first to sate that bloodlust, then we focus on whatever else needs to be done. It helps us after the change if we've eaten on the hunt, then we're not cripplingly hungry when we turn back to two legs.'

'Makes sense, but I'm still not going to try that any time soon.'

I thought it was a mistake, but not something we needed to argue about. We needed to be on the same page. Besides, he was probably right that now wasn't the best time to set his wolf free, not when we had guests scrutinising our every move. Sexy smile or not, I didn't doubt that Ace was watching our every move.

I changed the topic. 'What security do we have in place at the mansion?'

Manners grimaced. 'It's piss poor, to be honest. I was going to talk to you about an upgrade. There's a camera over the main entrance and exit, but that's it. Anyone can drop from the balconies to the ground below, even in human form.'

'Have you reviewed the footage?'

'Not yet, but I can do that now.'

'Can you order some new security for us?'

He considered my proposal. 'If I order it through a company, it'll probably take a week or two to be installed. If I utilise my connections in the brethren, I can get it done tomorrow.'

'I don't want to owe the brethren,' I said.

'I can get them to charge,' he suggested. 'It's just that then we can do it expeditiously with equipment I already know.'

I wondered whether the 'we' referred to Manners and me, or Manners and the brethren.

I weighed it up. I wasn't sure how well my pack would take to having brethren swarming all over the place putting in cameras, but it didn't feel safe and my job was to protect the pack. Finally I said, 'Get it done tomorrow. Make sure the brethren invoice for their time.'

'I'll put in the order now and review the existing footage. We've got a few hours before we leave for the hunt.'

'Clear the order for security with Emory first,' I suggested. 'I don't want to step on his toes.'

'He won't mind,' Manners reassured me. 'You're his mate's best friend.' He saw my warning look and held up his hands. 'I'll clear it with him.' As he went to the heavy door, he looked back to meet my eyes and a small smile tugged at his lips. 'Catch you later, Peach.' The absurd nickname startled a laugh out of me and he grinned as he shut the door.

I was alone again – as alone as I ever was in the Other. Something else had been pulling at my mind for days now, and I'd been too cowardly to deal with it. Today seemed to be a 'getting shit done' day, so I braced myself, pulled out my phone and dialled my mum's number.

She answered on the second ring. 'Lucy! How are you doing, my love?' There was a time when that question was just a greeting, but now I could hear her underlying anxiety. Mum still hadn't forgotten my brush with death. Without being able to tell her how I'd miraculously recovered by becoming a werewolf, my explanations had sounded somewhat hollow. I'd vaguely cited experimental treatment at the legendary Hoppas Centre, but my recovery was so fast that it was strange to ordinary humans.

Not that my mum is ordinary; she isn't, she's wonderful. She's the most caring person around, with an edge of no bullshit that she's refined to an art. Mum is a nurse, which was partly why she'd struggled to accept my miraculous recovery when she knew I'd been in organ failure.

'I'm good, Ma.' I hesitated. 'I've been meaning to talk to you about this for a while, but there never seems to be a good time.'

'Just spit it out, love.'

'My adoption papers. Can I have a copy? When I was sick, I wished I knew more about my birth parents. If I'd known their medical history, maybe it wouldn't have happened.' I knew that was bullshit; I'd been laid low by a succubus, not a mysterious hereditary condition I knew nothing about. But it had opened a can of worms I thought I'd sealed shut long ago.

'Of course you can,' Mum said instantly.

'It's not that I don't think of you one hundred percent as my mum, it's just that there's this void that hangs over me sometimes. I can't remember a thing from my first three years of life. I know I was young – but nothing?

You'd think I'd have a scent, or a sound, or a glimpse of a memory...'

Mum's tone was even. 'The human mind is an amazing thing, Lucy. It goes to great lengths to protect itself.'

'You think I came from an abusive home,' I said flatly.

'Not exactly, no. When we got you there was nothing in your medicals to suggest that. You appeared to be completely healthy and well looked after.'

I sensed the 'but'. 'But?'

'But it took you several months to speak to us. You took to Ben right away, and we'd often find you snuggled in his bed after we'd put you in your own room. We were told you were an only child, but that didn't seem right because you were so happy with other children. You were happiest snuggled with Ben by the fire, or in big playgroups and classes. You were sociable even when you were silent, but you were reserved with your father and me. For a long time.'

Mum had said in the past that I was a quiet child but we'd never talked frankly about my childhood. All I could remember were nights spent snuggling with Ben, and Mum and Dad being very kind. I didn't remember ever distrusting them or not liking them. 'That must have been hard for you,' I offered lamely.

'You were healthy and happy with Ben. Adopting a child is always a big deal, and you never really know what your child has experienced. We were prepared for it to be a hard road – and it wasn't hard for long, Lucy. You soon started to love us. You were shy with us at first, but you warmed up and we've never looked back or regretted it. You've been our daughter since you walked in our door. It just took a while for us all to settle.'

My heart constricted painfully in my chest. 'Thanks, Mum.'

'Now,' she said briskly, 'you can have the papers, though I'm afraid they won't be much help.'

'What do you mean?'

'Your birth parents' details are all gone.'

'Gone?'

'Yes,' she confirmed. 'It's the oddest thing. I remember seeing the completed papers quite clearly. The details are fuzzy but I'm *sure* they were completed. Anyway, when you were sick I dug them out and they were blank. I thought perhaps the ink had faded, but my details and your father's were there, so it seemed odd. I applied to the agency for another copy and they sent me the same document – complete with blank spaces. Your parents' names and dates of birth are gone. The agency apologised profusely, but it seems they haven't retained a complete copy of your papers.'

I slumped back dejectedly in my chair. 'So that's it?'

'As I said, you can have the copy of what I've got. Perhaps Jess could do some digging for you?'

I brightened. 'That's a great idea! If anyone can find out something, it's Jess.'

I changed the topic and we chatted about Ben and his latest love interest. Mum wasn't too fussed about her. We talked about Dad's latest baking endeavours, and it did me good to chat about normal things. Thankfully, Mum didn't harangue me about taking up my old job again. She couldn't wrap her head around my decision to quit being an accountant to become warden of an old mansion instead.

'How are you getting on with the mansion occupants?' she asked.

'Better,' I said happily. 'I think I'm making some headway.'

'I'm glad to hear it. You're a social soul, and you can win over anyone if you put your mind to it.'

Except grumpy werewolf packs. 'I'm trying,' I agreed.

'Trust isn't built overnight. I'd better go, darling. My shift starts in an hour and I need to get cracking.'

'Okay, Mum. Love you.'

'Love you, Lucy Caboosy.'

We rang off, then I blew out a breath and dialled Jess. No time like the present.

Chapter 11

'Hey!' Jess greeted me happily.

'Hey. You okay?'

'I'm great. I wrapped up a tricky case this morning.'

'Congratulations. Anything juicy?'

'A kiddie kidnap, actually.'

I winced. 'Ugh, horrible.'

'It was, but it all ended happily.'

'I'm glad to hear about it. Talking about kids – I want to look into my birth parents.'

There was a beat of silence on the other end. Jess had offered to dig into them for me many a time, and I'd said no just as many times. 'How come?' she asked finally.

'The whole dying thing has made me realise I want to know. I *need* to know. I was pretending to myself that it doesn't matter, but it does. I know who raised me, who loved me. I know Mum and Dad are my parents, and nothing will ever reduce what they have done for me, or who they are in my life. But I want to know more – who gave birth to me and why they gave me away.'

'Knowledge is a double-edged sword,' she cautioned. 'Once you know the truth, you can't unknow it.' She paused. 'Unless we get your mind wiped.'

'Let's not mess with my synapses. They hardly work as it is.'

Jess huffed. 'You're the brightest person I know, maybe with the exception of Fritz.' Fritz is a child prodigy who specialises in information gathering and hacking. There was no doubt in my mind that Fritz was brighter than me.

'The thing is, my mum said my adoption record is partially blank. She thought the entries had faded away, but when she hit up the agency they didn't have a complete copy either.'

'That's weird. Adoption agencies have everything in triplicate. A paperwork trail is essential. Leave it with me.'

'Do you need me to get the name of the agency from Mum?'

'Nah. I know your name and national insurance number. I'll be able to find it.'

'And why do you know my national insurance number?' I demanded archly.

'Just in case you ever gave me the green light,' she admitted.

'You're the best. Send my love to Gato and Emory. Oh, Manners is going to hit up the brethren for some security cameras.'

'I know. He already rang and spoke with Emory about it. I would have insisted that they fix you up with the security, but Emory had already sorted you out with top-of-the-line stuff. They'll be there tomorrow to hook it all up.'

'Thanks, Jess, and thanks to Emory, too. While I'm calling in favours ... I could do with having an informal chat with a dryad.'

'No problem. I'll ring Joyce and see if she'll meet with you.'

'That'd be amazing. Can the meeting be on the down-low?'

'Sure, I'll see what I can sort. I'll text. Love you, Luce. Better go – Gato's whining at the door.'

'Okay. Love you.'

'I'll be in touch with any news,' Jess promised before she hung up.

I sat thinking for a few more minutes then I reached out to Esme. *Anything else I need to know about this formal hunt?*

There should be at least nine of us, including our two guests. Ideally we want a show of strength and numbers for a first hunt. She hesitated. **Thirteen would be better – that's a full paw – but I'm not sure how many of the pack will answer our call to hunt,** she admitted unhappily.

Liam is warming to us. It's a start.

We should get Archie involved. If he comes, others will follow him. She didn't sound entirely thrilled about the prospect, but if we needed thirteen we weren't going to get it without Archie's help.

Mrs Dawes knocked and bustled in with a ridiculously huge platter of sandwiches for my lunch. She assured me that the council duo were settled in the guest wing.

'Will you come on the hunt later?' I asked her. That would be another one of my thirteen secured.

She beamed at me. 'I'd be honoured.'

'I understand I need thirteen for the hunt.'

'Yes, but with those two that's only an additional eleven.'

'What would Lord Samuel have done?' I sighed.

'He would have summoned the first thirteen in the pack.'

'Okay. Do that, and you can take Mark's place.'

'I'll round them up,' she promised. 'I don't think there will be too much resistance after the … incident with the succubus.'

I hoped not. If I couldn't inspire trust and respect, hopefully I'd at least earned a bit of caution and they'd think twice before refusing me. I didn't want to rule by fear – hell, I hardly wanted to rule at all – but needs must. After all, I *did* want to survive.

'Can you arrange a late dinner for us after the hunt?' I asked.

'Of course. I'll pop a half-a-dozen chickens in the slow cookers and get everything prepped, then we can have a feast when we're back.' Mrs Dawes seemed excited by the idea of hosting a formal banquet.

'Can you set us up in the dining hall?' I asked.

Her smile widened. 'Absolutely. I'll get Marissa and Elena to help me. I'd best go and get started.'

Elena was largely an unknown quantity. I'd seen the brunette a time or two in passing, but that was it. She hadn't shown me any friendliness or opposition, just total disinterest. If anything, she seemed a bit depressed.

I wasn't sure what her story was. She had transferred from another pack; they'd held a tourney for her and she'd settled in at thirteenth in the pack. Unlucky for some, but she didn't seem to mind. I was surprised that Mrs Dawes thought she was tractable enough to help to clear out the banquet hall.

The dining hall hadn't been used since I'd been turned as a wolf. It is straight from Edwardian times: red-panelled walls, heavy parquet flooring and dark wooden furniture. The banquet table extends to seat at least twenty.

I'd found the room in my first week when I'd been snooping around. It had been closed up and everything was covered in a fine layer of dust. I guess it didn't see much use, but I planned to change that. Eating together is a social thing that I hoped would gel the pack a little more – but it would take a while for Mrs Dawes to ready the disused room.

I thanked her again. 'Can you tell Archie I want to see him?'

Mrs Dawes excused herself and I ate one of the sandwiches. I probably should have given Archie a time to present himself, but I was at a bit of loose end. Manners' suggestion that anyone could jump from the balconies to the ground had stayed with me. I decided some sniffing around the grounds might be in order.

PROTECTION OF THE PACK

I stripped in my office and let the change roll over me. Esme immediately padded to the heavy door. With hindsight, it would have been easier if I'd opened it for her before I changed but I was still getting used to this.

She snorted. **I can open doors.** She reached out with a heavy paw and dragged down on the handle. The door opened a fraction and we used our nose to widen the gap so we could slink through.

We trotted through the corridor. Marissa was in the entrance hall and she started when she saw us. 'Alpha,' she greeted. 'Let me get the door for you.'

We inclined our head and she opened it for us. I wondered vaguely who she was waiting for but then refocused on our objective. I half-expected her to slam the door shut on our tail, but she didn't.

We trotted around the outside of the house, enjoying the fresh air and our body, which moved as effortlessly as a well-oiled machine. There is nothing like the joy of flying on four legs. We were itching to go for a run but we managed to restrain ourselves. We had a different objective in mind.

Esme cautiously scented the air around us, but there was nothing to suggest there were any predators around so we continued towards Mark's balcony. It hung over us, but Esme was confident that we could leap over the railing onto it. That was something to think about for the mansion's security.

We explored the area below the balcony. The ground was hopelessly trampled. Annoyingly, the rain had washed away any lingering scents. The grass and mud were so saturated, it was difficult to see any proper prints; even so, we had evidence that someone had been here, maybe multiple someones.

To my amateur eyes, it looked like Mark's killer had left via the balcony. That reinforced the idea the killer was a third party trying to avoid detection rather than someone from the pack. One of the pack could have sauntered back into the mansion whistling loudly, and no one would have been any the wiser.

We were busy smelling the grass for leads when a new scent drifted on the air. It was incredibly strong to our sensitive nose, an eau de parfum – the height of rudeness in the werewolf community. We sneezed to get rid of as much as possible of the scent and levelled an angry stare at the intruder.

Archibald Samuel: young, insolent and grieving. I'd cut him a lot of slack to date because I'd killed his father, but Esme was in control now and she wasn't feeling as generous. She stalked over to the eighteen year old and let out a low, menacing growl that, frankly, would have made me wet myself.

He blanched and suddenly looked a lot less sure of himself. 'Sorry,' he muttered. 'I went out with some mates from Common. I should have showered, but I was told to present myself to you ASAFP.'

His voice gained in defiance and Esme slunk closer, close enough to do real damage if she wanted to. Archie swallowed hard and we heard his heart hammering. He'd seen what we could do when we were annoyed; James's mutilation was still fresh in his mind. Esme held his gaze with our bright blue eyes until he looked away, then we stepped back and trotted towards the house. She yipped to indicate he should follow.

We paused by the heavy front door, waited for him to open it and went inside. As Archie followed me into the study, his eyes picked out all of the ways I'd changed what had been his father's room.

I let the shift roll over me and he jumped. 'Christ, that's fast,' he muttered under his breath, not intending me to hear.

I dressed efficiently but unhurriedly, then slid behind the huge desk. 'Talk to me about Mark,' I ordered.

'What's to say? He was a bully and an asshole.' Archie met my eyes defiantly. 'He was trying to persuade me to challenge you, but I knew it was only because he saw us both as competition and he wanted to use me as cannon fodder to see what you were made of.'

I smiled unpleasantly. 'Lucky for us both that you didn't take the bait. I don't like killing. My wolf does, but I prefer to resolve our issues like adults.'

'Sure, like ripping off someone's cock,' he mumbled, his eyes flashing.

I leaned forward. 'I'm new to the Other but I'm learning. If you raped someone then, sure, I'd order your cock to be ripped off. Better yet, I'd do it myself. This is a powerful realm full of powerful beings, and we need to deter bad behaviour. Justice needs to be served and the Connection doesn't seem that bothered about dishing it out. Even the officer investigating Mark's death was happy to palm it off on me. So yeah, a hands-on approach is needed and I won't hesitate to get my hands dirty. But that should be the last course of action, not the first.'

Archie slumped back into the chair. 'That's something my father would have said. He didn't believe in being animalistic just because we have animals riding around in our skulls.'

Esme snorted. She didn't appreciate his disparaging tone.

'I admired Lord Samuel,' I said. 'I didn't get to know him very well, and I regret that, but I respected him. When he ordered me to kill him to stop the pack going to Jimmy Rain, I did it because he asked me to, and because I'd just watched Jimmy Rain sadistically cut into him. I knew we couldn't have a man like that in charge here. He made Mark look like an angel.'

Archie shifted uncomfortably. 'Intellectually I know you're right, but it's taking a while for my emotions to agree. If I'd been in your position, I would have done the same thing. My father would have expected it of any of us, and he was a hard man to refuse.'

'I know. And you'd just mended things between you.'

'How did you—? Jinx. Jinx told you.'

I nodded. Jess and I had discussed Archie a time or two. 'She likes you,' I offered.

He grinned, a flash of teenage exuberance. 'Yeah, she digs me.'

I tried to hide my smile. 'She's mated to the King of Dragons. Maybe don't antagonise him by suggesting Jinx has the hots for you.'

His grin faded. 'Jinx is good people. She doesn't trust many people and you're on her list, so I'm going to make a real effort to be a good pack mate from here on in. It's what my father would have wanted. How can I help you?'

It was a shift in attitude quick enough to make my head spin. 'Tell me about Mark. What was he into?'

Archie snorted. 'He was shagging Seren, but she was only the latest one. He stepped out on Cassie when they were married. He went through a phase of Boosting.' He hesitated.

'Tell me.'

'He'd take Boost then go along to black tourneys.'

I raised an eyebrow questioningly.

'You ever seen *Fight Club*?'

Of course I had; it was a great movie. '"The first rule of fight club…"'

'"Is never to talk about fight club",' he finished with a smirk. 'Right. So you've seen it. Black tourneys are like fight clubs for werewolves and other creatures. There's two ways to fight, in skin or fur. Mark preferred fur.'

That made me feel a little sick. I couldn't imagine trotting out Esme like she was nothing more than a puppet gladiator and pitching her against other wolves for fun or sport. That wasn't how the pack was supposed to be; the pack was supposed to be family, our refuge. The idea of attacking each other nauseated me.

Archie continued. 'Sometimes the fights are against other werewolves, sometimes against other creatures.'

'That's disgusting,' I spat out before I could censor myself.

Archie nodded. 'Yeah, it's sick. And the worst of it is, it's all for the Others' entertainment. Anyone – vampyrs, ogres, wizards – with a bit of cash to flash can come along and watch the animals bait each other. The only rule of a black tourney is that the only blood spilled is the competitors'. There is some serious security in place to make sure that any other vendettas are left at the door. Rumour has it the venues are runed up. If anyone tries to start something, they'll be cursed so hard they'll wish the Connection had caught them.'

'You said "competitors". Is it always a wolf that fights someone or something else?'

'No. Anyone that wants to can, but werewolf on werewolf is the most common, especially amongst the younger wolves still trying to prove themselves. I saw an ogre versus troll match once – that was grim. It took over an hour because they could both take some real heavy damage before they tapped out.'

I was relieved to hear tapping out was an option. 'So it's not to the death?'

His expression was grim. 'It's not supposed to be, but all too often it goes too far.'

'And Mark was into this shit?'

'He loved it. He travelled to London most weekends to watch or take part.'

'And he killed opponents?'

'So I hear,' Archie said soberly. 'I never saw Mark fight, though he invited me to go with him to a black tourney and I went. It was during my ... rebellious phase. I never told my father.' His mouth turned down. 'I regret that now. Dad would have kicked Mark out of the pack faster than you can say "loner".'

I'd heard of loners. Lord Samuel had warned me early on what happened to werewolves who didn't toe the pack line. Loners are wolves who've been exiled from their pack. Without pack protection, they don't tend to last long in the Other and there are few repercussions if an unaffiliated wolf is killed, even with the Connection in place. Rumour has it that vampyrs still get together to hunt loners. Human hunting would be strictly punished, but lone-wolf hunting ... the Connection turns a blind eye.

'Anyone else in our pack go the tourneys?'

'Not that I know of,' Archie said, but he looked down and away evasively.

Before I could call him on it, there was a knock on the door and Ace Beckett popped his head round with an engaging smile. 'Just wanted to check what time the hunt is,' he said lightly. 'I wouldn't want to miss it.'

His eyes swept the office casually, but I couldn't help feeling he was noting the windows and exits. His eyes lingered for too long on my filing cabinet and I made a note to ensure it was locked before I left the room.

Ace looked curiously at Archie and quirked an eyebrow at me. I ignored his unspoken enquiry; it was none of his business what I was discussing with Archie.

'We'll gather at 7pm,' I said firmly.

'Great. I'll spread the word. We'll be ready.'

'Wonderful. I'll see you later.' I dismissed him and his eyes narrowed; he obviously wasn't used to being sent away. He managed to dredge up a tight smile, turned on his heel and left, shutting the heavy door behind him. I was making friends everywhere I went these days.

Archie stood. 'I'd better go,' he muttered. 'I'm going to Rosie's to get a quick recharge before the hunt.'

'Take someone with you. And Archie – we're not done yet.'

He looked at me and looked away again. 'I don't know anything else. You'll have to ask the others.' He walked out without a backward glance.

I may be barking up the wrong tree, but I think young Archie knows more than he's saying.

There was a heavy pause. **Why would you bark at a tree?**

I paused, flummoxed. *It means I may be mistaken.*

You would be mistaken if you barked at a tree, Esme muttered. **Clearly you'd have had too much sun as a pup.**

I didn't touch that. *I think Archie knows more than he's telling us,* I tried to explain.

Well, let's pin him down until he tells us what he knows. If he doesn't, we'll rip his throat out.

That can be Plan B.

What's Plan A?

We'll watch him and see if he gives anything away.

We stalk him before we attack, she said in apparent understanding.

Something like that, I agreed. Sometimes conversing with Esme was like trying to work out a Rubik's cube whilst wearing a blindfold.

Chapter 12

I got a text from Jess: *Joyce Evergreen is free to meet with you anytime. This afternoon if that works.*

I answered in the affirmative and Jinx sent me the address of her dryad friend. I grabbed my car keys from my desk drawer and headed out. Maybe informal enquiries with the dryads would help clarify a few matters and cross one issue off my Mark list. I was killing this detective shit.

Joyce lived in a well-to-do area known as Gerrards Cross. The houses came with a million-pound price tag and offered an easy commute into London. Joyce's was part of an estate; each house was the same and each house looked well-kept and clean. Lawns were mowed and their bushes well-tended. I snickered. Juvenile, I know.

What is amusing about cutting hedges?

It's another phrase for tending the hair between your legs.

Your fur is there to keep you warm. You'd think you'd want to keep what little you have. Humans are strange creatures.

That made me laugh more. She wasn't wrong. *It's tradition,* I explained when I'd finished giggling. I'd learned that Esme would accept anything strange if I told her it was a tradition. Apparently wolves are big on tradition, and it doesn't need to make sense.

Ah. Well then. Satisfied with my explanation, she settled down in my mind.

I raised my hand and knocked at the slate-grey door. A woman opened it. She was probably in her early thirties, with dark-green skin and contrasting blonde hair. She smiled warmly at me. 'You must be Lucy. Come on in. Jinx said you're in a pickle.'

A pickle seemed a mild way to describe the brutal murder of one of my pack mates, but we're British. We'd describe a torrential downpour as a 'spot of rain'.

'Just a little pickle,' I agreed. I kicked off my shoes and followed her in. 'No kids about?' Jess had mentioned that she had two little ones.

'My neighbour has them for me sometimes to give me a short break.' Joyce led me into the lounge, absently picking up toys from the floor as she went.

Jess had been hired to find Joyce's husband's killer; she'd got the job done and found Joyce the answers and closure that she needed. Even so, Joyce had been left a single parent to young kids. I could only begin to imagine how hard that must be.

'I'm sorry for your loss,' I said awkwardly. 'Jess mentioned you'd lost your husband.' The phrase 'losing your loved one' always makes me think you've accidentally misplaced them, like you've lost track of them on a walk in the hills, but these trite phrases were expected. I felt a genuine sympathy for Joyce; I'd seen grief destroy Jess, and it was only recently that she'd truly put herself back together.

Joyce gave me a stiff smile. 'Thanks,' she replied. 'How can I help you?' She got straight to the point and I appreciated that. She probably could sense my awkwardness.

'I'm new to the position of alpha of the Home Counties pack. I gather there's some tension between my wolves and the dryads at the moment.'

She tucked a strand of hair behind her ears. 'I don't know how frank to be,' she said finally.

'As Frank as Sinatra.'

She sent me a faint smile. 'Your younglings have been straying into dryad territory at Black Park. We're normally fairly flexible about these things, as long as no harm comes to our trees, but...' She hesitated.

'Go on.'

'They've been daring each other, egging each other on. We shrugged it off at first – harmless younglings screwing about, kids will be kids no matter what species they are. But just recently they came into our heartlands and one of them urinated on our elder tree.'

Her outrage was palpable; she was ramrod straight in her chair and her cheeks were flushed with anger. 'The elder tree!' she repeated indignantly. 'The dryad commune reported it to your pack. Lord Samuel would normally have smoothed out such issues and the younglings would be taken to task so that no one would dare transgress again, for a few months at least. But this time Lord Samuel didn't come. Mark Oates came instead.' Her eyes narrowed. 'He walked right up to the elder tree and he also pissed on it.'

My mouth dropped open. 'He did *what*?'

She nodded, her mouth set in a grim line. 'He urinated on the elder tree. When he was finished, he spat on it. He said the younglings could go where they liked in Black Park, and then he walked out.'

Joyce met my eyes unhappily. 'The commune is due to meet and the pack's fate will be decided. I fear our truce is at an end. There have been enough tensions lately between the humans and the creatures, but to have your second relieve himself on the elder tree... That is not a youngling's infraction.'

'No, it is not,' I agreed hotly. I shot to my feet. 'Can you take me to the commune, or to the elder tree, or to whoever I have to apologise to?'

Some of the tension left her shoulders. 'Let me make some calls.' She stepped out of the room and shut the door. Her landline phone was in the hallway; my wolf-enhanced hearing is so good, even when I'm in human form, that I could hear her side of the conversation even through the closed doors. It was clear that she was begging on my behalf for them to meet with me, but the outrage ran deep and they didn't want to give me the opportunity to apologise.

I texted Jess. *Can you ask Emory for the proper way to apologise to some dryads? A real grovelling apology. x*

What did you do? X

Not me. The dead guy literally pissed on their elder tree. I don't know what an elder tree is but it seems like a big deal. X

Oh jeez. Emory says you couldn't manage a worse insult for a dryad, other than spitting on it too. They water the elder tree with blessed spring water – there's a whole ceremony. They believe the tree guides and protects them. They marry and honour their dead in the shade of the elder tree. Emory suggests the only thing that can even start to help is to take a young sapling to plant in recognition of the insult. And you must offer to tend it. If the sapling takes, then the insult is forgiven. If it dies…x

Oh man. Mark spat on it too. What happens if the tree dies? x

War probably.

Shit. I'll take a hardy tree. x

You do that. x

I pocketed my phone as Joyce slipped back into the room. 'They'll meet with you,' she said.

'When?'

'Now.'

'Sure. We'll need to swing by a garden centre first.'

Chapter 13

Armed with a silver-birch sapling, we were en route to meet with the dryads. Joyce had stayed in the car whilst I selected the young tree, and she'd looked pleased with my selection. The garden-centre assistant had assured me that silver birches symbolise renewal and purification in Celtic mythology, so it seemed like a good choice. Plus, silver birches are native to the UK and very hard to kill. All entries in the plus column.

Now I needed to do some grovelling and, believe me, I was totally fine with grovelling. Pissing on other people's property, let alone their holy tree, was absolutely not A-okay. My mum would have had the reprobates scrubbing it clean. She's a stickler for the rules, and respecting other people's property is a big one that she drilled into me.

And to have the dryads reach out to resolve the issue and Mark compound the insult... If he wasn't already dead, I'd be kicking his ass. I'm a businesswoman, and this is *not* how you handle a valid complaint. I don't care how dog-eat-dog the Other Realm is, I have standards.

We parked in the main car park and got our ticket for the dashboard. I followed as Joyce led me confidently through the dense park. We soon veered off the wide gravelled and paved paths and into the dark forest. It was fairly mild for February, but I still regretted not wearing a jacket – and not just because I missed its warmth. Once again, I was out on serious business covered in flamingos. I kind of get why Emory is always dressed in black suits: he's always perfectly dressed for any occasion. Whether it was the death of a pack mate or grovelling to another species, black is appropriate. In neither of those scenarios are flamingos apposite.

I tucked the sapling under my arm and did some quick Googling on my phone as I followed Joyce. I was careful not to walk into any trees; I didn't need that indignity on top of everything else.

Eventually Joyce brought me to a huge clearing, in the centre of which stood the most enormous tree I had ever seen. Its trunk was thick and broad, and its branches stretched far higher than the surrounding trees. The clearing was quiet, as if even the birds didn't dare intrude on its solitude.

It is ancient, Esme murmured, her tone respectful. Age is a big deal to wolves; if a wolf lives to old age, it will have learnt a fair few tips and tricks to pass down to the young pups. Pack elders are revered; it is this reverence that allows an elderly alpha werewolf to step down when the time comes.

I set down the young sapling and started forward to the ancient tree. The clearing was still empty; I guessed we had time before the other dryads made an appearance. I stepped up to the old tree and touched a hand to its rough bark.

'I'm very sorry,' I murmured, my tone heartfelt. I didn't even feel the tiniest bit silly for apologising to a tree.

The ancient tree groaned and its leaves shook over my head in a movement that had nothing to do with the wind. Goosebumps pricked my skin. And then something *old* reached out its consciousness to mine. I had time to shout a warning to Esme before my self-awareness was lost, swept into the vast awareness of the tree. No, not a tree singular, but all the trees, *all* the trees in the forest.

Most of them were slowly awakening after a long cold winter, and they were lethargic and snuggly, like I felt after an accidental afternoon nap. Buds and leaves were forming; new life was growing. Birds were building nests in the heavy boughs, and the trees welcomed taking charge of new, precious life. They offered berries and protection and looked on them with warm affection.

All around the forest, the trees were humming with hope and renewal. I could sense where humans were strolling, where dogs were running and where the deer were bounding. Through it all, the trees greeted me in turn; they accepted my presence amongst them as if it were ordinary. But like everything Other, it wasn't ordinary, it was magical. Their strength grounded me, their hope lifted me up, and I felt so young in the face of their collective years.

The ancient tree tugged me, gently corralling me back to the clearing. Its awareness took me to a spot of earth that had recently been dug up. I didn't understand its significance because I knew too little about the dryads. I knew too little about everything.

I could see myself kneeling by the ancient tree, touching its rough-hewn bark. Dark had fallen. How long had I been floating with the trees? Another awareness reached out to me, frantic with worry. In turn, I reached out to her and she grounded us. Reluctantly I let the elder tree deposit me back to where I belonged.

LUCY!

I'm okay, I assured Esme. I blinked, disorientated. I could still feel the bark upon my hands and the trees in my heart. I took a shuddering breath. 'Thank you,' I said to the elder tree. Leaves fluttered around me, falling with a soft rustle and landing in a perfect circle.

You've been gone for hours, Esme whispered. She was trembling and I could feel her fear for me, and for herself, that I had been lost forever.

I'm okay, I reiterated. *The tree just took me on a little journey.* I sent her waves of love and reassurance.

A journey? To where? Her curiosity was helping to steady her, but I could see in my mind's eye that she was still taking gulping breaths, trying to recover from her panic. It was something she had never felt before.

To the other trees, so I could better understand them, I think. I still couldn't explain if the trees were sentient or something else, but I think my magic as a piper allowed me to communicate with them on a deeper level.

I gave Esme one last mental hug and stood up. Having been prone for hours, my muscles protested at the movement. I turned away from the ancient tree and found three ancient dryads facing me instead, two men and a woman, all green skinned and grey haired.

'Hi,' I greeted them a bit inanely.

'You have communed with the elder tree,' the male nearest me whispered.

I nodded. 'Yes.'

'You are blessed.' The other male gestured to the perfect circle of leaves around me.

'I feel privileged,' I admitted. 'I came here to apologise and came away with something else entirely. But I *am* sorry.'

The female dryad waved away my apology. 'It is done. The elder tree sees no insult from you.'

I pointed to the sapling on the ground a few feet away. 'I brought you an apology tree.'

The female smiled. 'We will take care of her.'

'I will speak with the wolves and make sure that no further infractions occur. If one of my wolves steps out of place, you must call me directly and I will resolve the issue.'

All three nodded, eerily synchronised.

'We will be coming to the park, to hunt later.' I didn't want to ask permission, but they needed to know. I didn't want them to think it was an invasion.

'So mote it be. Enjoy the renewal of the hunt,' the female dryad intoned.

As she turned to leave, I cleared my throat. 'I would like permission to bring the pack here, if I may, to make a point.'

The three dryads exchanged long looks before the female finally nodded. 'It may be done on this one occasion. But if any treat the elder tree with disrespect, there will be repercussions.' Her voice was heavy with warning and I inclined my head in acceptance.

With that, she turned and walked *into* a tree at the clearing's edge. It subsumed her – she literally disappeared into it. I let out a strangled gasp. Both dryad men followed suit, sinking into two trees next to hers and disappearing. Right: magical realm, dryads recharge in trees and their bodies can somehow combine with the organic material of a tree. Who was I to judge? I have a wolf in my head.

I touched the elder tree one last time. 'Thanks,' I whispered. I stepped out of the ring of leaves and walked towards the edge of the clearing, where Joyce was waiting for me, eyes wide. 'I'm sorry,' I said. 'That took a lot more time than I expected. Are you still okay for childcare?'

'No problem.' She gave me a hesitant smile. 'I rang the neighbour and asked her to give the kids dinner and start their bath.'

I blinked. 'What time is it?'

'6.30pm.'

'Shit.' I pulled out my phone; I had fifteen missed calls from Manners. *Shit.*

I called him. 'Alpha,' he answered, his tone courteous. He must have had company, otherwise I suspected he'd be swearing at me. Fifteen missed calls don't usually make for a calm and collected conversation.

'I'm already at Black Park. I'll meet you all at the main car park,' I suggested.

'Very good, ma'am,' he said. 'I'll arrange it. We'll park on the road and walk in to meet you.'

'You're mad at me, aren't you?'

'Absolutely,' he responded, his tone still even and respectful.

'I'll explain everything later.'

'Indeed.'

I bit my thumb and rang off. He was *so* mad at me. 'Hey,' I said to Joyce, 'what should we do with the sapling?' I didn't want my apology tree to die; that seemed like bad juju.

She smiled. 'Just leave it here. One of the others will find the perfect place for it. You don't need to worry about tending it – we'll look after it.' The affection in her tone was unmistakable. Dryads really do love trees. If they'd all had an experience like mine, I could see why.

'Thanks,' I said. 'You can take my car home and I'll wait until the pack arrives. Someone will give me a lift home later.' She hesitated, her duty as a dryad warring with her duty as a mum. 'Go,' I insisted. 'It's fine. Thank you for all your help today.'

'I've never in my life seen the elder tree commune like that for so long. That was amazing. Was it ... uplifting?' She was curious and envious in equal measure.

'It was,' I admitted. 'It was amazing.' I couldn't even begin to explain the experience, but it felt like a vast weight had been lifted from me. Something in me was ... looser, like someone or something had untied a knot that I hadn't known was there.

I passed Joyce my keys. She climbed into my car and gave me a friendly wave as she drove off, leaving me to await my pack and a very grumpy Greg Manners.

Chapter 14

I didn't have long to wait before the pack started arriving on foot. Archie came with Liam and Marissa. Seren trailed behind them, her eyes still red and her face puffy. From what I'd learnt of Mark, he didn't seem worthy of the grief she seemed to be expressing, but what did I know? Maybe he was a cute and fluffy kitten when he was with her.

Marissa was whispering with Liam and Archie, and I could just make out her words. 'Steve says both of their alibis check out. Manners was getting some, and Lucy never left Rosie's.'

I tried hard to keep my face neutral. Steve had made quick work of confirming our alibis and leaking it to Marissa, for which I was grateful. So why did I suddenly feel so damn miserable?

Brian, Noah and Ethan strolled in together, giving me looks that were both cautious and curious. David and Elena walked in with Mrs Dawes, and I smiled warmly at the housekeeper. Tristan slunk along at the back.

Triumph rose within me, lifting me out of my funk, and Esme crowed with delight. I had an actual full house. Everyone who'd been asked to the hunt had turned up. It felt like progress.

Bringing up the rear was Manners, together with Ace and Lauren. His face was carefully neutral – too neutral. I couldn't tell if his annoyance was directed at me or at our esteemed council members.

'Archie!' I called. 'Lead the way while I talk to our guests.' I dropped back to smile at Ace and Lauren. As an accountant I'd done a lot of schmoozing in my fledgling career, and it is one of my strong points. I needed to do some damage control after dismissing Ace earlier.

'How are you getting on?' I asked him.

'I managed to speak to some of the pack about your turning,' he said lightly.

Panic seized me. My turning had been anything but normal. Esme took over our body for a split second so I didn't miss a step. *Thanks.*

'Oh?' I said lightly. 'It's really not an interesting story.'

'Mrs Dawes saw you that night, but other than that you were sequestered. With Lord Samuel having passed, it makes it difficult to dig into what happened.'

I smiled winningly. 'I guess it will just have to remain a mystery.'

'The report said you had no recollection of the event or the circumstances of your turning.' It was a statement, but I could hear the question in his voice.

'That's right,' I said easily. 'I was very ill.'

'And then an unknown third party stabbed you?'

'Exactly,' I lied.

'Any idea why someone would want to stab you?'

'Nope. None. I'm a very lovable person.' I gave him a winsome smile.

Manners snorted and Ace smiled. 'You are,' he agreed with a wink. Ugh.

As we walked on through the undergrowth, I noticed that Ace was watching me with cool, assessing eyes. All hint of flirtation was gone but, when he saw me looking at him, he gave me a warm smile. His dimples flashed in his ridiculously chiselled jawline. I might not have trusted him, but yum.

Lauren appeared openly scornful; she clearly wasn't buying the BS that I was peddling. That made it pretty likely that Ace wasn't, either. Never mind. I didn't need them to believe it, I just needed them to rubber stamp it and leave. With Lord Samuel dead, there really wasn't much investigating for them to do. They'd been ordered here weeks earlier whilst he was still alive. The bureaucratic red tape just hadn't caught up yet.

'Since we're here,' Ace said, 'I'd like to offer our services in investigating the recent death of Mr Oates.'

My smile in return was a little more strained. Refusing might not be an option, but I was going to try. 'How kind of you. Luckily, my own investigations are underway, and I doubt it will be long before the culprit is found. We can discuss it further after the hunt.'

'Still, I insist. We're trained pack investigators. I'm sure we can help by dividing the interviews between us.'

'Let's discuss it later,' I reiterated. If in doubt, delay, delay, delay. 'For tonight, let's just enjoy the hunt.'

'Of course,' Ace agreed. 'I can't think of better company for it.' He flashed me another smile, which made my insides warm despite myself. Damn him for knowing how attractive he was.

Archie led us all to a small clearing with a wooden lodge. He unlocked the pine door and the first five of the pack went in to change, not out of any sense of modesty but because it was a convenient place to store our clothes and ensure they stayed dry regardless of any inclement weather.

I watched as they stripped and changed. They left the hut door open; there was no modesty in the pack. As Elena stripped, I struggled to keep my face neutral. She had a ragged scar across the back of her shoulder that was puckered and silvered – an old scar and a nasty one. It must have happened when she was young, before she'd moved packs. It looked horrific, poor girl. I wondered what she'd gone through.

Ace was standing near me and he was also watching Elena, but his gaze was dark and predatory. I swallowed a little; he was far more dangerous than his dimples and smiles portrayed. He used his good looks like I did, as a shield and a smoke screen. That was something to remember.

As Elena emerged on four legs, she left the hut on the other side of her two companions, keeping as much distance between her and us as possible. She wasn't the only one bearing scars; Mrs Dawes had a wicked looking one up her forearm that I'd never seen before. No wonder she always wore long sleeves. Like me, she hadn't been a werewolf long, and I wondered whether she had acquired it before or after her turn. It would probably be rude to ask.

Manners, Lauren, Ace and I were the last ones to shift. I hoped that my esteemed guests would be too preoccupied with their own shift to notice how rapidly mine took place. Manners obviously had a similar thought because he stood in front of me, blocking the others' view with his muscular frame.

I whipped off my clothes and put them in a neat pile in the nearest locker. When I looked up and caught my reflection in the mirror, Ace was looking at me. His gaze was openly admiring as he ran his gaze down my body. Ugh: that was just plain rude.

I wanted to let the shift rip over me and get me safely into fur, but I waited patiently for Manners. When I was sure he was ready too, I let the shift roll over me. In seconds I was on four legs.

Esme waited calmly for the others to complete their transformation. Ace's change took a mere two minutes, one of the fastest I'd seen, perhaps only beaten by Marissa's. Ace's head whipped towards me when he noted I was already on four legs, his eyes widened and his jaw dropped fractionally. *Wow*, he mouthed at me in the mirror before smiling in open admiration. He was impressed at the speed of our transformation. Esme gave a wolfish grin back.

When everyone was ready, we headed out. Esme took the lead and I settled down to let her run the show. She was eager to show the pack what she was made of. Letting out a yip that meant 'follow me', she dived into the dense woodland without looking back.

She stretched out our legs and joy flowed over us as we effortlessly covered the land and cleared the obstacles in our way. Esme pulled the pack on mile after mile, and they followed us with happy yips. We reached out our senses – not just sight and smell and hearing, but something *other*. As I had with the elder tree, we felt everything that was around us.

We could see where the deer were quietly grazing and resting. Not far now. Not far at all. We called a command to slow down because we needed to conserve some energy for the final sprint when we brought down our targets. Someone queried us – Lauren – wondering why we were slowing down. We gave a warning growl and she dropped back. We knew what we were doing, and we guided the pack forward slowly and carefully.

Finally we scented our prey, and so did the rest of the pack. Excitement swept through them as the anticipation ramped up. Esme gave some quiet commands and the pack split into three smaller groups – paws – that separated to flank the deer herd. There were no yips, barks or growls, no noises at all as we slunk closer to our quarry. The deer would scent us soon enough and the game would be afoot.

Esme and I approached the clearing with Manners to our right and Ace and Lauren to our left. They held back respectfully, letting us take prime position. When we were close enough, we burst out of the undergrowth, our heart racing as we exploded towards the unsuspecting deer. The left flank did the same, led by Marissa and Seren with Brian, Noah and Ethan. The right flank was a little slower, just a half beat, but it made all the difference.

Archie led that paw, with David, Elena and Mrs Dawes. The fractional delay gave their quarry the head start it needed to survive, but our target wasn't so lucky. We approached from behind and leapt onto its back to bring it down. As we laid the deer low, Manners leapt in and ripped out its throat, ending a potential struggle before it could begin. Parallel to us, Ace and Lauren effortlessly corralled and killed the deer nearest to them.

Marissa and Seren had a slightly longer chase with their prey, harrying it and nipping at it before eventually bringing it down. We all started to feast on the three deer. Archie's paw returned from its hunt empty handed.

Manners was sharing the carcass of our kill with me, but I stepped back and let Archie and his cohort take a turn. Manners followed my lead and did the same. All around us, the pack was making happy noises and ripping enthusiastically into the feast. I even saw a few wagging tails.

Esme and I were satisfied; the hunt had exceeded our hopes. Everyone we'd called to hunt had turned up and, by working in paws we'd brought down three deer. It had been a monumental success.

The wolves devoured our ill-fated prey and we stayed there until we were all-but picking the bones clean. With dinner over, we dragged the remains – such as they were – into dense undergrowth where they would never be found. There was no need to advertise the pack's presence, even though it was us that constantly replenished the deer herd. It wouldn't do to let dinner go off.

All done, Esme and I called a commanding bark and led the way once more. With our Other sense stretched out, it wasn't hard to know where we were going. We could feel the ancient tree like a pull on a magnet. It wasn't too far from our location, so we set a relaxed pace and let our food settle as we ran.

Tension ran through the pack as we broke into the clearing and they realised where we were. Esme moseyed forward to the elder tree and bowed to it – not a sign of submission, but one of respect.

Shit. I hadn't thought through this part. I needed to address the pack, but to do so I'd need to shift, meaning the council members would see my lightning-fast change. Well, Ace already knew it was fast; let them see it and wonder what it meant.

I called the pack to gather round and then I faced them with the elder tree at my back. Esme and I let the change roll over us. I stood in a power stance with my legs akimbo, like I wasn't even a little bit awkward about being completely naked.

I glowered and met the eyes of my pack until they all looked away. 'It is not okay to urinate on the elder tree.' My voice was hard. 'If *ever* catch wind of another packmate being so disrespectful to our neighbours, you will be out on your ass before you can say "lone wolf".' I glowered some more. 'Have I made myself clear?'

The wolves ducked their head, tails tucked in close. I noted Archie, Noah and David were cringing most. David often seemed to be looking down at the ground or out the window, and it surprised me that he was eleventh in the pack. He seemed far more subservient than I'd have expected an eleventh to be, but what did I know?

'Excellent,' I continued. 'On this occasion the dryads have forgiven us the insult, but if they had demanded blood I would have given it. Your actions reflect on the pack. To act so disgustingly, so shamefully, brings all of us into disrepute. I'm not just angry, I'm disappointed. Lord

Samuel would have been disappointed. I will not allow this behaviour to stand. This is the only warning you will get.'

I glared a moment longer and some of the gathered wolves let out whimpers of distress. 'Good.' I nodded and slowly smiled. 'Let us remember the joy and success of the hunt. Today we have hunted and fed, and I'm proud to have you all with me. Now – fastest to the lodge wins!'

I let the change snap over me and Esme and I bounded off. Calls of excitement rang in the air as the pack leapt into action. But we had the advantage; we could sense the most direct route like it was a map in our mind, and we sprang towards the lodge. We *needed* to win this.

Esme was confident of our success, but Ace and Lauren would not hold back out of a sense of respect and they were in prime condition – but then, so were we. The race was on and nothing would stop us. We gave it our all, pounding through the forest like Satan himself was on our tail.

We heard the pack behind us, but the sounds were happy and joyful, washing away the scolding of a moment before. I hoped the lesson would stick, but I needed the pack to have this positive night together to start to cement some bonds.

We arrived at the lodge first. Our chest was heaving as we gulped in air, but we made it a full twenty seconds before Manners joined us, then Ace, then Liam. I wondered if

Tristan would be annoyed about Liam beating him back; time would tell.

I shifted back into human form once more, opened the lodge door and grabbed my clothes. I dressed swiftly whilst the others started their shift back, then waited patiently. Some were so slow that it was hard to believe the shift was enjoyable.

As I stood ready to go, Ace joined me. 'That's some shift you've got there.' His tone was openly admiring.

'Thanks. It's handy.'

'I'll bet. I've never seen a shift that fast. You're remarkable.'

I like compliments as much as the next girl, but his voice was distinctly smarmy and his interest in me not even slightly disguised. He was attractive and clearly used to his open leer getting him results.

My polite smile grew strained, and I hoped Manners' shift would hurry the heck up. I cast around the room and found it had just ended. He met my eyes and read something in them that had him striding over to my side, nudity be damned. 'That was a great hunt, alpha,' he said calmly, pulling on his trousers.

'It was!' I agreed brightly, resisting the urge to sidle closer to him.

Ace glared at him, Manners glared right back. Esme gave a yip of happiness: two virile males were fighting over her. I had no doubt it was all a show on Manners' part, but I was grateful nonetheless.

Finally, all the pack members were human and dressed. We locked up the lodge and went back to the cars.

Liam flashed me a grin and a thumbs up as he climbed into his car with Marissa and Seren. Brian gave me a nod that showed begrudging respect, even if there was nothing friendly about it. Ace had brought his own car and Lauren slid behind the driver's wheel. No one offered me a lift.

I climbed into Manners' car. The air was stony. Nuts; I'd forgotten he wasn't terribly happy with me. I was fairly sure that the pack weren't the only ones who'd get told off tonight.

Chapter 15

After a few minutes of silence, I was squirming. 'Okay, just do it already.'

Manners kept his eyes on the road. 'Do what?'

'Tell me off. Go on, I'll get you started.' I dropped my voice an octave. "Lucy, there's a killer on the loose, and you just disappeared without telling anyone where you were going, and what you were doing. That was irresponsible at best, reckless at worst. You could have been killed and I wouldn't have even known where to find the body'.'

I returned to my normal speaking voice. 'But I didn't know I was going to be gone for hours! Honestly, it was a total accident. Jess hooked me up with one of her dryad friends and I went to go and find out what their beef with Mark was. She told me he'd pissed on the elder tree—'

'He *what*?' Manners interrupted, aghast.

'He urinated on their sacred elder tree. Even worse, he'd been called there because a few of the pack's younglings had infringed on dryad territory as a dare, and one of *them* had pissed on the elder tree. Mark strolled in and made it worse.'

'Christ,' he muttered. 'Mark was an idiot.'

'Of the worst sort,' I agreed. 'He didn't even know he was an idiot. And that's not all I learnt about him today. Have you heard of black tourneys?'

Manners turned to stare at me before jerking his eyes back to the road. 'Tell me he wasn't into black tourneys.'

'Hip deep,' I confirmed. 'He used to take part regularly, and at least once he took Archie along to see one. At least, that's what Archie tells me.'

'Lord Samuel would have skinned Mark alive if he'd known,' Manners said darkly. 'This opens up a whole new can of worms. Black tourneys are illegal for good reason. If the Connection gets wind of one, they shut it down and turf the participants into jail, sometimes with a judicious mind wipe. As far as I know, the tourneys only take place in London or Liverpool – but if Mark regularly took part in them, he'll have killed plenty of people. Restraint wasn't in his nature.'

'And the victims may have relatives who wanted revenge.'

'Enough to torture him with silver,' he agreed.

'We need to go see a tourney.'

Manners' jaw tightened. He didn't like the suggestion.

'We can ask questions subtly.' I pointed out. 'We're not
going to find out anything here.'

'I'll see if I can find out when and where the next tourney
is, and we'll take it from there. In the meantime, there are
people I can ask about the tourneys without too many
repercussions.'

'Who?' I asked nosily.

'I know a few griffins.'

'What do griffins have to do with them?'

'Rumour has it the tourneys are run by one of them,
unsanctioned by Shirdal.'

'Shirdal is the griffins' head honcho, right?'

Manners hesitated. 'Yeah, basically.'

'And you know a guy.'

'I know *the* guy. Bastion has worked with me for years,
albeit I thought he was just another brethren member...'

'You've known Bastion the deadly griffin assassin for
years, and you didn't know it?' My tone may have been a
tad more mocking than the situation called for, but Greg

Manners always seemed to know *everything*. It was nice to find out he was fallible.

'Yeah,' he muttered. 'Not my finest moment. But I'll speak to him and see what I can dig up.'

'Cool.' I didn't tell him about the whole being-one-with-the-trees thing. I don't know why exactly, but it felt a bit … special, something that was just for me. Besides, I couldn't work out how to explain it without sounding like a total dope. I cleared my throat. 'So, are we alright?'

He slid me a long look. 'You pull that shit again and we'll have words. Next time you go off site, I need to know. You're alpha now, you've got a target on your back. You always travel with backup.'

'I did,' I insisted jokily. 'I have my wolf with me at all times.'

'I'm serious. For now, your backup is just me. When we work out who we can trust, you'll always need a second with you. Liam is looking promising now that Mark's influence has been removed.'

I nodded soberly. 'Let's hope so.'

'The hunt tonight was a good idea,' Manners admitted.

'The night is still young. I can't wait to dive into a roast chicken.' My stomach gave a well-timed rumble.

He flashed me a grin. 'You're not the only one. I'm starving, even after a good helping of deer. And Mrs Dawes bakes a killer cake. I smelled it in the kitchen earlier.'

'You have a sweet tooth?'

'My one flaw.

I snorted. 'If cake is your worst flaw then you're doing okay.'

'A moment on the lips, a lifetime on your hips,' he said *sotto voce*.

'A moment on the lips is a *second* on your hips when you're a werewolf,' I grinned.

'So far, that's been my favourite thing about being a wolf – the ridiculous metabolism.'

'And, of course, hanging out with my fabulous self.' I batted my eyelids outrageously and his lips curled up in a smile.

'Yeah, that too.'

It was times like this that I wished I had Jess's skill of being a human lie detector. I changed the topic. 'Do you think Mrs Dawes has ice cream?'

'Ben and Jerry's,' he confirmed.

'Shut up! What flavour?'

'I had Phish Food yesterday.'

I punched a fist in the air. 'Yes! That's my favourite.'

'I ate the whole tub.'

I glared at him. 'If that's the only tub, you're going to be so sorry, mister. I'll make you pay.'

His lips twitched. 'Yeah? You and whose army?'

I folded my arms. 'I don't need an army. I'll get a certain acquaintance to turn your hair pink again. Or maybe green this time.'

'Then for both our sakes, let's hope Mrs Dawes has a second tub. I'm easier on the eyes when I'm blond.'

'You rocked pink,' I disagreed.

'Yeah?' Manners slid a sideways glance at me and I flushed a little. I turned on the radio to prevent further conversation, and he smiled but let it go. I sang along to Mariah Carey with gusto.

'Is there anything you can't do?' he asked. 'You're a social butterfly with model good looks and an amazing singing voice. Not to mention you were an accountant, so presumably you're pretty damn smart.' Then he muttered under his breath, 'Despite evidence to the contrary.'

I decided it would be more diplomatic to focus on the first part of his statement. 'You think I'm model pretty?'

He kept his eyes on the road. 'You know you are.'

Hard to dispute that. I use my good looks like a warrior wields armour. They protect me. Men think I'm out of their league and rarely bother approaching me. Women fall into two camps: the first wants to hang out with me, as if my genetic good looks could somehow be catching, and the second type of woman assumes I'm a bitch and leaves me well alone. My innate need to please means I've spent a fair amount of my life winning around the second camp. Just because I'm pretty, doesn't mean I have to be evil.

I focused on Manners' first question. 'I'm a terrible knitter. My mum is really into her knitting but I just suck at it. I tried but my tension changes constantly and I'm forever dropping stitches or adding extra ones. About the best I can do is a scarf, and even that would be full of holes,' I admitted.

'It's not the most fatal flaw I've ever heard of,' he commented lightly.

'Yeah, well, yours is your love of all things sweet.'

'That's a proper flaw,' he protested. 'For years I had to work really hard not to eat that second doughnut – or I had to work out extra hard.'

I held a hand to my forehead dramatically. 'Woe is me.'

He ignored me; probably for the best. We drew up to the mansion. 'Game-face on,' he advised softly.

I nodded and wipe away the last trace of humour. 'Let's go feast.'

We went straight to the formal dining hall. Mrs Dawes' helpers had started setting out food and the smells were so good they made my stomach cramp with hunger. It took genuine self-restraint not to rip into the nearest chicken leg.

Let's eat, Esme urged. **I'm hungry, and we're alpha.**

We're human now. It's tradition to wait for the others.

She subsided, but I could feel her petulance. *They won't be long,* I assured her.

Luckily they weren't and the hall soon filled up. To my surprise, other pack members who hadn't been on the hunt turned up, including Cassie and a man she was draped all over. Rather uncharitably, I thought that her broken heart had made a rapid recovery. Maybe Steve wasn't far wrong in his suggestion to look at the spouse first.

I waited until the doors were shut then stood and raised a glass of wine that I really wished I could down in one. 'Today was an excellent hunt, the first of many,' I said in a clear voice. 'The Home Counties pack will continue to go from strength to strength as we work together.'

'Hear, hear,' called out Archie, nodding solemnly.

'Aye,' said Liam, thumping his fist on the table.

To my surprise, it was Marissa who joined in first. Before long, almost everyone was banging their fists on the table in a cacophony of noise. I tried to note who remained silent: Tristan, Seren and Brian.

I held up my hand and the banging fell silent. 'Let's eat!' I called.

The room exploded into whoops and we all dug in. Unlike Manners, I've always had a good metabolism. I can eat and eat without fear of putting on a pound. Sometimes it's a pain because bitchy comments are chucked my way about how I *must* be anorexic. But nope, just a crazy metabolism that I can't beat. I don't know whether it's from my biological mum or my dad, nor if the metabolism has an expiry date, but I guess now that I'm a werewolf it doesn't really matter.

The feast went on and the wine flowed. That amazing metabolism has a downside: it is hard for a werewolf to get truly inebriated. Despite that, the younger members of the pack were giving it their very best shot.

Archie staggered away from the table, ignoring his mates' protests and saying loudly that he was calling it a night. I frowned. He looked really pissed, but I'd only seen him drink two glasses of wine, which was nothing for a wolf. I knew he'd been a druggie before he was blooded; drugs are the only way a wolf can get a real high, and even they have a much shorter effect than they do on our human counterparts. I didn't think Archie was using again, but he was staggering. I watched him bounce off the doorway, giggling to himself.

I went over to Ace and Lauren, who were slowly circulating around the pack and questioning them. They were following protocol, business after the hunt, so I had no right to stop them, but they were impinging on the party atmosphere I was trying to create. Time to give them a new target.

I crossed the room with a ready smile, a weapon as sure as our claws.

Less deadly, Esme muttered mutinously. She wanted to deal with them head on.

We must observe pack law, I reminded her.

Yes, she agreed grumpily. **For now.**

Lauren greeted us with a nod; there was no hint of warmth in her. Brian gratefully made his escape as attention turned to me. 'The hunt has been conducted. Now let's discuss business,' I said to Ace.

'You know why we're here,' he said. 'The council want us to investigate two matters. The first is the circumstances of your ... unusual turning. Unfortunately, with Lord Samuel's untimely demise, there is no evidence beyond what he placed in his report. You've already said you have nothing to add. We've questioned most of the pack and no one else was present. The council therefore considers this matter closed.'

I tried to keep the relief from my face. 'And the second matter?'

'The second matter bears further investigation: it is the death of Lord Samuel and your ascension to the role of alpha.'

'You have my report,' I said calmly.

'Yes, but there's plenty missing from it,' Lauren bitched.

Ace glared, his eyes flashing in warning. 'Why was Lord Samuel sent to Liverpool in the first place?' he asked.

I shrugged. 'You'll have to ask the council. All I know is that it sent him.'

'Why did Lord Samuel fight with the alpha of the Cheshire pack?'

I needed to tread carefully. The real reason was that Lord Samuel had been helping Jess by trying to stop a bunch of daemons from entering our realm, but that wasn't common knowledge for a good reason. There was no need to advertise that there was a daemon realm, and that a portal could be created to it. The bad guys already had enough weapons in this realm; they didn't need anything else in their arsenal.

'I understand there was a lot of animosity between Lord Samuel and Rain,' I said finally.

'The conflict was personal?'

I shrugged. 'Apparently their mutual dislike was well known.'

'And why did Lord Samuel take you, an unseasoned werewolf, as his second if he was going to challenge Rain?'

I widened my eyes innocently. 'I have no idea. You'd have to ask him,' I said unhelpfully.

I'd kept Jess out of all of my reports to keep her safe and off the radar, but I really couldn't explain without bringing her into it. Lord Samuel and I had travelled together; I'd gone because Jess was in trouble, and Lord Samuel had come along for the ride. He'd been sent by the council to investigate Rain in a cloak-and-dagger operation. I didn't know how far the secrecy went, or if Ace knew who'd sent him.

'Talk me through the battle.'

I did, omitting the witches and the daemons. I included the fact that Bastion and the elves had been involved.

'Why were the elves involved in pack matters?' Ace questioned.

I shrugged again. They'd been there to seal the daemons into containment charms. 'Maybe they just didn't like Rain,' I said finally. 'I'm told he's a bit of a brute.'

Ace was watching me like a hawk. There were so many holes in my story you could have limboed through them. It was time to call it a night. I yawned. 'If you'll excuse me, as the alpha I should duck out soon so that the pack can let their hair down.'

No one ever gets their party on properly when the boss is there, and I'd seen frequent glances my way. Dammit, I *like* parties. I really wished Jess was there so we could crank up some music and dance on the tables. Maybe I'd arrange a night out with some local friends soon – I needed to let my hair down, too, alpha or not.

'Of course,' Ace said with a friendly smile which had been missing during our chat. 'I'll continue to speak to other members of the pack.'

'No one else was there,' I pointed out with a warm but unhelpful smile. 'I'm afraid you may be wasting your time.'

He smiled back, just as warmly. We were both so full of shit. 'No doubt the council members questioning Rain's pack will get more answers.'

Shit. 'We can hope,' I said brightly.

Ace gestured for Lauren to drop back and give us some privacy. As she did so, a sour expression crossed her fine features. 'You look ravishing tonight,' he complimented me. The shift in gears was enough to give me whiplash. And who says 'ravishing' these days?

'Thanks. I rock jeans and a T-shirt,' I said jokingly.

'You rock anything,' he agreed. 'You're not what I was expecting, Luciana.'

'Oh, it's just Lucy. Nothing so exotic for me.'

'There's nothing *just* about you. You're not what I was expecting for the first female alpha in decades.'

'What were you expecting?'

'A raging, bra-burning-feminist.'

'I'm that, too, minus the bra-burning bit. I like bras too much.'

'I'm a fan of them too,' he smarmed. Yuck.

'I bet you'd look great in one.' I winked cheekily and his eyes tightened in anger. His flirtation was only skin deep. 'Anyway, goodnight. I'd best go so the party can get started.' I nodded farewell to Lauren. She watched me leave without a change of expression.

I looked around as I excused myself. Manners was talking to Liam, so I left him to it. I joined Mrs Dawes, who was on her third glass of wine and looked pretty happy. She was talking with Marissa, who gave me a reserved smile as I approached.

'Thank you for all of your hard work,' I said to Mrs Dawes. 'And the rest of the team. You've done us proud.'

She blushed. 'Aren't you kind, my alpha? It is my honour to serve you.' She said it formulaically, like it should mean something to me.

You need to reply 'It is my honour to protect you', Esme prompted.

'It is my honour to protect you,' I parroted. How the heck did Esme know all this stuff? Surely wolf packs didn't have the same rigmarole as werewolf packs?

Mrs Dawes beamed at my response and directed a pointed look at Marissa. I didn't want to pressure Marissa into saying some sort of magical oath that she didn't mean, so instead I said, 'Can I have a quick word?'

Marissa followed me off to one side of the room, leaving Mrs Dawes frowning after us. 'Mark took Boost,' I started. 'Tell me about it.'

'I really don't know much,' she said with a simpering smile.

'Bullshit. It's late and I'm tired. Just tell me.' I'd used up the last of my patience with Ace.

'There's really nothing to say. He took Boost. I think a couple of the others might have done, too.'

'Who?'

'Archie and Noah, maybe.'

Jess had told me that Archie hadn't touched Boost, and since she's a truth seeker her information is golden. But Noah? That surprised me. He seemed like a good kid, and I was pretty sure his dad was fairly high up in the pack hierarchy.

I questioned Marissa some more but she only gave me innocent wide eyes, which frankly pissed me off. I knew what she was doing because I *invented* vacuous; she was a smart girl playing dumb. Sooner or later I'd trip her up and rip off that façade.

After I let her go, our council guests withdrew from the party and the atmosphere lightened, but looks were still being cast my way. With an inaudible sigh, I left the room. I was only a little bit grumpy. It was for the best, and I was pleased the pack was having some fun under my rule – even if I was excluded from it.

Chapter 16

I went into my office and checked the time. It was nearly 10pm which was a little late for calling my mum, but I decided Steve would probably be awake. He answered on the second ring. 'Hey Lucy. How is it going?'

I considered. I'd managed to repair some of the damage to the relationship with the dryads, and the hunt had gone well, but Mark's killer was still on the loose. You win some, you lose some. I settled on, 'Not too bad. You?'

'Busy day here. I got called to a suspected arson. Someone thought it was an elemental flaming up, but there was enough lighter fluid present to set fire to a small country.'

'So just your garden-variety arsonist then?'

'Looks like it,' Steve agreed. 'And there was a bit of a stir amongst the vampyrs, but I haven't got to the bottom of that yet.'

'A stir?'

'There was a public gathering of a good few of them. Very unusual – they're usually more subtle than that. The gargoyles put in a formal complaint.'

I frowned. Lord Wokeshire had a mansion that was a little older than ours; he definitely had space to entertain, so that made me think the gathering wasn't Clan Wokeshire. But if the gathering wasn't the Wokeshire clan, their rivals weren't being very discreet about it. Were they challenging him?

'I mention it,' Steve continued, 'because it was at the park just around the corner from your land.'

I blew out a breath. Wonderful. Prowling vampyrs right on my damn border. Exactly what I needed. 'Great.'

'I'm sure it's nothing.' His tone didn't match his words. 'The pathologist came up trumps, though. It's been a quiet week, so he got to Mr Oates straight away. The only thing that stands out, besides the silver poisoning, was that he'd been drugged by a potion. A highly regulated one. It's an agent that confuses the recipient, makes it easier to question them, and it makes it harder for them to co-ordinate their limbs so they're less likely to pose a threat. I'm told it's quite unnerving. The Connection has been known to use it to subdue violent prisoners during transport. No sign of a hypodermic needle puncture, so it was likely to have been imbibed willingly.'

'You think he trusted his drugger?' It made me think of Cassie and the man she'd been draped over tonight.

'That, or his food or drink was spiked without his knowledge. Anyway, that's all I've got. How are things your end? Anything new to report on Mark Oates?'

'He was an asshole,' I reported flatly.

He snorted. 'That was the consensus. I haven't spoken to a single person that liked the guy.'

'He was an asshole that took part in black tourneys,' I expanded.

Steve let out a low whistle. 'Now that's not in any of the information I've got on him, so he must have kept it off the radar. The Connection always comes down hard when they find a tourney, but they're too well organised and it's too easy to change the location at the drop of a hat. We've had a team of inspectors digging into black tourneys for years with very limited results. A couple of raids here and there, but we've never managed to snag anyone important.'

'I'll dig into it and let you know what I find.'

'Tread very carefully, Lucy,' Steve warned. 'The guy that runs these things is known as Ghost, partly because he's damn hard to find but also because that's all that's left of his enemies.'

I snorted. 'Sure, but when you've been raised on Thanos and Magneto, Ghost seems a bit tame.'

He paused and when he spoke his tone was incredulous. 'Lucy – the difference is that Ghost is *real*, not make be-lieve.'

'Potato-tomato.'

'That's not how that saying goes.' He sounded exasper-ated.

'Why does everyone think I can't handle myself?'

'Because you're a skinny, privileged little white girl who was an accountant until a few weeks ago?' He had a point.

'I'm a werewolf now,' I protested. 'An alpha werewolf. I'm totally tough.' Well, Esme is.

'Uh-huh. Just take back up, keep me in the loop – and don't do anything stupid.'

I hung up without giving any assurances. Jess has always had an aversion to lying and my long association with her had made me less quick to fib.

I appreciated Steve's candour but I was a bit bummed out that everyone seemed ready to write me off. I'd ripped off James's man parts; I'd parlayed with the dryads. I felt like I was doing a pretty good job. I wished that everyone else – hell, *someone* else – agreed.

I decided that ice cream might help. Manners had said that Mrs Dawes had Phish Food and that was exactly what a pity party called for. I went through the pack's communal lounge and down the dormitory corridor. As I walked past Mark's room I contemplated doing another search, but the red tape was still up and my need for ice cream was strong.

The kitchen was empty. I headed straight for the chest freezer and rooted around for a solid minute, muttering to myself and swearing a little. I really needed Ben and Jerry's; if Manners had eaten the last tub, I was totally kicking his ass.

I lifted some peas out of the way and did a happy dance as I spied what I needed. It was cookie dough, which isn't my favourite, but it would do in a pinch. The tub was brand new and unopened. I grinned and dug out a fork. It's so much easier to dig into frozen ice cream with a fork than a spoon, and I don't care how many people find that weird.

The kitchen was a little chilly and it was pack space, so I decided to take my treasure and head back to my bedroom to indulge in private. If no one saw me, no one would ask why I was eating ice cream with a fork. And I wouldn't need to share.

Why are you so excited about this small carton? Esme asked curiously.

Just you wait. This is better than fresh deer, I promised. I felt her doubt. *Honestly, you're going to love it.*

We scootched our way back down the corridor past Mark's room.

Wait, Esme called suddenly.

What?

Listen, she hissed.

I froze and listened. There was a muffled sound of pain, so faint that we had to strain to hear it. It was coming from Archie's room. He'd been drunk but this didn't sound like an early hangover.

'Archie?' I called through the door. 'Are you okay?'

There was half a beat of silence then the sound of shattering glass. 'Archie?' I shouted louder. 'I'm coming in.' I tried the door handle but it was locked. 'Stand back from the door.'

I kicked the lock mechanism with all my strength, then cringed as the door flew inwards. The force from my kick was such that it was ripped from its hinges and the frame. Luckily Archie was off to one side, but the door struck his desk and broke into two. Sheesh. I really didn't know my own strength.

I sneezed violently as something assaulted my nose but we ignored the urge to follow the scent and looked at Archie. He was tied to his desk chair, just like Mark had been. Unlike Mark, Archie was still alive, but he wouldn't stay that way for long – he had a huge slice up his sternum which was bleeding heavily. I thought I could see entrails poking out. It looked horror-movie fake, which was probably the only reason I didn't vomit.

He needs to change! Esme said urgently. **Free him from the chair.**

The thick ropes binding him were tied in tight knots. Luckily, I had my girl-guiding badge in knot tying and made quick work of undoing them. I hauled Archie off the chair and laid him carefully on the floor, whipped out my phone and dialled Amber.

'I'm not healing anymore cocks today,' she said wearily.

'I need you, now! Archie is badly hurt,' I hissed urgently.

'I'm on my way.' She hung up.

I compressed Archie's wound. I didn't dare leave him, but frustration was roaring through me because I couldn't follow his attackers. I dialled Manners and prayed he'd pick up.

'Ma'am?'

'Archie has been attacked. Get to his room now! See if Mrs Dawes has any emergency potions from her friendly witch.' I hung up.

He needs to change, Esme reiterated.

I know that, but he's unconscious. What can we do?

Archie is unconscious, but his wolf is not. Pipe the wolf. Quickly.

Keeping my hands on Archie's gruesome wound, I closed my eyes and reached inside myself like Lisette had taught me. I imagined a deep well of magic, reached into it and drew up the power lurking there. It was slippery and hard to grasp, and I struggled to haul it up. I kept as much as I could balled up in my hands, and then I pushed. It flowed it out from me and into Archie.

Wolf, I called urgently. *Archie needs you!*

What need have I of him? came a snarling response.

If he dies, you die.

I will return to the Great Pack, he said indifferently.

CHANGE! Esme snarled at him. **Your Alpha commands it.** Power whipped out from her and the wolf cringed.

What is this? he said, but he spoke with wonder. **It will be done.**

The change started over him, but it was too slow.

Faster, Esme urged, and again something happened between the wolves that I didn't follow.

Archie's body shuddered and transformed. In seconds, he was panting in his wolf form. He gave a low whimper. The change had kickstarted his rejuvenation abilities, but the wide slice was still vicious and open.

It's alright, Esme reassured Archie's wolf. Her voice was gentle now. **The healing has already begun. Lie down. The humans will help you.**

Archie's wolf let out another low whine but he lay down carefully.

A witch will come to help you. Let her treat you both.

I will allow it, he agreed. **No other is to approach.**

Agreed.

Agreed.

With the immediate panic over, I turned. Behind me, Manners was keeping everyone out of the room, but the corridor was full and I could hear whispers.

'Did you see his eyes? They were gold – he's gone full wolf!'

'The wolf lay down! Did you see that?'

'It's like the wolf recognised her as alpha!'

'Has Mrs Dawes got anything to help him?' I asked Manners.

He shook his head and I swore. Even with a werewolf's ability to heal, I wasn't sure if he'd survive long enough for Amber to arrive. 'Keep everyone back. The wolf will let Amber DeLea heal him, but he won't tolerate anyone else approaching. Keep it locked down.'

Manners agreed, and then I let the shift roll over me. In my haste I'd forgotten to remove my clothes and they tore, disappearing entirely as we shifted. Rest in Peace, inappropriate flamingo shirt.

Esme and I scented the air around us, but the burning candle on Archie's bedside table overwhelmed our delicate nose. We sneezed rapidly to clear it but to no avail; we couldn't scent the attacker.

Archie's assailant had fled though the balcony door. The glass was smashed; it looked like the door hadn't opened and they'd panicked and burst through it instead. That suggested the balcony wasn't the point of ingress.

I'd done everything I could for Archie. It was time to go hunting. With a growl of agreement, Esme leapt through the ragged hole in the balcony door, landing briefly on the balustrade before using it as a springboard to leap down.

We took a moment to look around, but night had fallen and any tracks were hidden under the veil of darkness. We sneezed rapidly, clearing the cloying scent of the candle from our nose, then sniffed again. This time we caught a scent – it smelled like lavender, but there were no lavender plants on the estate.

With our tail straight up with excitement, we followed the scent. We pounded across the estate, pausing to sniff now and again as we charged forward. If it started to rain it would be game over.

We ploughed forward. Once we'd left the estate and were on the streets, we slowed down and tried to be a little more unobtrusive. Hopefully, we'd be mistaken as a big dog if we just kept trotting on.

The smell led us straight to the Black Park. We started forward – and then we saw the gang of vampyrs.

They were unmistakably vampyr. Firstly, they were dressed in black leather, which is so on trend for them at the moment, and secondly, they were all absurdly attractive. They made me look plain, which on any other day in a bar might have been quite nice. But a group of five vampyrs hanging around a children's park at night struck me as questionable.

Esme is tough, but even she agreed that hiding was a good idea. Vampyrs and wolves have a hate-hate relationship that spans eons; they wouldn't hesitate to slice us into small pieces if they saw us.

We ducked and hid under a climbing frame. We clung to the shadows and cursed that the lavender-scented one was getting away, but if we tried to back out now we'd be sashimi. Bitterness pulled at us as we sank down low.

Chapter 17

'Bloody vampyrs,' groused another voice. 'Mon Dieu, I knew I shouldn't have come out tonight, but I just wanted a little stretch from the church.'

My eyes picked out a stony, grey shape almost perfectly camouflaged by the shadows. A gargoyle! I'd never actually *seen* a real gargoyle; I'd gone to a church to meet one but we'd been derailed by a huge, rampaging ouroboros. That's a whole story for another day.

Esme was relaxed, which told me she wasn't worried about him. That was good because *I* was. He was squat, with pointed ears and a mouth full of sharp, spikey teeth. His short wings extended above him.

He saw where I was looking. 'I know. Wings are a pain in the ass. They're too small to carry me far, and they itch like a bitch.' He scratched his crotch. Thank goodness it appeared to be covered in some sort of loincloth – but that was *all* he was wearing.

Curiosity finally got the better of me and so, making sure I was tucked tight into the shadows, I turned back to human. Fuck. I'd forgotten it was cold and I was naked. I was crouched in a teeny-tiny ball so the gargoyle couldn't see much of me but – man, I missed my fur right then.

He blinked, his yellow eyes flashing in the night. 'Well now. It's good to see you again. That's a lightning-fast shift, wolfie darling. I haven't seen one that fast in a few decades.'

I blinked in confusion. 'Have we met?'

The gargoyle smiled, a maw full of sharp spikes which looked less than friendly. 'My mistake.'

I guess I looked like another naked blonde woman he'd seen lately. 'Aren't you worried about them hearing us?' I whispered.

'Not really, wolfie, no. Super-speed, super-healing, super-bitey, but no super-hearing. Sounds like they're bitching amongst themselves. Looks like Alessandro stood them up. Hopefully they'll mince on out of here before you can say crushed windpipe.'

I grimaced at the mental image. 'How come you're hiding, too?'

'New to the Other, are you, my snarly darling? Wolves and vamps don't get on, it's true – but gargoyles and vamps are something else. Mostly the vamps see us as caviar. We may be ugly little fuckers, but apparently we're a tasty little morsel. Didn't fancy my chances at five to one.'

'Can't you fly away?'

'About as fast as a fat duck, lovey. They'd be on me faster than I could shit my pants.'

I pulled a face; that wasn't an image I needed.

'Of all the sodding nights to go for a stroll.' He sighed dramatically. 'I'll have to haul ass back to the church before the sunrise. It's hard for the human tossers to explain away a stone gargoyle in a kids' park. And I'd probably get covered in stinking spray-paint, too. Teenagers have no respect for French masonry these days.'

'You're French?'

'I was, a long time ago. Now I'm British. We're an inclusive cosmopolitan society these days, not like the good old days.' He sighed.

Despite myself, I found myself liking the rude little thing. 'So that's a real thing? Struck by daylight, and you're turned to stone?'

'For at least a week. Let me tell you, your joints ache like a motherf—'

'I'm sorry to hear that,' I interrupted quickly.

'Delicate constitution, have you, my bitey pup?' he asked with an amused look.

'My mum is anti-swearing. She thinks it shows a small mind.' I hadn't exactly stuck to her no swearing rules, but certain phrases have never made it into my vocabulary. One rhymed with hunt and the other rhymed with ... mother-clucker.

'Nothing small about my mind, love, just my stature. I don't remember my mum. Too many centuries gone.' He scratched his bald head. 'Shame that. I bet she wasn't a cumberworld.'

I blinked. 'A what?'

'Cumberworld. Someone that is so fecking useless, all they do is take up space. The youth of today have no education.'

'To be honest, we just say waste of space.'

He snorted. 'And your mum would say *my* vocabulary is limited?'

I'd clearly touched a nerve. I tried to change the topic. 'So was your mum a gargoyle, too?'

'Certainly not. Gargoyles are *made,* my sweeting. I was something else once. Back in the days where every breath wasn't agony.' He shrugged like it didn't matter. 'Here, the loiter-sack louts are muttering rude shit about Alessandro, but they are finally leaving.'

I decided to leave loiter-sack alone. I wasn't sure I wanted to expand my vocabulary anymore.

He's right, Esme spoke up. **They're going.**

'Of course I'm right, my four-legged friend. I'm not often wrong.' His gleaming yellow eyes looked off into the distance. 'At least, I don't think so. It's hard to remember these days.'

He heard me? Esme asked.

'Course I did. Loud and clear, my canine culver. You're shouting.'

'Can all gargoyles hear a werewolf's wolf?' I asked curiously.

'I don't rightly know, my dove. I don't rightly know.' He gave me a toothy grin. 'It's been lovely gabbing with you, but the path is clear and I must skedaddle to my destination before the sun starts its twatting rise again. I'll see you anon, deary.'

'Wait! I still have questions. Did you see anyone else besides the vampyrs?'

'Aye, there was a wolf that stepped along. She didn't hide though, just kept going in a right old hurry.'

'You're sure it was a she?'

'I said she, didn't I?' He glared at me; he was a sensitive little chap.

'Right. Which way was she headed?'

He shrugged. 'I didn't see. It was about then that the vampyrs arrived and I made myself scarce for survival reasons.'

'Sure. Thanks for all your help, Mr...'

He laughed. 'It takes more than a flash of boobs to earn my name. Take care of yourselves, my mamtams.' He nodded and lumbered out.

He was right: he wasn't fast, but he was determined. His little legs hurried, though his wings stretched behind him were undoubtedly making the whole thing a lot more difficult. He cursed and swore, like he couldn't help but blister the air with all the words that he'd managed to hold back from our conversation. I winced at some of the particularly colourful phrases. Frankly, I wasn't sure they were anatomically possible.

What on earth was all that about? How come he could hear you? Can he pipe?

Esme was oddly silent.

I didn't feel any magic directed at me.

It would have been directed at me, Esme pointed out.

Well, did you feel anything?

No.

What do you know about gargoyles?

They're called the dark ones, but we don't need to fear them, she said finally.

Why?

It's not talked about. It was the first time I could recall her admitting to not knowing something. For some reason that made me feel better. She wasn't *all* knowing.

She snorted into my mind. **Of course I'm not, Lucy.**

It feels like you are sometimes.

I'm of the Other, I know the Other. You are of the Common, you know the Common. Let's go home. The trail has gone cold, she admitted grumpily.

She didn't like admitting defeat any more than I did. Mum raised me with a can-do attitude and not-doing pissed me off. I like achieving. I'm told I was inseparable from my sticker star-chart when I was a kid.

We shifted into four legs and trotted home, keeping a wary eye out for straggling vampyrs. When we returned to the mansion, we headed straight for the scene of the crime. Esme let out a bark of dismay when we arrived; Ace and Lauren were near the balcony, along with Tristan and Noah. Any tracks and traces were long gone, blasted to oblivion by thoughtless idiots.

I shifted so I could yell. 'What do you think you're doing?' I shouted. 'Get back inside. You've destroyed the bloody crime scene.'

'We're checking for clues,' Noah explained.

'You're obliterating them!' I snarled. 'Inside, now. All of you.' I directed my glare at the council members, too. They might have investigatory powers, but they weren't here for Archie, they were here for me. This was not their ambit.

Ace threw me an easy smile. 'Sorry, Lucy. I thought I'd help out. Noah and Tristan were here first, so the damage was already done by the time we arrived.'

'That's very gracious of you,' I said through clenched teeth. 'But you're not here to investigate Archie.'

'No,' he admitted, one dimple flashing. 'We're here to investigate you.' He gave me a wink as if I shouldn't worry about it then slunk off after the others. I swore darkly and followed them. I needed to check on Archie.

A rush of warmth swept over me as I stepped into the mansion; God bless central heating. Manners stood at the entrance, his face carefully blank. I sighed. I didn't want to be yelled at for running off – I'd made an impulsive decision, but I didn't think it was the wrong one. If I'd caught the culprit, I would have solved Mark's death and Archie's attack, and secured the safety of the pack. Risk versus reward. It was worth it.

Manners said nothing, but he ducked into my office and came out a moment later with a white dressing gown. I blinked: I'd forgotten I was nude. How quickly nakedness had become normal. I wrapped myself in it. It was soft, oversized and very fluffy, so it probably undermined my snarls a little, but I'd been so cold in that damn park that I was willing to put up with a little embarrassment to be warm again. 'Archie?' I asked.

'He's doing okay. Amber is with him – thankfully she came really fast. She must have broken a few speeding laws to get here. She said the change saved his life. He wouldn't have lasted that long if the shift hadn't kick-started his healing.'

'But he's going to be alright?'

'She thinks so. Physically.'

'But mentally?'

'He's gone full wolf. She's not sure if his wolf will relinquish the hold on him enough for Archie to re-establish control.'

That seemed nuts to me because my relationship with Esme was nothing like the battleground Manners was describing.

Thankfully, Esme murmured. **We will teach him.**

I wasn't sure we could teach what we had, but I guessed it was worth a shot.

'Did you manage to find out anything?' Manners asked.

'The assailant was a female werewolf, but that's all I got.'

He looked surprised and a little impressed. *Ha! Take that.* 'That narrows things down significantly. With the black-tourney angle, we could have been looking at all manner of beastie.'

I shook my head. 'Both times ingress to the room was through the mansion. We were always looking at an inside job.'

He looked at me appraisingly. 'You're good at this.'

'Could you sound less surprised?' I asked drily. 'It's a logical deduction and I'm a logical soul – it's one of the reasons I love maths. But my ability to reason extends beyond mathematics.'

'You were gone for quite a while,' he fished.

'There were some vampyrs in the park.' I filled him in on my conversation with Steve, including the drugging angle.

Manners frowned. 'I thought Archie was drunk when he staggered out of the feast.'

'Me too. Don't beat yourself up, we couldn't have known.'

'He'd been spiked – targeted.'

I nodded. 'And what did he have in common with Mark?'

Manners swore viciously. 'The black tourneys.'

'Bingo. Call your eagle and let's dig into this.'

He flashed me a grin. 'I dare you to call him an eagle to his face.'

I blanched. 'Erm, maybe not.'

'Good call.'

'Get the brethren security guys in first thing tomorrow,' I ordered. 'If we'd had cameras installed, we'd already know who attacked Archie.'

Manners almost stood to attention. 'You got it.'

'Are gargoyles always ... vulgar?' I asked abruptly.

He looked at me curiously. 'When did you see a gargoyle?'

'One of them hid from the vampyrs with me,' I explained. 'In a kids' park, under a climbing frame.'

He grinned. 'Yeah gargoyles are all pretty offensive. Why do you think I left you outside while I went in to speak to them at the church?' He was referring to one of our first battles, when we fought the giant ouroboros together.

'Oh, so *that's* why. I just assumed you wanted to take control of the situation.'

'No, I didn't want to get told off by Emory for taking you in to meet the Other's most obnoxious creatures.'

'He wasn't *that* obnoxious.'

'Then he was on his best behaviour.' He coloured a little. 'Trust me, they can be obscene.'

'That sounds like a fun story.'

'Another time maybe.'

'I guess. I'd better go and check on Archie,' I said. 'Have you called Steve about the attack?'

'No. Should I have?'

I thought about it. I was info sharing with Steve, but this wasn't a murder, just an attack, and pack politics were at play. Bringing in the Connection undermined me, like a child hiding behind her mother's skirts. 'No, that's fine,' I confirmed. 'Let's go see the patient.'

Chapter 18

Archie was being treated in his room and we had to cross the communal living space to reach it. The room was packed and it fell silent as I walked in. I glanced around. As far as I could see there were pack wolves, more than had attended the feast, and wolf pups dotted amongst the adults. The pack had rallied and come together in the face of an attack. It said something that they had rallied for Archie but not for Mark.

Mark had been number two in the pack, and he may have had their respect or even their fear, but they'd had no great affection for him. I looked around the room and was pleased when many wolves made eye contact and inclined their heads. It was a vast improvement over my first large pack gathering, which had been met with stony silence and glares. Of course, at that time I'd been explaining that Lord Samuel was dead by my own hands so I hadn't exactly expected a warm fuzzy welcome. Lord Samuel had been eccentric but well liked.

I couldn't see the council wolves, for which I was grateful because this felt like a moment just for the pack. However, there were still too many wolves that I couldn't recognise and put a name to; I would have to do better.

As I was chastening myself, Liam slid abruptly from the sofa and knelt before me, head bowed. There was an audible gasp around the room, then everyone seemed to hold their breath until Marissa copied Liam and Seren followed. It started off a Mexican wave of kneeling.

One of the kids, Bobby I think his name is, remained standing. 'Kneel to your alpha,' his mother, Sonia, whispered to him. He frowned in confusion.

'But I thought we didn't like her,' he said loudly into the silence.

Sonia blushed bright red. 'We respect our alpha. Kneel!' she hissed and pulled him down by his sleeves. A titter of laughter went around the room, easing the tension.

The last standing wolves finally knelt; they trusted Liam's and the others' judgement of me. Even Tristan knelt, though he kept his eyes locked on mine in challenge.

What the hell? I asked Esme, stunned.

They are acknowledging us as alpha! she crowed triumphantly. **Let's turn, so we can howl acceptance of their offer.**

Their offer of what?

Loyalty.

I slid off the beautiful dressing gown reluctantly. As I went to pass it to Manners, I was startled to see him kneeling too, right next to me. And now I was naked. Which put his eyeline at... Thank God his head was bowed.

I let the change rip over us. The instant we stood on four legs, we tossed our head back and let out a long triumphant howl. All around me my pack looked up, exchanging smiles, looking pleased. Once again, I'd passed a test I had no idea existed.

Enough of this. We need to check on Archie and his wolf.

We do, Esme agreed, but happiness was bubbling through her at the pack's acceptance. I didn't fully get what had happened, but I gathered it was a big deal.

We padded out of the room and down the corridor. Outside Archie's room, a Ben & Jerry's carton lay on the floor with a discarded fork nearby. Delicious ice cream lay in a milky puddle, sticky and nowhere near as good as when it was frozen.

It turns out that even in wolf form you can sigh a little.

I moved past the foregone treat and slunk into Archie's room. It was a mess; the door I'd kicked in hadn't shattered cleanly, and there were shards of wood everywhere.

Archie – or rather his wolf – was lying prone, panting. His golden eyes were wide with fear.

Esme reached out to him instantly. **It's alright,** she crooned.

I can't move. Panic laced his thoughts.

Amber needs you to be still to heal you. She's making you better, Esme reassured him.

'Nearly done.' Amber said wearily. 'One last rune.' She pulled out a pot of potion from her ever-present black tote bag and snapped on fresh disposable gloves. The smell of the potion was vile, and we recoiled.

'Sorry,' she said absently. She dipped her paintbrush into the tar-like substance and smeared it liberally on Archie's wolf's belly. It glowed for a moment, then the wolf leapt abruptly onto his legs and growled at her.

'Stop it,' Amber growled back firmly, not batting an eyelid. 'I saved your life. You owe me.'

The wolf subsided but watched her flintily with golden eyes. Amber ignored him as she packed her bag. She addressed her comments to me. 'I'll invoice you. Your "get here quick" carries an extra fee. But it saved his life – as did his shift.'

She slung her tote on her shoulder and looked again at Archie's wolf before turning to us. 'You need to deal with this.' She gestured to his golden eyes. 'But we need to talk before I leave. I'll wait in your office. Don't be too long, I'm tired.'

We inclined our head in acknowledgement and she left us alone with the feral wolf. I reached inside myself for the magic to pipe, but Esme stopped me with a gentle paw. **We don't need it while we're like this. We can talk to him because he is pack.** She turned to him and I felt the shift of her focus.

How are you known?

I have chosen Fred, he said finally.

It is a worthy name, Esme agreed, even though I was giggling in our head. **I am Esme.**

You are alpha.

***We* are alpha,** Esme corrected him. **Neither of us can rule alone. Together we can command respect. So must it be with you and Archie.**

He does not let me out, Fred said sulkily. **I am forever locked in chains.**

We will tell him to let you out, Esme promised. **But you must let him return.**

Why?

You know what will happen if you do not. An image of complete darkness flashed in my mind.

I do not want that. Fred shuddered. **But I want freedom.**

We are alpha, Esme pointed out. **We will make Archie let you loose, as long as you promise that when the time comes to relinquish hold you will do so.**

Fred considered it. **I will agree to this. On your oath so mote it be.**

On my oath so mote it be, Esme agreed solemnly.

Fred bowed his head in submission. When he looked up, his eyes were blue. Archie was back.

I shifted into my human form and reached out to him. 'You need to turn back to human Archie.'

He considered me for a long minute before he bowed his head, eerily echoing his wolf of moments before, and his shift started. It was a long five minutes until he stood before us as human once again. He looked pale and shattered, and his expression was shuttered. 'What *are* you?' he asked me.

'Naked,' I answered, deliberately misunderstanding his question. A blanket lay on his sofa so I picked it up and wrapped it around myself. 'Get dressed.'

I sat on the sofa. Archie stared at me blankly for a long moment before he tugged clothes out of his chest of drawers and pulled them on slowly, moving as if his whole body was aching.

Before I gestured for him to sit on the sofa with me, I brushed off some splinters of wood and eyed the open doorway. It couldn't be helped. I couldn't hear anyone in the corridor so we were alone for now. 'Tell me what happened,' I demanded.

He sat down gingerly on the sofa. 'I have no fucking idea,' he said, frustrated. 'The last thing I remember is the feast after the hunt. Next thing I know, I'm ... lost. So fucking lost. And then my wolf found me.' He frowned and scratched his head. 'He pulled me back, and then *he* let *me* take charge. He's never done that, not once. What the hell is going on?'

'You were attacked. You were drugged at the feast and you excused yourself. You were staggering like you were drunk.'

'I don't get drunk,' Archie muttered.

'No. I was concerned but I thought you were just letting off steam,' I admitted. 'I excused myself from the party to grab some ice cream. When I was walking along the corridor, I heard a sound like you were in pain. I called to you and you didn't answer. There was shattering glass, so I kicked down the door. Your assailant had left via your balcony door. She'd left you sliced from navel to sternum and you were bleeding badly.'

'She?' He frowned. 'I don't remember.'

'We've had intel that it was a female,' I confirmed. 'You were tied to a chair, so I undid the knots and laid you down. You were unconscious but your wolf wasn't, and I convinced him to turn. He took over. The shift started your healing and I called Amber DeLea for the rest.'

'How did you convince my wolf to turn?'

I shrugged. 'A bit of snapping and snarling. I followed your attacker's tracks, but I lost her near a group of vampyrs. I spoke to a witness who saw a female werewolf pass that way.'

'One of my pack mates drugged and attacked me,' he said flatly.

'It seems that way. Do you know who?'

He shook his head. 'I don't remember anything past the feast.'

'Where you ingested the drug,' I surmised.

'My wolf... He let me back in control,' he said wonderingly. 'What's going on?'

'We'll talk about that another day,' I reassured him. 'For now, pack some stuff. I don't want to leave you here as a target.'

He shook his head. 'I don't know why I'd be a target. It doesn't make sense.'

'Someone thinks you have something in common with Mark – and the only thing I know about is the black tourney you attended.'

He blanched, then sighed. 'I downplayed it a little when we spoke earlier. I attended a couple of them with Mark.'

'A couple or a few?'

'A few,' he said reluctantly. 'But it was before my blooding and before I took my place in the pack. I was high a lot of the time in those days, as much as a werewolf can be. I was rebelling against my dad's authority – teenage shit. Dad would have been so mad if he'd known.' He sighed. 'Mark paraded me like a badge, the alpha's son at a black tourney. Eventually I got the vibe that I was being used and I stopped going.'

'But not before everyone linked you and Mark,' I pointed out.

He winced. 'Yeah.'

'Whatever Mark was into, it looks like his killer thought you knew about it.'

'I don't,' he promised.

I wished I had Jess with me – then I remembered. She could truth seek on the phone if she were in Other.

I stood and pawed though the remains of my clothes, but I couldn't see my phone in the remnants. 'Where's your phone?' I asked Archie.

He blinked at my sudden change of topic. 'There.' He pointed. 'Charging by my bed.'

I powered it on and passed it to him to unlock. When he passed it back, I dialled Jess's number, which I knew by heart.

'Lucy? Are you okay?' Her voice was sleepy, like I'd just woken her.

I realised the time: it was nearly 11pm. 'Sorry to ring so late. Archie has been attacked.' Jess had warmed to Archie the last time they'd hung out; he'd saved her bacon by letting her ride his back away from a horde of ravening unicorns. Since then, they'd been kosher.

'Do you need me to come?' she asked urgently.

'He's fine – Amber healed him – but I need to ask him some questions. Can you listen and tell me if you think he's telling the truth?' The last line was purely for Archie's benefit. He didn't know Jess was a truth seeker; she kept her skills hidden for good reason, but it made sense that I would trust her more experienced judgement.

'Sure. Put me on speaker.'

'Repeat what you just told me,' I ordered Archie.

He ran through his whole story, from the feast to waking up to discussing the black tourneys.

'Okay,' said Jess. 'Take me off speaker.'

Mindful of a werewolf's superior hearing I walked out to the balcony, careful not to tread on the shattered glass. 'Go.'

'He was lying when he said he didn't know his attacker, but I rephrased the question, and he was telling the truth when he said he couldn't remember who attacked him. He was telling the truth when he said he didn't know why Mark was killed, or by whom. He knows something about his attacker, but not consciously. Amber might be able to scry the image out of his mind.'

Or Fred's mind, Esme suggested.

You clever little wolf! I praised. *That's a brilliant idea.*

'Thanks, Jess. That's been really helpful. Sorry to wake you. At least you weren't busy with Emory when I called.'

'We were busy earlier,' she said cheerfully. 'And you can call me any time, you know that. While I've got you, I've been digging into your adoption papers but the copies I received were incomplete. I've made an appointment to go to the offices in a couple of days.'

'Thanks, Jess. I owe you.'

'Don't be silly. I'll keep you up to date. Love you, Luce.'

'Love you. Meditate yourself back to sleep. Night, Jess.'

'Night, Lucy.'

We rang off. 'Jess believes you,' I said to Archie. I'd speak to Amber before I raised scrying as an option. People don't tend to like others screwing with their minds, so I'd check if it was possible first. 'Let's get you somewhere safe.'

He grabbed a few things, shoved them into a duffel and slung it on his shoulder. I glanced at the candle on his desk. 'The candle – is it yours?'

He shook his head, frowning. 'No. I'm not a candle guy.'

'Chicks dig candles,' I said lightly. 'Let's go.' I moved the candle mentally into the evidence column. I'd been too hasty to dismiss it from Mark's crime scene, but I'm a quick learner.

We went through the communal lounge, where I slipped on the dressing gown instead of clutching a blanket around me. Archie was swamped as the pack moved round him, touching and hugging to make sure he was alright. Their concern and affection was palpable and nice to see. It would have been nicer if some of that affection had been directed at me but, in a pinch, I'd take the new respect they were showing me instead.

I turned to Liam. 'I want you to take Archie to Rosie's tonight and stay with him. I'll see if Maxwell can provide some elemental support.'

Liam nodded. 'No problem. I charged two days ago, though.'

'You're not there to charge, you're there to keep Archie safe. It's best if you do it in wolf form.'

Liam puffed out his chest. 'I'm on it,' he said proudly.

Manners came to my side. 'Are you okay?' His eyes swept over me analytically.

I nodded. 'Yeah, but I can't find my phone.'

'I took it out of your clothes.' He slid it out of his delightfully large man-size pockets. 'Here.'

'Thanks,' I said, relieved. I tapped out a message to Maxwell asking if two of my wolves could come to recharge and get some protection. He answered in the affirmative almost straight away. Phew.

'Can you chauffeur Liam and Archie to Rosie's, then head back when they're safe? I could use a little back-up here tonight.'

'No problem. I'll go now.' He didn't quite salute, but I could see the urge bubbling away.

'You can salute if you want,' I said with a cheeky wink.

He slid me a wry grin. 'Old habits die hard. Emergencies bring out the soldier in me.' Then he collared Archie and dragged him away from his adoring fans.

I took advantage of the kerfuffle to slip away to my office. I'd kept Amber waiting long enough.

Chapter 19

Amber was sitting in my chair with her feet on my desk, snoozing. She had no doubt stolen my seat as a power play, but now that she was fast asleep and drooling it was hard to be mad at her. Sleep had softened the lines on her face, making her look more approachable. When she was awake, Amber's eyes permanently glinted with suspicion and distrust, and she gave the impression that she was all sharp edges. I knew a defence mechanism when one slapped me in the face.

I contemplated letting her sleep longer, but I knew she'd definitely get a crick in her neck if she slept like that and she'd be happier in her own bed. I cleared my throat loudly and she started awake. She blinked and calmed herself; I saw the moment her usual collectedness swept over her.

She removed her feet slowly from my desk and rubbed her eyes. 'You took your sweet time,' she muttered. 'I told you I was tired.'

'You did. I'm sorry I kept you waiting,' I said honestly.

She shot me a reproachful look. 'Lord Samuel never kept me waiting.'

I tried to hide my irritation but, from her slight smirk, I guessed that I failed. 'I'm here now. What would you like to talk about?'

'The candle in the room. Did you notice it?'

I nodded.

'It's a potion in solid form. The candle, when lit, is used to deliberately confuse a wolf's senses. Its strong scent ensures that the werewolf can't smell anything else, like illegal drugs, dead bodies or familiar scents.'

'Great. Does it work on any other species?'

'It works as a lovely, scented candle for the rest of us. No one else has super-scenting abilities that need to be interfered with. It's illegal, of course. But there you go.'

'Mark was given a highly regulated potion used by the Connection to discombobulate prisoners during transport. Apparently it affects their ability to control their bodies.'

'I know the one you mean. It also affects their memories and makes them more susceptible to suggestion. It's a nasty potion, known catchily as 3418. Only a handful of us are licensed to brew it, and we can only sell to the Connection.'

'So someone is selling it illegally.'

'Or someone is stealing it from the Connection's stores,' Amber pointed out. 'It's not always the witch that's in the wrong you know.' She glared, affronted.

'Sorry. But can you give me those names?'

'No. I'll look into it myself and let you know what I find.' She moved as if to stand up.

'Archie doesn't remember his attacker, but there's a chance his wolf might. Can you scry the wolf's mind?'

She sat down again. 'I'm not sure that's ever been done,' she said finally. 'Let me do some research. Scrying hurts. The wolf needs to be prepared and willing for that. I won't do it without his full consent.'

'I'll speak to him.'

She grabbed her bag from the floor. 'I'll be in touch,' she said as she swept out of my room without a backward glance.

I slumped onto my desk and put my head on my arms. I was tired but still a bit antsy. The mansion didn't feel safe anymore, and that pissed me off not just for my own sake but for all of the wolves that lived here. It was a stronghold;

it was *supposed* to be safe. I'd patrol tonight and see if I could keep it that way.

There was a quiet knock on my door. I sat up and tried to look alert. 'Come!'

The door opened and I relaxed again as I encountered Manners' baby blues. 'Hey,' I greeted him.

He shut the heavy door. 'Hey,' he smiled. 'I come bearing gifts.'

He slid a plastic bag across my desk, and I opened it eagerly. My eyes almost filled with tears when I saw the contents. 'You brought me Ben and Jerry's!' I exclaimed in delight.

'Phish food,' he confirmed. 'Your favourite.'

I beamed at him. 'Thank you so much. You're the best.'

'No problem. I saw you'd dropped the tub in your haste to rescue Archie.'

That made me sound rather heroic and I quite liked it. No one had ever accused me of doing anything heroic before, apart from offering some excellent tax advice.

'Thank you,' I repeated, meaning it with all my heart. It was such a kind gesture.

'No problem, doll.'

I grimaced. 'No. Not doll, either.'

'Doll face?' he suggested, with a teasing smirk.

'God, no.'

'I'll work on it,' he promised.

I rolled my eyes at his continuing efforts to find me a suitable nickname then pulled the lid off the tub and peeled back the cellophane. I frowned. How was I supposed to eat it? Manners pulled out a fork from the side pocket of his combats. I grinned. Having a soldier as a number two was the best thing ever: they were so observant. 'Perfect,' I said, digging in happily. He watched with open amusement as I chowed down.

This *is* good, Esme admitted. **What is it called?**

Phish food.

I never thought I would enjoy fish food.

I giggled. Manners looked at me questioningly. 'Esme didn't think she would enjoy food that fish eat,' I explained. He laughed.

I do not get the humour, Esme complained

It's too complicated to explain, Esme. Sorry.

She mentally shrugged and decided to ignore our human weirdness. She sat down to lick and groom our fur.

'I've a few updates,' I said to Manners. I ran through my chat with Archie and my call to Jess. He knew she was a truth seeker, so that made it easier. I told him about the candle and what Amber had said, including that she might be able to scry something from Fred's mind.

'You've been busy,' he praised.

'I need to sort this. I hate that the mansion doesn't feel safe.'

'New security will be in first thing tomorrow,' he promised.

I nodded. 'But for tonight, most of the pack is here and we can't have another attack. I'll patrol the grounds.' I grinned. 'After all, I need to run off this ice cream.'

He studied me seriously, his face giving away nothing. 'I'll patrol with you.'

'That would be great.' I could use the companionship; besides, he would be a huge asset if trouble came knocking.

'Give me ten minutes and we'll head out together,' Manners said. 'I just need to make sure there are beds and blankets for everyone who wants to stay human.'

'Is everyone staying?' I asked, surprised.

'Strength in numbers, and comfort in them too. The majority will bunk down in the pack lounge.'

'Shouldn't *I* sort the blankets and stuff?' I asked.

He shook his head. 'No. The Prime doesn't hand out food, he just orders it to be given out. You ordered the blankets.'

I blinked. 'But I didn't.'

'You delegated it to me. Relax, I'm your second. That means more than just patrolling with you, it's about helping you succeed as a leader. I've got your back.'

I didn't need Jess's truth-seeking abilities to know that he meant every word. 'I know you were happy being brethren, but I'm really glad you nearly died and had to be turned into a werewolf,' I said.

He laughed. 'Me too, honeybunch. Me too.'

I snorted. 'No. Veto.'

He stood. 'Back to the drawing board. I won't be too long.'

When he left, I had a goofy smile on my face. I told myself my happy was from the ice cream. I didn't need Jess to tell me I was lying.

Chapter 20

I shivered a little as the rain continued its steady downpour. It was the slow kind of rain that soaks you to your core.

Manners and I had started the patrol by ourselves. We'd circled the mansion together, then taken it in turns to duck into the house and check the corridors and the slumbering occupants of the living room. Our patrol had been noticed; before long we were joined by Marissa, Seren and, far more surprisingly, Tristan and Brian. Brian almost looked at me with grudging respect too. Almost.

We split into three teams of two: two of us inside, two of us around the mansion, and two of us patrolling the outskirts of the grounds. The cold February weather was making the experience arduous, but the sun was rising.

Soon the other packmates would be up and we could fall into the welcoming warmth of our beds.

Even with our thick fur, the constant chill and dampness had us shivering any time we paused in our patrol. Better to keep moving. Half of me wanted to stop and roll into bed, but Esme was focused on the safety of our pack. She was in charge, and there was no way she'd let me shirk, no matter how much I wanted to. She pulled our weary body on, her eyes and ears primed and searching. She was like a machine.

I hadn't tried to speak to Manners' wolf while we were patrolling because it seemed like something I should do with permission. He and his wolf seemed content with the job of securing the pack, and they worked in harmony. His wolf didn't seem as angry as Fred had been, but then Fred already had a lifetime of subjugation.

It wasn't long before noises from the mansion started to disturb the air around us. The occupants were stirring.

The front door opened and Ace leaned against the heavy wooden door. 'Everyone's up,' he called. 'You can stop patrolling.' He looked at me approvingly, but Esme and I didn't need his approval; we needed our pack to be safe.

Esme gave a headshake; we'd stop when the brethren arrived to set up additional security. As if I'd summoned them with our thoughts, three black Ford Escapes rolled up the driveway and parked in the drive. I was about to change to talk to them when it occurred to me that, although nakedness might be par for the course for the pack, it could cause a different reaction in the brethren.

Esme agreed, and she trotted past Ace and into my office. I changed to human and grabbed the white dressing gown – not my most authoritative outfit, but it would have to do. I was so happy to be warm. I grabbed Manners' combats and T-shirt and took them out.

He had already started to shift, and it was only another minute or so before he stood before me in human form. I held out his clothes and averted my eyes. He threw on his combats quickly but, despite the chill, he didn't seem to be in a hurry to pull on the T-shirt. He had a magnificent torso, tanned and full of rippling muscles that I couldn't help but admire. I hoped my stare looked calm rather than ogling – but man the guy was cut. Yum.

He and Ace seemed to be having a moment. Their eyes were locked in a staring contest. I let out a barely audible huff. 'Thank you, Ace. This is a pack matter. You can go.'

He hesitated a beat too long, and Esme started to get riled. Finally he nodded and ducked back inside. Ace might be council, but we were alpha.

The occupants of the black cars decanted and started unloading enough hardware to secure Fort Knox. One of the occupants sauntered over and Manners gave him a hard look. 'Sam. I didn't expect to see you here.'

'The Prime Elite sent me, and so did Jessica Sharp. I'm to help in any way I can.'

A little of Manners' anger died, but there was still something bubbling away. I was missing the context. Who was he, that Jess would send him? 'There's something I need to talk to you about in private, but let's get this building secured first.'

'Agreed,' Sam replied coolly. 'A glass company is on its way to replace the broken balcony doors, courtesy of the Prime.'

'And he got the measurements of the doors how exactly?' Manners huffed.

Sam smirked. 'Fritz found some blueprints and Google Earth images. He sorted it.'

Manners nodded. 'Well then, it will be right.'

'No doubt.' Sam stalked back to one of the cars and opened the door. 'We're here, kid,' he said.

The skinny black kid, who'd been snoozing away, rubbed his eyes. Seeing Manners, he fumbled excitedly with his seatbelt and bounded out. He flashed Manners a huge grin and bounced into his arms. 'Greg!' he cried, hugging him tight. I watched as Manners returned the hug just as warmly.

'Fritz,' he murmured. 'It's good to see you, kid. Thanks for coming.'

'I wouldn't miss it for the world. We can hang out and sort out a control centre for you, just like old times.' The young boy pulled back, searching his face. 'You didn't even say goodbye,' he accused softly.

'Had to skip town before my mother got wind of me being there,' Manners said lightly, ruffling the kid's tight black curls. 'Besides, saying goodbye to you is just too hard.'

'I missed you,' the lad said in a small voice.

'Back at you.' Manners pulled him in for another hug.

'Is there a reason you're still shirtless?' Fritz asked with a mischievous grin.

'Showing off my guns.' Manners winked, making Fritz laugh. 'Come on, I'll show you where we need to set up.' He turned back to me. 'I'm going to set up in your office. It's the most secure room and it makes sense for you to have primary access.'

'Sure.' I knew nothing about security, but they could do whatever the hell they liked if it would make the mansion more secure. I did *not* want another incident. I was aware that the attacks had probably been carried out by a pack mate, but hopefully the cameras would make them think twice about launching another. 'Manners,' I called. 'Hallways and entrances and exits. We don't want cameras in every single room. People are entitled to some privacy.'

He grimaced a little but nodded, then headed inside.

I was exhausted and I needed some down time. The mansion was crawling with strangers, and they were already banging and hammering and drilling. It was not conducive to a good sleep.

I knew just where to go. I got changed, grabbed a duffel of spare clothes and headed off to Rosie's. It was early morning, and the breakfast trade and portal trade were booming.

I nodded to Maxwell, who was serving behind the counter. 'Your boys are upstairs,' he called.

I nodded. *See you on the other side,* I whispered to Esme, feeling a little morose.

I always come back, she reassured me gently. **Sleep well, Lucy.**

As I stepped into the portal, Esme faded from my mind and my triangle disappeared from my forehead. I went upstairs to the apartment and was admitted by an elemental I recognised from my last visit.

Archie and Liam were at the breakfast bar eating toast with a huge pile of scrambled eggs; they must have raided a farm. My tummy rumbled loudly. I'd been in wolf form all night and my hunger was crippling.

Liam pushed his plate towards me. 'You get started on that. I'll make some more.'

I didn't need to be invited twice and sat down next to Archie. 'Hey, Archie. Hey, Fred.'

Archie blinked. 'Who's Fred?'

'Your wolf. He calls himself Fred.'

Archie's mouth dropped open. 'Fred?' he said wonder-ingly. 'That seems so ... nice.' He shuddered a little.

'Fred *is* nice, he's just a bit grumpy that you never let him have the reins.'

'Because I'd be lost!' Archie exclaimed. 'He'd never let me regain control!'

'Yet here you sit,' I pointed out. 'In control again.'

Archie looked confused. 'He was in charge?'

'He was. When you were injured, he took control and made you both change. He saved your life.'

'Why?'

I shrugged. 'I guess he might like you a little after all.'

Archie scratched his head. 'I don't get it. My whole life I was told never to trust my wolf, that he'd ravish and destroy everything if I let him.'

I snorted. 'Most of the time our wolves are more civilised than we are. Humans have always been the real monsters in this life.' I dug into my scrambled eggs and let Archie think on it.

Liam was looking at me speculatively across the kitchen. 'What's my wolf called?'

I shook my head. 'I don't know, we haven't met yet.'

'We hunted together,' he pointed out.

'Sure, but you were still in control. One day, when all this is over, I'll see if I can say hi to your wolf.' I guess I wasn't keeping my piping ability so quiet anymore; only time would tell if it was a huge mistake.

'How?' Liam asked.

'I'm a piper.' I shrugged casually and carried on eating. They were both looking at me aghast, as if I'd casually announced that I was the devil incarnate. I ignored them, finished up my toast and eggs and washed them down with some orange juice.

I picked my duffel. 'I'm going to get some sleep. I was up all night patrolling. I'll see you both after a few hours' kip. Stay here and watch my back, would you?'

They both straightened and gave firm nods. I walked into the room I'd used last time. I wanted to fall straight into the fresh sheets on the bed but I really needed a shower. I peeled off my clothes and turned on the shower to hot. I could almost imagine Esme wagging in my head – she loves a hot shower.

I washed quickly but found my eyes sliding shut under the warmth of the spray. I dragged myself out of the shower and towel-dried my hair but I couldn't be bothered to dry it. I needed sleep. I tumbled towards the bed, and in minutes I was out.

Chapter 21

I awoke feeling refreshed and ready to roll. I checked the time: 1pm. I'd only had just over four hours sleep, but being a werewolf sure has its upsides.

My tummy was rumbling again, so I got dressed and took a minute to French braid my blonde hair out of the way. I moisturised my face, swiped on the barest brush of mascara and counted it as a good job.

I rang my mum for a quick chat. She was on her way back in from a long shift so we didn't talk long, but it was nice to hear her voice. She always has such unwavering faith in me, and it always helps me feel stronger.

I headed into the kitchen feeling pumped and ready to face the day. The boys had been talking but they fell silent when I walked in. Jeez, it was enough to make a girl paranoid. 'Morning,' I greeted them cheerfully.

'Alpha.' Liam nodded. 'You look well rested.'

'I am, thank you. Is there anything up here to eat?'

'Bacon sandwich?' Liam offered.

'Yes, please! That'd be great. Is there any coffee on the go?'

Archie went to the kettle to make me a coffee whilst Liam turned on the grill and started sorting out some food. There are definitely benefits to being the boss.

Archie slid me a glass of OJ. 'How do you like your coffee?' he asked.

'Milky and one sugar.'

'My dad always called that wussy coffee,' he mumbled.

I smiled. 'Then one wussy coffee over here, please.'

'Coming up.'

A few minutes later I was eating a sandwich and drinking a hot, wussy coffee. I was feeling positive; yes, there'd been another attack but I knew it was a female werewolf, and right this minute the mansion was being converted into Fort Knox by a host of hunky brethren men. All for mate's rates. Plus, my pack had done that kneeling thing, and it seemed like I was finally making them realise that all I wanted was for them to be happy and safe. Small goals in life bring the most happiness, possibly because they're so achievable.

After I'd eaten my fill, I was eager to head downstairs, step through the portal and feel Esme again. I felt vulnerable without her, as if I were missing a limb – an important one, like my right arm.

Archie, Liam and I packed our duffels and cleaned up. It wouldn't do to leave the apartment in a state, though no doubt Maxwell has it cleaned professionally between occupants. It's always spotless.

The lunchtime crowd had rolled in and there was a queue for the portal. Liam was still in the Other, which was reassuring; I felt vulnerable in Common when so many Others undoubtedly had access to the full range of their powers.

We queued for a long ten minutes. Some dryads walked in and nodded to me in recognition. I didn't know them from Adam, but I guess being alpha means everyone knows you.

The tension in the room ratcheted up when the five vampyrs I'd hidden from in the park walked in. From the looks they were getting – a mix of curiosity and caution – I guessed they weren't local. 'What do we have here?' The leader stalked forward and sneered at me.

'A queue,' I responded, gesturing behind me. 'Perhaps the concept has passed you by. What you do is stand in a line and wait your turn. Or is common courtesy beyond vampyrs?'

He sneered some more and opened his mouth to deliver an undoubtedly witty response. Maxwell sauntered over. 'Problem?' he asked the vampyr coldly.

'And you are?'

'I'm master of this hall,' Maxwell narrowed his eyes. 'You must not be in need of a portal.' He leaned against a table, arms folded, and levelled a hard stare at the vampyr.

The vampyr faltered and exchanged glances with his pals. He cleared his throat. 'No disrespect was intended.'

'I should hope not, because the nearest portal is thirty minutes' drive away. And you're about to enter Common, and she is about to enter the Other.'

'She stinks of wolf,' he snarled.

'You must be young,' Maxwell said insultingly. 'The sanctity of the halls stands. Either you respect the rules, or you can go to another portal.'

The vampyr leader grimaced but appeared to simmer down. 'Fine,' he muttered.

'Fine,' Maxwell agreed. 'The back of the queue is over there.' He put half a dozen witches and dryads between us.

'Thanks,' I murmured.

Maxwell winked. 'As special as you are to me, I'd do that for anyone. No fighting in the halls. You all need to know that if you try anything, the elementals will rain fire down on your heads. Literally. Retribution is swift and decisive when the sanctity of a hall is broken. It's been a while since I've rained hellfire, but I'd be happy for the excuse.' He spoke loudly so the whole café could hear. We all took the hint: Roscoe might be away, but Maxwell was stepping up to the plate.

He gave the barest of nods to two of his elemental cronies and they strolled past the vampyrs. The elementals wouldn't *bring* trouble, but they had no issue with ending it. I took out my phone, surreptitiously got a shot of the asshole vampyr and sent it to Jess.

He's a vamp with a chip on his shoulder. Can you find out who he is? X

I got a quick response: *On it x*

I know that Maxwell is a big, bad fire elemental but he always comes across as friendly and easy going so I sometimes forget the power he wields. I reminded myself that people are like onions, made up of many layers, and that the Other is *dangerous*. That was something I'd realised as soon as I became aware of it, but recent events had superseded that awareness and I'd been more focused on pack issues than Other issues. This was a timely reminder that I couldn't bury my head in the sand.

Luckily, politics are something that come naturally to me, so I could bump them up my priorities' list. I made a mental note to amend my spreadsheet later. Pack relations were important, but so was securing more allies. It would also be helpful if my pack could have a unique selling point, a USP, that made us a desired ally. It was something to think about.

When I strolled through the portal, Esme joined me on the Other side. *Hey!* I greeted her joyfully.

Hello, Lucy. She felt my annoyance and I flashed up the memory of the vampy asshole.

She asked eagerly, **Can we go and taunt the vampyrs some more?**

Best not. I sighed reluctantly. *We don't want to piss off Maxwell.*

No, she agreed. **He is an admirable hunter.**

Let's go home and see what the brethren are doing.

Securing our den, no doubt. Esme is so literal.

No doubt, I agreed.

I waited for Archie to pass through the portal, then we went out to my car. As I drove home, I made light conversation. 'Still no idea who attacked you?' I asked.

'None. I'm sorry. The last thing I remember is the feast in the hall.'

'No problem. We'll work it out,' I offered reassuringly.

'He can bunk with me until we work out why he's a target,' Liam suggested.

'Good idea. Strength in numbers. Both of you be careful who you accept food and drink from. Archie, do you remember who brought your drinks?'

Archie shrugged helplessly. 'I'm sorry. I was a bit excited after the hunt. We took turns organising rounds of drinks. No one sticks out in my memory, but I'm sure Mrs Dawes and Elena served most of them. They often do.'

'Never mind. We'll work it out.' I repeated. I'd wait until I'd heard from Amber about whether it was possible to scry a wolf before I raised the idea with Archie.

'Elena didn't get on with Mark, did she?' I asked casually.

Archie frowned a little, catching my drift. 'Elena had no love for Mark, but she couldn't ... wouldn't hurt *me*.' He laid emphasis on the last word. So he didn't doubt she could have hurt Mark. Interesting.

'She looooves Archie,' Liam teased, nudging him in a juvenile fashion.

Archie glared at him. 'Shut up,' he muttered.

Liam sobered. 'Actually, maybe she would hurt you. You broke her heart. It took ages for her to start hanging out with us again. I blame Archie for dating a friend – don't mix business with pleasure.'

Archie coloured. 'We dated for all of three months. Things ended – it was fine.'

Liam snorted. 'Eventually.'

I raised an eyebrow. 'How did things end?' I asked Archie. 'Did you dump her?'

Archie winced. 'Dump is such a shitty term. I liked her, but I'm not ready for something serious and that's what she wanted. She's also pretty messy, she always had to come to my room. It got to be a bit much.' I tried not to condemn him for dumping someone for being a little untidy.

He was red faced and embarrassed so I directed the conversation back to Mark. 'She didn't like Mark?'

'She seemed to like Mark well enough when she joined the pack,' Liam disagreed.

'I know she wasn't always part of the Home Counties pack. Do you know where she came from originally?'

'She was a born werewolf. She used to talk about her family a lot. I think she petitioned the council to move from a southern pack – Cornwall or Devon.'

'Any idea why?'

Liam shrugged. 'It's not unusual at her age. It's hard to find a werewolf mate if everyone you know grew up with you and thinks of you like a little sister.'

It was my turn to frown. 'And is it always the women who are displaced?'

Archie rolled his eyes. 'Don't go all feminist on us! It's the way it's been for centuries – it's tradition.'

'Traditions can change,' I growled. 'Back to Elena and Mark. She liked him but they had a falling out – over what?'

Archie shrugged and Liam shook his head; they didn't know, or they weren't sharing, I wasn't sure which. I'd have to ask Elena herself.

As we drew up to the mansion, Archie let out a low whistle. 'They've been busy.'

He wasn't wrong. There were new metal installations above every window and door. Metal shutters? That felt a bit overkill – but what did I know? One pack mate was dead and another had been attacked. I wasn't sure if the shutters were to keep intruders out if we hit a panic button or to keep them in.

There was a team of witches on ladders painting runes on every surface. The marks looked a little ugly, but you wouldn't see them if you were in Common.

'Go and mingle,' I said to Archie and Liam. 'Reassure everyone you're okay. I'm going to talk to the witches and then the security guys.'

I approached Amber. She had a clipboard and was marching up and down like a military commander, checking all the runework was perfect. 'Hey, how's it going?' I asked.

'All but done.' Amber confirmed. 'We're just finishing up the last few sets.'

'Are there any anti-vampyr runes?'

She raised an eyebrow, 'Most people are content without them if it's a residential property.'

I thought of the five vampyrs meeting in the park around the corner. It might be overkill, but paranoia was fast becoming a good friend of mine. 'Can you do one or two? I'd feel better.'

She raised an eyebrow but nodded and stalked over to one of the witches who was still up a ladder. 'Shauna,' she called, 'we need another protection rune.'

'Against what?'

'Vampyrs.'

'I'm on it,' Shauna promised.

'Anything else?' Amber asked me impatiently.

'Nope, that's great. Thanks.'

'Pay the invoice promptly. That's the thanks I prefer,' Amber said brusquely.

'Sure thing.'

I left them to it and went into my office. The room had been transformed: on my side was my mahogany desk, bookshelves and cosy leather chair; on the other side was a security station. It somewhat ruined the ambiance.

What's up? Esme asked.

They've made our den look horrible, I grumped.

I felt her amusement. **It keeps the pack safe,** she pointed out.

At times, she's a better person than me. *Yeah,* I sighed. *Okay.*

There were numerous CCTV screens, computers and keyboards, and two swivel chairs. The screens were wall mounted and the computers were set up on a sleek modern desk. Manners was sitting at it with the kid, Fritz.

Sam was lounging in my leather chair, looking casual and deadly in equal measure. Something about the guy screamed predator, and he made both Esme and me uneasy. He *looked* normal but there was a deadly alertness to him that he couldn't quite hide. He made Manners look soft, which was ridiculous because Manners was the toughest guy I'd ever met. It was the eyes. Sam had deadly eyes.

'Toodles,' I called into the room. 'How's it going?'

'Toodles?' Fritz giggled. 'You're not very scary for an alpha.'

'I can alpha your ass off, but this is my office and I refuse to be cowed.' I met Sam's eyes and the tiniest smile tugged at his lips. I was amusing the terrifying guy – great.

'What's with all the metal shutters?' I asked. 'Are they to keep intruders in or out?'

'Both,' Manners confirmed. 'We've situated panic buttons in a couple of places. Hit one of those and the mansion goes into lockdown – no one in and no one out. If we're attacked, we can roll down shutters to make it harder for our enemy to gain entrance. And don't worry – the Prime has already dealt with the planning permission and it's been granted.'

It hadn't even occurred to me that planning permission would be required. Emory had greased some palms to get all of this done so quickly. I got the feeling that I was going to owe my best friend's partner big time. 'And the runes?'

'Amber sent a team.'

'At the Prime's request, I assume,' I said drily.

'He looks after his friends,' Manners said with a hint of pride. He idolised Emory and it wasn't hard to see why. Emory is head of both the dragons and the brethren in the whole of the UK, and he knows a thing or two about inspiring loyalty. Maybe I could ask for his Spark Notes.

'What precisely do the runes do?'

'A few things. Primarily, we got ones to keep the Common realmers away, to help prevent humans stumbling on a house full of wolves. We've also got anti-fire runes, which will stand up to even a level-one fire elemental – for a short period at least. And we've got anti-spy runes. You could have a conversation with your window open in this office and someone standing outside won't hear a word.'

Now that would be handy. I'm a big James Bond fan, and I loved the cloak-and-dagger vibe. Life was so much more exciting now I was a werewolf. 'Cool. I asked them to add some anti-vampyr runes as well.'

'It's probably overkill. Vampyrs can't gain access to a residential house without permission anyway.'

'I'd rather go over than under. What about our land?' I asked. 'Can vampyrs gain access to that?'

'They can get onto our land,' Manners confirmed. 'But we've set up perimeter cameras and motion detectors.'

I thought of Archie's shattered door. 'Can we arrange a master key for all the bedrooms in case of emergency?'

'That was already sorted,' He pulled out a keyring with a wolf head on it.

I blinked. 'It was? So, I didn't need to break down Archie's door?'

'No, but you were pretty impressive. You certainly made an impression on the pack.' He grinned. 'I heard a few people talking about it afterwards.'

I was such a doofus; I'd had access to a key the whole time. I groaned aloud and changed the subject. 'Who is going to monitor this?' I gestured to the cameras and screens.

'In down times we don't need to worry too much, but when we're on high alert like now, we'll set up a rota. I'll ask for volunteers, run some training and get some six-hour shifts in place. We shouldn't need to maintain that level for long.'

'I've set alerts,' Fritz piped up. 'When the external motion detectors are triggered, it sends a notification to Greg's phone. He can log in and monitor remotely wherever he is.'

'Nice work,' I complimented him.

Fritz flashed me a grin. 'I'm good at this stuff. Now I'm going to spend the next day trying to make your security system as un-hackable as possible.'

'I appreciate that,' I said, like it didn't fluster me that my system might be hacked. This realm was something else, and I needed to learn fast or I'd fall behind.

Fritz nodded, turned back to his computers and started to type rapidly.

Manners watched him for a minute and called his name a couple of times. No reaction. 'He's in the zone, so now we can talk freely.' His tone was ominous and I didn't think I was going to like what was to follow. Serious Manners was a troubled Manners.

Chapter 22

'What's up?' I asked easily, like I wasn't nervous of the answer.

Probably death and destruction, Esme commented. **He's always so serious when there's death or destruction. He doesn't know anything about how to have fun.**

Sam's lips twitched a little. 'I like her. She's funny – for a wolf.'

I froze. He could hear Esme? First the gargoyle, and now him? I frowned. 'All right, what are you?'

'I'm known in some circles as Bastion,' Sam confessed.

I froze. There was only one Bastion I'd heard about. 'Bastion the deadly assassin griffin?'

Amusement flickered in those deadly eyes. 'That's the one.'

'We've met before. You were at the battle of the daemons when Manners was turned wolfy.'

'I was.'

'We didn't get a chance to chat, but I know Jess was grateful that you flew in to wreak havoc.'

'I'm always ready to wreak havoc.' He said it levelly, with no hint of amusement. He wasn't kidding.

'Yeah, I get that. You're a pretty scary dude.'

He was looking at me analytically. 'You've adjusted well to the Other.'

There was something in his tone, something almost familiar. Maybe a hint of affection? Jess had told me that the deadly griffin assassin thought of her like a favourite niece, that he watched over her. Jess and I were BFFs; if he knew Jess, he knew me. I wasn't sure if that was creepy or reassuring.

He watched understanding flicker over my face and gave an approving nod. 'You were always a quick girl, Lucy.'

'I'm missing something,' Manners interjected, an edge to his voice. He didn't like not being in the know.

I resisted the urge to shout 'Ha! Now you know how it feels!' because that would have undermined the calm authority figure thing I was trying to rock. I cleared my throat instead. 'Bastion here has watched me grow up.'

'Into a lovely young woman.' Bastion winked.

A noise almost like a growl emanated from Manners, and Bastion's smile widened.

'Watch it, Sam,' Manners snapped. 'She's alpha. Show her some respect.'

'I assure you I have nothing but respect for Lucy Barrett.'

'Then stop trying to give Manners a hernia,' I said, giving Bastion a pointed look.

Bastion smirked but didn't reply.

'We're getting off topic,' Manners said finally. 'Bastion knows where a black tourney is taking place, but there's a small problem.'

'There's always a problem.'

'It's tonight. In London.'

We were forty-five minutes out from London and I failed to see the issue. 'So?'

'So, we don't have much time to prepare.'

I blinked. 'We go, we pretend to be bloodthirsty spectators, we poke around. What else do we need to prepare?'

'Anonymity is essential for the tourney's audience. We need to disguise ourselves.'

Bastion shrugged. 'I'll sort masks. They're easier than glamours, and they expect one or the other at the tourney. Besides that, wear black and look rich. They like rich patrons.'

I could do rich – I have a dress for every occasion. I'm a girly-girl, so sue me. I don't have much black, though; I'm a pink girl. 'Why black?' I huffed.

'It hides blood splatters,' Bastion said blandly.

I wished I hadn't asked. 'Cool, cool, cool. What time do we need to rock and roll?'

'We'll leave here at 10pm. The tourney doesn't get going until midnight.'

'And the location?'

Bastion shook his head. 'That's need to know.'

'Um, I kind of need to know...'

'No, you don't,' he said firmly, meeting my eyes with a steely gaze.

'But how am I going to get there if I don't know where "there" is?'

'I've arranged transport. Be ready at ten.' He rose lithely from my leather seat and stalked out of the room. The guy had presence.

Fritz didn't even look up as Bastion left.

The day was still young, even factoring in some much-needed primping and pampering time. It was time to track down David and Elena, two people I knew had issues with Mark. David was lower on my suspect tree, given that he was male, but I hadn't ruled out the possibility that my gargoyle friend had been wrong. Besides, the female werewolf may well have had an accomplice so it was best to keep an open mind.

I tracked down Elena in the kitchen with Mrs Dawes. They were busy preparing dinner and Noah was mucking in as well. There were several huge pots of beef stew bubbling away, and Noah and Elena looked like they were making bread from scratch. I itched to join them – I love making bread. That yummy, yeasty smell gets me every time. 'Shall I make another batch?' I offered to Mrs Dawes.

She smiled her warm, maternal smile. 'Bless you, Lucy, you don't need to. I'm sure you have more important things to worry over.'

'What could be more important to the pack than food?' I asked, only half-joking.

I didn't wait for permission but grabbed the flour bag and weighing scales from Elena and started weighing ingredients. I didn't need a recipe: a basic white loaf was something I'd made with my dad hundreds of times, and there was something homey and familiar about the activity. In my angsty teenage years, pounding the shit out of the dough had helped me work through my issues in a healthier manner than drugs and promiscuity. Though I'd dabbled in those as well – what teen didn't?

I focused on the task at hand, careful not to mix the yeast and the salt – they like each other about as much as vampyrs and werewolves. I oiled the worktop because that keeps the consistency better than flouring it, then turned out the dough and started working it.

I looked up; the others were frozen, watching me aghast. 'Is it really so shocking for the alpha to bake?' I asked, exasperated.

'I've never seen it happen before,' Elena volunteered.

'You came to us from another pack, didn't you? No baking alpha there?'

Her expression grew guarded. 'No, no baking alpha there.'

'Where were you from originally? Your accent isn't really West Country.'

'Devon,' she admitted.

'Ah, so you know our esteemed council members. Anything I should know about them?'

She looked at me seriously. 'Don't trust any of them. At best, Ace is a serial womaniser.' I'd got that vibe already.

'And at worst?' She looked away so I tried a different tack. 'Most people seem to think Mark was a bit of a dick, too.'

PROTECTION OF THE PACK

She snorted. 'I know I shouldn't speak ill of the dead, but he was a wanker. He toned it down when Lord Samuel was about, but any other time he'd go full asshole.'

'Like what?' I asked curiously.

Elena shrugged. 'He was a brawler,' she said finally.

'So I've heard.' On a gamble, I met her eyes. 'I hear he was into black tourneys.'

Mrs Dawes gasped, Noah looked down, but Elena didn't bat an eyelid though her jaw tightened. Bingo. Of the three of them, only Mrs Dawes seemed surprised.

'Did he ever try to get you to go to one?' I asked.

'No, not me,' Elena replied, keeping her eyes on her baking. She covered her rolls with some oiled clingfilm. 'These need to rest for an hour,' she said to Mrs Dawes. Then she washed her hands and walked out without another glance at me.

She is upset, Esme noted. **We should bring her a carcass.**

Maybe ice cream would work better, I suggested.

The little tub was good, she agreed, **but a rabbit would be better. Just a small token of our concern.**

Ice cream is a human tradition, I explained.

Ah, well then. In my head, she settled down to groom herself.

I looked up to see Noah looking at me oddly. The best defence is good offence; at least that was what Sun Tzu or someone said. I went with it. 'Did you like Mark?'

'He was okay, better with the lads than the ladies. He was more comfortable throwing on some sport and drinking a beer than trying to make conversation.'

'Girls can enjoy sport and beer too.' I tried to keep the annoyance out of my voice.

'I know, but Mark didn't. He didn't really see the sexes as equal, even though werewolf females have so much more strength than human women.'

'Equality is about far more than strength,' I pointed out flatly.

'Hear, hear,' Mrs Dawes murmured almost inaudibly. If I hadn't had werewolf hearing, I probably wouldn't have caught it.

'Did you know about Mark attending black tourneys?' I asked Noah, going straight for the jugular.

'No, I had no idea, but with hindsight it makes sense. He was a fighter, always ready to take an insult and resort to violence to solve it.'

I'd have bet my bottom dollar that young Noah was lying to my face.

He hesitated then said, 'Honestly, I think he was biding his time to challenge Lord Samuel, and I think Lord

Samuel knew it. That's why he let so much of Mark's crap slide. In the last year or so, Mark got bolder and bolder. He never disobeyed Lord Samuel's wishes, but he dealt with stuff in a way that Lord Samuel would never have approved of – but always when he was away. I saw Mark with bruises and stuff, but I just assumed it was because of his pugnacious nature. I never made the connection to black tourneys. If I had, I'd have told Lord Samuel my suspicions and that would have been enough for him to act. He could have called the council. He wouldn't have needed to fight with Mark one-on-one.'

'And you, Mrs Dawes?' I asked. 'Did you know what naughty Mark was getting up to?'

She shook her head. 'The tourneys, no. I did hear he was taking drugs. He went through a phase of using Boost – I found some pink bags in his room when I was cleaning. I had a word with him, but he promised it was an experiment and said he was done with it.'

'Did you tell Lord Samuel?'

'I – no. I believed Mark, and Lord Samuel was a bit tetchy about drugs. Archie had just gone through a rebellious phase. Lord Samuel had given him enough rope to discover who he was and that drugs weren't good for the Others.'

'He didn't want to give Archie enough rope to hang himself?'

'No, not that much rope,' she agreed. 'Lord Samuel seemed to be giving Archie the freedom to do what he liked, but I know he kept tabs on him. He knew who Archie's dealers were and where he was going when he went out.'

'But he didn't keep similar tabs on Mark?'

'No, Mark wasn't his son. He was barely his second and certainly not a trusted confidante, not like you and Manners. It's good to see an alpha and beta bond working in harmony as it should.'

Noah agreed. 'Yeah, that's what it should be like.'

My dough was elastic and soft, so I plonked it back into the ceramic bowl for its first proving and covered it with a clean, damp tea towel. 'I'll be back in an hour to knock it back and shape the rolls,' I said to Mrs Dawes as I washed my hands. 'Any idea where I can find David?'

'He's our resident gardener. You'll find him out by the roses, I should think. He's often there when he's upset.'

'Why would he be upset?'

'Well, with Mark and Archie and everything,' said Mrs Dawes lamely and looked away. I couldn't blame her: she was the cook, housekeeper and resident counsellor. Everyone seemed to confide in her and the pack needed to know that she held on to their secrets as carefully as her own.

Noah was lying to me, and Mrs Dawes wasn't being up front. I sighed; perhaps I hadn't made as much progress as I'd thought. I made a mental note to take another crack at Noah when we were alone.

'I'll be back,' I reiterated. Noah gave me a friendly smile that the optimist in me added to my 'positive progress' column. Maybe I'd been wrong when I'd thought that cookies weren't the way to the pack's heart – bread sure had worked a treat.

Chapter 23

The brethren group were still working away, but the witches had packed up their paintbrushes and scarpered. There was no sign of the runes I'd seen them painting on the mansion. 'How come the runes are gone?' I asked the nearest man dressed all in black.

He raised an eyebrow, as if the answer were obvious. 'If the runes are visible, you give your enemy the opportunity to counter or nullify them. For these runes to reappear, a witch would need to touch the walls of the mansion. If the enemy has sneaked in a witch close enough to touch the walls, then the witch and her runes are the least of your problems.'

'Invisible runes. I bet they're pricey.'

He snorted. 'Runes are expensive – but invisible runes break the bank.' He looked me over. 'You must have done the Prime Elite one helluva favour.'

I smiled noncommittally. Nope, he was just a millionaire dragon shifter in love with my best friend. I sent Jess a quick message, letting her know that Emory had really gone the extra mile in making sure I was safe. I was sure she'd ensure he was adequately rewarded for his kindness. Kindness should be encouraged, after all.

I went into the grounds to look for David. From what I knew of him, he was a quiet guy. He wore glasses, which were obviously an affectation since the first change healed minor issues like poor eyesight or poor hearing. That made me wonder if he was like me, a rare human who'd been changed into a werewolf, rather than being born one. If so, his human family might still expect the specs, though he could have told them he'd started wearing contact lenses.

Less than five percent of wolves are changed; the rest are born. Because the survival rate for the change is so low, the council don't like too many humans to try to change. It leads to too many bodies that they have to explain away.

As I'd expected, David was out by the rose garden.

Why is he cutting bushes? Esme asked in confusion.

I didn't know how to explain topiary to a wolf, so I fell back on an old favourite. *It is tradition.*

Ah, well then.

I called out a greeting. Startled, David whipped his head towards me. 'Alpha,' he welcomed me when he'd recovered.

'David, I wondered if I might have a few words with you. I understand Mark wasn't your favourite person.' There was no point in pussy-footing around.

'That's not a crime,' he said defensively. 'Mark wasn't a lot of people's favourite person.'

'So I'm beginning to gather, but your name keeps coming up and I'm under an obligation to investigate. I don't believe you killed Mark.'

His shoulders dropped. 'No. No one thinks me capable of anything.'

I was startled by his defeatist attitude. 'It's a *good* thing that I don't think you killed Mark,' I pointed out.

'In a werewolf pack, someone believing you're capable of violence is a good thing. No one thinks I'm capable of saying boo to a goose.'

I felt Esme's confusion. **Why would one say boo to a goose? It is better to stalk it silently and snap its neck.**

I struggled to contain my laughter. *Yes, thank you, Esme. I'll note that the next time I hunt a goose.*

'You're eleventh in the pack,' I pointed out. 'That's an impressive rank in a pack our size. I'd say you've shown you've got plenty of capacity for violence, when pressed.'

'I did well during my first tourney, but since then I haven't had a need for violence. I was a gardener before my turn, so it makes sense that I fulfil that role for the pack. But everyone sees me as little more than a green-fingered dryad. I'm a wolf, dammit.'

I considered his problem. 'Okay, so next hunt we make sure you're the one given the opportunity to kill our quarry, then everyone will be reminded that you're still part of the pack. But David, you're often sitting off to one side. You need to mix.' At the recent hunt, he'd been part of Archie's paw and they'd returned empty handed. I understood now why that had galled him so much.

'Easier said than done. I'm shy – and apparently I'm boring.' He sighed.

'Who called you boring?'

'Seren, when she dumped me for Mark.' Ah. Now we were getting to the heart of the issue.

'That can't have been easy for you.'

'I thought I was in love. I thought Seren was the one. Apparently, she thought I was boring and shy. Thankfully, she dumped me before I proposed. That would have made it a hundred times worse. I told my parents I dumped her.'

'Were you changed by Lord Samuel?'

'I was changed by the Berkshire pack after a near-fatal car accident. The driver who caused the accident was a werewolf. He didn't want me to die and land him with a manslaughter charge, so he hauled my body away and changed me.'

'I imagine that didn't go down well with the council.'

'No. He was incarcerated for six months, but that was still better than anything he'd have received in the Common penal system. When he returned to the Berkshire pack, I decided it was time to move on. I didn't want to go too far, so I petitioned for the Home Counties pack. Lord Samuel accepted me. He was very kind.'

'He was,' I agreed. 'So... about Mark...'

'What is there to say? I hated him. He was vile and rude, he stole my girlfriend, and he thought that might was right. He was an asshole and I'm not sorry that he's dead.' David winced. 'Maybe I am, a little. I wish he'd moved to another pack or something. Death is so final. He didn't get a chance to redeem himself.'

'Do you think he wanted redemption?'

'No, but everyone deserves a chance to improve. He was raised in the Cheshire pack, in a world full of brutality where Jimmy Rain rules with blood and violence. Half of his pack live in fear and the other half are brutes, like him. Mark was the latter. He was a staunch supporter of Rain's, but he wanted to be top dog. He would never have dreamed of challenging Rain, but everyone knew he was biding his time to challenge Lord Samuel.'

'So why didn't he just challenge him? Mark was a fighter and he was far younger. I don't understand his reticence.'

David snorted. 'We've always speculated that Lord Samuel had some sort of hold over Mark – it's the only reason Mark would have held back. He treated Lord Samuel with barely concealed disdain. If he could have moved against him, he would have done. But he didn't and no one knows why.'

Perhaps it was time to do some more digging in Lord Samuel's office. Maybe there were some records that could shed some light on the matter. 'So, you didn't hurt Mark?' I asked.

'I wasn't strong enough to hurt Mark, even if I'd had the inclination to – which I didn't.'

I didn't think that was technically true. The potion in Mark's system and the candle burning in his room were both designed to disorientate and incapacitate him, then he'd been tied down. I was confident the killer was significantly weaker than Mark, or why use the potion?

David didn't seem like a likely candidate, though; mad as he was at Mark and Seren, he wasn't someone who revelled in violence. Mark's murderer had taken their time killing him, slowly cutting into his flesh and gradually poisoning him with silver. Whoever had killed him had enjoyed it.

'Who do *you* think killed Mark?' I asked.

David was startled by the question. 'An outsider,' he said finally. 'Mark did some drugs, including the new fancy one, Boost. It was crazy expensive and Mark was just a park ranger. There was no way he could afford that drug on his wage. I reckon he owed the wrong person money.'

It was a viable theory. Steve Marley had told me that Mark had finished with Boost a few months ago, but he could have been wrong. More likely, Mark had funded his drug habit with money he earned from dabbling in the black tourneys.

'What was Elena's problem with Mark?' I hoped an abrupt change of topic might startle an honest answer out of him.

David wasn't so easily manipulated. He pulled off his tortoiseshell glasses and cleaned them on his T-shirt before responding. 'I don't know the full story but it was something to do with her brother.' He pushed the glasses onto the bridge of his nose. 'Her brother got killed and she blamed Mark for it. I don't know why. Her brother was from a different pack.'

'And Noah? What was his problem with Mark?' Marissa had suggested it was something to do with drugs, but I wanted to hear what someone else had to say before I approached Noah.

David hesitated. 'No one pays attention to me so I hear things,' he said unhappily. 'From what I gather, Noah took some Boost at Mark's suggestion – Mark gave him his first hit. Noah got addicted and his parents had to pay a healer an arm and a leg to get him clean again. Noah said Mark used his position as second to pressure him into it. I don't know how true that is, but Mark was a bully and I'd believe it of him.'

We talked for a few more minutes, and David told me more than I'd ever need to know about roses. It was clear he was passionate about his calling. There was nothing wrong with that and I silently vowed to help him make some friends in the pack. His problem wasn't dissimilar to mine – he just didn't fit in yet. I'd help him get there. Maybe we could do a regular pack film night when things settled down and give everyone more opportunity to mix and mingle.

When I returned to my office, a muscled brethren dude was guarding the door. He paused just a moment too long before stepping aside. Great: even non-wolves didn't re-spect me.

The room was empty except for Fritz, but he was in the zone and didn't even acknowledge my greeting. I guessed the brethren guard was there to keep Fritz safe. It would be frighteningly easy for someone to hurt the spaced-out whizz kid whilst he was lost in a world of code.

I spent a good twenty minutes tearing apart my office looking for Lord Samuels' secret journals. I had seriously expected some sort of locked drawer or hidden compartment – a room behind the bookshelf would have been epic. But no, it was just an office. A locked cabinet held files on each pack member, but all they contained were names, addresses, current occupation and a photo. That was it: no handy notes scrawled in the margins telling me that Lord Samuel knew about the black tourneys and was blackmailing Mark into not challenging him; no notes about Mark taking Boost. Zip. Zilch. Nada. I was feeling less James Bond and more Nancy Drew by the second.

I gave up and called a farewell to Fritz, which was duly ignored. I took the long way to the kitchens rather than going through the communal living room. The kitchen was empty, so I happily knocked back the bread and shaped it into a dozen rolls. I left it for a final prove and checked the time. I needed to start getting ready, but first I wanted to get Noah alone and see how he responded to David's accusations.

I spotted him in the lounge, chatting quietly with Archie in the gaming area. The consoles were off and the two of them were slumped in the beanbags. 'Can I borrow you for a minute, Noah?' I asked with a friendly smile.

Noah was young, perhaps not much older than Archie. 'Sure,' he said finally, giving Archie an 'ugh what now?' look. His cheerful friendliness in the kitchen had dissipated, but I understood about presenting a different front to different people. Noah was playing it cool in front of Archie.

Archie shoved Noah up from the beanbag. 'Don't be an ass. Lucy's nice.'

'Thank you,' I smiled. 'I am very nice – when I'm not mutilating people.' I gave Noah a wink. Perhaps he needed a timely reminder that I wasn't just a pretty face and a surly attitude was going to get him nowhere fast.

Noah paled a little at the reminder of the de-manning of my succubus ex.

'Follow me,' I said brightly. Since my office was still occupied by the brethren, albeit by Fritz and his guard, I took Noah to my living room. The cheerful yellow room wasn't your normal interrogation setting, but it would have to do.

I gestured for him to sit but I remained standing. I'd take any advantage I could. 'How old are you, Noah?'

'Eighteen.'

'And were you born a wolf?'

'Yeah.' He was being loquacious all right.

'Are your parents in this pack?' I ignored his wilful lack of conversation.

'Yeah, my dad George is fourteenth, and my mum Sally is forty-second.'

'You've done very well to get to ninth at your age.'

His chest puffed out and he grinned. 'Yeah, it totally grinds Dad's gears.'

'I bet. So did you get a helping hand?'

He faltered. 'What do you mean?'

'Rumour has it Mark gave you some Boost, and you used it during the recent tourney to hop up several ranks.' It was pure conjecture on my part but Noah looked away and hung his head. I'd hit the nail on the head.

'You can't prove that,' he muttered finally.

'I don't need to prove it, I just need to call another general tourney and watch you slide back down the ranks. Boost supply has been permanently disrupted. You couldn't get more if you tried.'

'I don't want anymore.' He shuddered. 'It was horrible.' He met my eyes. 'I didn't want to take it, I swear. Mark made me. He said if I didn't, he'd make sure something fatal happened to my dad when he fought him.'

I blew out a sharp breath. If Mark hadn't already been dead, I'd have killed him myself. Okay – beat him up a little.

Vile, Esme spat. **To threaten his family like that. Mark Oates did not know the meaning of pack.**

No. I agreed. *He did not.* He'd left Cassie when they couldn't have kids together and moved on to a younger model. He'd threatened the younger pups and he'd pissed on the elder tree. I was glad I hadn't known him better. At least this investigation had helped me discover his character and a few issues within the pack. Now I could get on with doing some fence-mending.

I'm excellent at finding people's common ground, and I'd frequently organised social events for my old firm. I was going to glue this pack back together if it killed me. And if I didn't do a good job, then it very well might.

Chapter 24

Once the dam had broken, Noah's story poured out. Mark had cornered him, threatened him and plied him with Boost. Afterwards, when he was high as a kite, Mark had turned Noah lose on the pack's tourney where the increase in his strength and speed had shot him to an undeserved ninth place.

After the tourney, Mark had cornered Noah and shown him a video he'd taken of Noah taking the drugs. He said that if Noah didn't do as he ordered, he would tell Lord Samuel all about his terrible 'drug habit'.

'He was blackmailing you.'

'Yeah,' Noah said miserably. 'At first it was small things. He made me go with him to a black tourney, just to watch, he said. It was horrible. You could see the fighters weren't there willingly. He made me strip and parade around the tourney with nothing but a mask on, and he made me turn in front of the other patrons just for shits and giggles. He—' Noah broke off, looking upset and angry in equal measure.

'The next time he took me, he made me let a vampyr feed on me.' He shuddered. 'Then the next time I went out alone, I got set upon by the same vampyr and some of his mates – he'd got a taste for me apparently. Mark dealt with the vampyr attack and he got some compensation from them, but he kept it all. And I haven't been attacked again since, but it...' He trailed off. He didn't need to finish the sentence; the attack had knocked his youthful confidence.

I sat next to him, resisting the urge to throw my arms around him. His teenage pride probably wouldn't welcome a hug from me. 'That's horrible. I'm sorry.'

'He was bragging to some wolves at the black tourney that I was his little sub-bitch, that I'd do anything he said. It was horrible. It wasn't long after that that he made me go to the elder tree and piss on it. I don't know why, but I got the impression he was deliberately trying to screw pack relations with the dryads. I got scared about what he'd make me do next, and I finally got up my nerve and told my parents. I've never seen my dad so angry – not at me, at Mark. Mum had to talk him down from challenging

Mark then and there. My dad's fourteenth, but he's not in the same league and he would have died. Mark would have made sure he died.'

'Mark was an asshole,' I said before I could censor myself.

Noah grinned and the smile chased away the shadows in his eyes. 'Yeah. He really was.'

'So what did you do?'

'I went to Mark and told him that I was done, I wouldn't do his bidding anymore. He said that if I wasn't his entertainment then I'd be his nest egg and demanded monthly payments of £250 to keep quiet. It wasn't much, so I agreed. Mum and Dad have been paying him for the last month or two.'

He looked up at me. 'But neither of them would have hurt him. They were trying to gather evidence to have Mark kicked out. They would never have hurt him, that's not who they are.'

I nodded. 'Of course not. They're not like Mark.'

'No.' He relaxed a little. 'No one else in the pack is like Mark. With him gone, the atmosphere is much lighter. I know we're not supposed to speak ill of the dead, but I'm glad he's gone.'

'I'm not surprised.'

He looked down at his toes. 'Are you going to take away my rank?' he asked in a small voice.

'I'm probably going to hold a general tourney soon,' I admitted. 'With Mark gone, things need a shuffle around. But the pack doesn't need to find out about your Boost incident. Mark took advantage of you. As far as the rest of the pack are concerned, in the last tourney you just got lucky. We'll see where you end up. You might surprise yourself.'

'The truth is, I don't want to be in the top thirteen. We're supposed to be the pack's first line of defence and I'm just not good enough.'

'We'll see,' I said lightly. I squeezed his shoulder. 'Thanks for telling me the truth.'

'My mum thinks you'll be good for the pack. She's never wrong.'

'She seems wise.' I winked. 'I like her already. You can go now.'

Noah left like a shot, closing the heavy door behind him. Our conversation had made my heart ache a little.

I called my mum. 'Hey, love,' she said when she answered her phone.

'Hi, Ma. Are you alright?'

'I'm good, thanks. I just had a busy shift and I'm ready for a cuppa and a biscuit.'

'Sounds good.'

'I'm a woman of small pleasures. Lucy, you need to call your dad and your brother. Call and make small talk. Your dad is worried you're growing up and growing apart.'

I snorted. 'Mum I'm twenty-five! I *am* grown up!'

'You know what I mean. Call him and talk about baking or something.'

'Noted. I wasn't actually calling for a telling-off.'

'You never do, but sometimes you need it. What's up?'

'If I were being blackmailed, what would you do?' I asked.

There was a knock and Manners popped his head around the open door. I nodded to say he could come in and held up five fingers in the universal 'I'll be five minutes sign'. He shut the door and sat on the sofa opposite me.

Mum said, 'Do you promise this is hypothetical? Because if you're being blackmailed, we'll go straight to the police. I don't care if you've been in a porno or—'

'Mum! I have *never* been in a porno!' Manners' head snapped towards me and I flushed bright red. 'I swear we are talking hypothetical here, but I need a parent's take on a situation. If someone made me do something – like take drugs or something – blackmailed me with video evidence, and then made me do worse stuff, as my mum what would you do to my blackmailer?'

'They forced you to take drugs and do things against your will?'

'Hypothetically.'

'Then hypothetically, I'd hypothetically kill them,' she said, her tone matter-of-fact.

'You would?' I was surprised and a little bit pleased. Mum is a nurse with a Hippocratic oath, yet for me she'd kill someone. Motherly love.

'Yes. And your father would help me hide the body. No one on this green earth is going to hurt either of my babies.' She paused. 'Now if someone has nude photos of you, we can hire a private eye or something and steal them back.'

I groaned. 'No naked photos, no pornos. This is hypothetical, I swear. Man, winning a bet is not worth this conversation.'

The last line sold it and Mum's tone lightened. 'Well, if you're not being blackmailed then you'll be coming to dinner this weekend, won't you?'

'And if I don't?'

'Then I'll cry all day, certain in the knowledge that my little darling has flown the nest and left me behind without a second thought.'

I laughed; we both knew I was still surgically attached to her. 'That's *emotional* blackmail,' I pointed out.

'It seemed to fit with our conversation.'

'I love you, Mum. If I can, I'll be there.'

'Okay, Lucy. Stay safe. Love you.'

'Love you, Ma.' I rang off and buried my head in my hands in mortification. 'Can we go back in time to just before you walked in? And this time I'll tell you to go away?'

Manners grinned. 'No can-do, cupcake. That is now a cherished memory. I didn't know you could blush so red.'

I groaned.

He sobered abruptly. 'Why were you asking your mum about blackmail?'

'I've learnt all sorts of things about Mark since our last catch-up. He was quite the snake in the grass. He forced Noah to take Boost, then blackmailed him with the drug use and made him attend the black tourneys. He made Noah stroll around naked, be dinner for a vampyr and piss on the elder tree, amongst other things.'

'Humiliating him.'

'Yeah. Mark was a real shit. It also turns out David was dating Seren, and Mark stole her from him.'

'David doesn't seem the type to tie someone to a chair and bleed them slowly to death.'

'There's a type for that?'

'Yeah – the Marks of the world.'

'Hmm. David thought Lord Samuel had a hold over Mark because that was the only explanation as to why Mark hadn't challenged him yet. I searched the office but didn't find anything helpful.'

'It's not the only explanation.' Manners frowned.

'What other explanation have you got?'

'I'd say Mark wasn't calling the shots. Someone was making him bide his time.'

'His former alpha?' I suggested. 'Jimmy Rain?'

'Maybe he was former in name only. There was always a real beef between Samuel and Rain, though I don't know what it was. I was surprised when I learnt that the council had sent Lord Samuel to investigate Rain, albeit secretly – their enmity was well known. Very well known, if even the brethren were aware of it. No one would trust Samuel's report as being unbiased. It seems odd. Let me think about it.'

I sighed. 'The more we investigate Mark, the more the suspect list increases. Isn't it supposed to decrease?'

'Do you have an actual list?'

'Of course I do. I have a spreadsheet.'

Manners flashed me a roguish grin. 'Another spreadsheet?'

'What?'

'You sure love spreadsheets.'

'Who doesn't?' I asked rhetorically. Surely everyone loved a spreadsheet. That's how you stay organised. 'I feel about spreadsheets how you feel about guns.'

'Like they're an essential part of my being?'

'Exactly.'

'Let's talk it through. Who's on your list?'

'Shadowy black-tourney guys are number one, but Noah's mum and dad are now up there. My mum said she'd kill to protect me from an abusive blackmailer.'

'Sure – but why the attack on Archie?'

I brightened. 'That's right. That doesn't make sense, does it?'

'We should still investigate the parents. Archie is a druggie, so maybe the murderer blamed him for bringing drugs into the mansion in the first place. There's something there, but it's thin. Who else?'

'Mark stole David's girl, so *he's* got to be in the mix, though I don't really see it.'

'No. And again, why attack Archie?'

'To move up the ranks? To prove himself? Because it turns out he liked violence?' I spit-balled.

'Maybe,' Manners conceded. 'Who else?'

'Elena. She knows something. Maybe she only knew about Noah being forced to the black tourneys, but she's been acting oddly. David said she blames Mark for her brother's death.'

'What do we know about the brother?'

'Nothing,' I admitted grumpily.

'And her beef with Archie?'

'They dated and he dumped her, broke her heart. She had the means and opportunity to dose Archie with the potion. He remembered getting drinks from her and Mrs Dawes.'

'Is Mrs Dawes on the list?'

'Hell, no! Besides the fact that she's an actual saint, she loves Archie and treats him like a son. Jess told me she thought Mrs Dawes held a candle for Lord Samuel. I could *maybe* see her doing something about Mark, but it would have been a report to a higher power, not tying him to a chair and slicing and dicing him. And *definitely* not attacking Archie.'

'I agree,' Manners said. 'We have a few suspects but no one that rings all the bells – though Elena might work if we can dig up more about the brother. For now, we're back to the black tourneys.'

I sighed. 'Great, that means we've got to mingle with the assholes tonight.'

My phone pinged and I pulled it out to read the message. It was from Jess.

No luck on identifying the vamp, everybody has been weirdly tight-lipped. They all know him but they're lying about it. Nate's out of town and not answering his phone. I've managed to persuade a local vampyr to talk to you in all your wolfish glory. He owes me, so I hope he'll tell you the truth. You free now for a cloak-and-dagger rendezvous? X

I replied: *Sure, when and where? X*

Black Park, by the lake. In 20 mins. I'll arrange an impartial third party to adjudicate. He'll keep you safe. You take Manners, and he'll take his daughter Mererid. X

I recognised the name; Mererid wasn't especially common in these parts.

You managed to persuade the head of the local clan to meet with me?! Lord Wokeshire?

Yup. You'd better get moving.

On my way.

I looked up from my phone. 'We have a date with a vampyr lord.' Primping and pampering would have to wait, and I mentally removed the face mask from my beauty routine. Dammit, I love a mask.

Manners raised an eyebrow. 'Do we? Okay. I'll meet you outside in two minutes. I just need to grab some more weapons.'

Doesn't he realise he is a weapon? asked Esme, confused.

It takes him a while to turn to wolf. Guns and knives are pretty instantaneous, I explained. It was easier than pointing out that for the first thirty-odd years of Manners' life he'd been a soldier and his weapons of choice had been man-made. He probably wasn't used to his wolf being an option.

Ah, Esme said in understanding.

I went outside to the drive. Bastion was leaning against a white Land Rover Discovery. He opened the passenger door for me. 'Um. I'm on my way out,' I said lamely.

He sent me an amused look. 'I know. I'm the impartial third party Jinx has sent to ensure good behaviour. I can rip wolves or vampyrs to pieces in seconds if you misbehave – and you all know it.' His dark eyes looked threatening and his whole being screamed predator. I wasn't foolish enough to disagree.

Manners strolled out in time to hear Bastion's explanation. 'If you're acting as a neutral party, we should take separate cars.'

'Just hop in,' Bastion growled. Manners hesitated then climbed in and Bastion started the car. As we drove off, he clarified the situation. 'We're taking my car because yours has been compromised.'

'What do you mean "compromised"?' I demanded.

'Your car has been bugged.'

'What the hell?' I exclaimed. 'This is real life. People don't bug shit in real life.'

Bastion slid me a patronising glance and didn't reply.

Why should a bug distress you? We can squash and eat insects, if we like. I doubt they are tasty, but we can do it.

Not that kind of bug. A device used to listen to us.

That is sneaky, Esme observed.

You sound like you approve, I said huffily.

A good hunter uses everything at her disposal.

'Who has it been bugged by?' Manners asked.

'That's the million-dollar question,' Bastion replied drily.

Chapter 25

The question of who had bugged our car and why was really annoying me. I tried to think back to any conversations I'd had with Manners in his car. 'We talked about the dryads and Mark pissing on the elder tree,' I said.

He nodded, looking grim. 'And we talked about Mark being hip deep in the black tourneys. If the car is bugged by Mark's killer, our number-one suspect is someone linked to the black tourneys and now they're going to know that we know.'

'But they don't know that we know that they know.' I parroted the famous *Friends* episode. Manners looked blank. 'You never watched the TV show *Friends*, huh?'

'No.'

'It's a classic, you're missing out.'

He shook his head and still looked grim, despite my attempts at levity. 'We could be walking into a trap.'

Bastion made a small noise of disagreement. 'You'll be in disguise and they wouldn't expect you to track down a tourney so quickly. They'll be prepared for you to show up to the next one, not this one. Plus, you have me with you. We'll be fine.'

'Is the organiser, Ghost, a friend of yours?'

Bastion shook his head. 'No, we're not friends. Griffins don't do friends.'

'That must be lonely.'

He met my eyes in the rear-view mirror. 'We kill people for a living. Most people struggle to accept that.' I noticed that he didn't deny being lonely. Poor murderous assassin guy.

'Sure, it's a toughie,' I agreed. 'But a lot of things in the Other realm kill. Everything seems pretty violent. Common rules go out of the window.'

Bastion chose not to comment. 'Everyone will be busy staring at me. You'll go under the radar.'

'Why will they be staring at you?' I asked.

'We'll split up outside and I'll enter in my griffin form. That's fairly rare, so I'll draw attention away from the two boring humans. Ghost usually takes human form.'

'Hey! We're not boring,' I protested.

'You're not human either,' he pointed out dryly.

Fair point.

We drew up to Black Park. 'Let's go and see what the vampyrs have to say for themselves.'

We moved quickly to the lakeside. Bastion gave a solemn nod to the handsome man sitting on a bench. A few steps back was a lady, who was presumably his daughter. They looked like chalk and cheese: she was fair to his dark and she was glaring at us, contempt written all over her pretty features.

I gave her a wide smile and a finger wave, just to screw with her. Her gaze darkened and I resisted the urge to snigger.

I turned my attention to Lord Wokeshire. I remembered Jinx telling me that a vampyr could alter his age at will, so he obviously fancied playing the silver fox today. His dark hair was streaked with grey, but that didn't detract from his good looks. It isn't fair: men with grey are sexy, women with grey hair are crones.

Vampyr! Esme hissed vehemently.

Hush. He has information we need.

Rip the answers from his body, she suggested.

Wow, she really didn't like vampyrs. I guessed it wasn't just werewolves that had issues with the vampyrs but the wolves themselves.

So many dead, she mourned. **So many pups gone at their teeth. And they didn't even eat their carcasses.** It wasn't the deaths but the sheer waste that upset her. Death for death's sake made no sense to a wolf, whereas death to survive – to eat – was fine.

Settle down, I pleaded. *I need to focus.*

Fine. Filthy blood-letter. But she did turn around three times and settle down in my mind. I sent her a kiss and she sent me a nuzzle with a wet snout in response.

'Lord Wokeshire,' I greeted the vampyr neutrally. 'Thank you for meeting with me.'

'I owed Jinx,' he said finally.

'Me too,' I admitted. 'So we already have some common ground.'

His face remained impassive. Not the friendly crowd, so I decided to warm him up before going straight for the real issue. 'Some of your vampyrs attacked one of my wolves,' I started.

'That has already been dealt with,' he said coldly. 'Reparations were paid, as set out under the Connection law.'

'To whom were reparations paid?'

'To the pack.' His tone said 'well, duh' even if his words didn't.

'Who received the money for the pack?' I clarified.

'Mark Oates.' Of course it was Mark. 'And the vampyrs who carried out the attack?'

'They were punished.'

'How?'

'That is a vampyr matter. They were punished and that is all you need to know. I do not intend to go over old ground. The attack has been dealt with and it will not be repeated.' He stood as if to leave; he was hasty for a dead guy.

I grabbed my phone and pulled up the picture of the vampyr who'd been rude to me and who'd been lurking near the scene of Archie's attack. 'Do you know who this is?' I asked.

Wokeshire froze before sitting back down. His face didn't change, not so much as a blink, but it was so stony and impassive that I knew he was shocked. He was controlling every muscle not to reveal his surprise. His daughter, however, didn't have as many centuries of practice as her father and her eyebrows shot up before she mastered her shock.

Lord Wokeshire continued to study the photograph as he worked out his response. 'I can't tell you about him,' he said finally.

'Can't or won't?'

'Can't. Each species has their own secrets and he is one of ours. What I *can* say is that whatever he's digging into, you need to stay far away from it.'

Not gonna happen. I changed tack. 'Is he a newly turned vampyr?'

Lord Wokeshire seemed to consider whether he should respond. 'No,' he said finally. 'He's old.'

'He acted like he didn't know what a hall was,' I said, thinking of his rude behaviour in Rosie's.

'That's all it was,' he replied dryly.

I shook my head, not getting his meaning.

'Acting,' Lord Wokeshire clarified.

'Why would he need to pretend to be young?'

'I suspect you weren't the one he was trying to fool. He used you as a smokescreen. Everyone expects us to snarl at wolves.'

'You haven't snarled once,' I pointed out.

'There's a griffin here to see that I don't.' He slid a wary look at Bastion.

'If the griffin weren't here, would you be trying to kill me?' I asked curiously.

Lord Wokeshire sent me a wry smile. 'You're as direct as Jinx.'

'We're sisters from another mister,' I said. 'We grew up together.'

'In Common.'

'But no less for it,' I rejoined snarkily.

He held his hands, signalling peace. 'With the Connection ruling the roost, even I wouldn't kill a wolf for no reason,' he admitted finally.

'Maybe we can build some bridges,' I suggested. 'Let bygones be bygones.'

He barked a laugh that had no humour in it. 'There's too much blood under the bridge.'

'Water under the bridge,' I corrected.

He shook his head and sent me a dark look. 'For our two species, it's blood. Rivers of it.' He smirked. 'Maybe change will come in a vampyr's lifetime.'

I sighed. 'Is that a joke, a vampyr's lifetime? Is it code for never?'

He smiled, and I suspected I'd hit the nail on the head. He stood and inclined his head respectfully to Bastion. Bastion didn't acknowledge him but continued to watch his every movement with unsettling sharp eyes.

'Vampyrs have been going missing,' Bastion asserted.

Lord Wokeshire stilled. 'I cannot discuss that with you. How did you hear about it?'

'I have my sources.'

'No doubt. It is clan business. Tell your sources that if I find out who they are, I'll kill them myself.'

Bastion smiled in a way that had no warmth. 'No.'

Lord Wokeshire grimaced but didn't dare push it further; instead he looked appraisingly at me. 'It has been interesting meeting you, Lucy Barrett, alpha of the Home Counties pack. You're smart. Maybe you'll even survive for a while.' He stood and Mererid followed. They melted into the shadows and disappeared.

I let out a low whistle. 'Holy crap on a cracker, that's a cool way to make an exit.'

'It's a pain in the ass when you're fighting them.' Manners grimaced, remembering his near-fatal battle with a vampyr that had culminated in his shift into a werewolf.

'Yeah. That would be tough to fight.'

'You think they're there and then, bam, they disappear into the shadows and reappear somewhere else. Not to mention their speed.'

'I guess with the change we've inherited both a wolf and some tough enemies.'

Manners shrugged. 'Dragons and vampyrs have always been enemies, even more than wolves and vampyrs. With wolves, the vampyrs know they'll always win. They just need to sit pretty while we age and die.'

'Damn, that's heavy.'

'It's true. We're mortal, they're not – and nor are dragons. It's why their enmity is particularly strong. They're fighting over an insult that took place three thousand years ago.'

'Yikes! What was the insult?'

'No one can remember. They may be immortal, but their memories aren't infallible.'

'I bet it was a "your mama" joke,' I muttered. 'They never go down well.'

Manners laughed. 'Imagine centuries of feuds because of a comment about the wrong MILF.'

Bastion was silent and statue like, his stony expression giving nothing away. 'What about you?' I asked. 'Griffins are long lived, right?'

'Long lived. Not immortal,' he responded finally.

'How old are you?'

'That's a rude question in any realm,' Manners said to me reproachfully.

'What was all that about missing vampyrs?'

'It may be nothing,' Bastion shrugged.

'But it may be something.'

'The new vampyr, the one he won't tell us about, he's been asking about missing vampyrs.'

'So what, he's a vampyric Sherlock Holmes?'

Bastion looked at me flatly. 'I will dig into it further,' he said finally. He wasn't willing to speculate. 'We're done here.' Bastion turned and walked away. We scrambled after him – after all, he had the car.

The afternoon was drawing to a close as we returned to the mansion. New gates secured the front drive, but they opened as we approached. As we drew up, there were no black Ford Escapes in sight and it became clear that the brethren were gone. The balcony door had been restored to its full glory, and I knew that invisible runes covered the house. The metal shutters were ready to slam down at a moment's notice, and cameras covered every entrance and exit. We weren't Fort Knox, but we were a helluva lot better than we'd been before.

'Grab some dinner and get ready,' Bastion advised. 'We'll leave at 10pm.' He walked away without looking back. He was a hundred yards from us when he shifted into his griffin form; his clothes melted away and he became fifty percent lion, fifty percent eagle and one hundred percent deadly. He spread his white wings and flew off.

'The vampyrs aren't the only ones who can make a good exit,' I muttered to Manners. 'We need to work on ours.'

He threw me a grin and shook his head. I was being entertaining again.

We separated. I intended to go to my rooms when something occurred to me. *If* Mark's death was somehow linked to the black tourneys, then Archie's attack may have been related to them too. Maybe he saw someone he shouldn't have; if that were true, then Noah might well be the next target.

The mansion was secure, but against *outside* forces; something in me the whole way along had said this was an inside job. I didn't like my suspect list, and I didn't want to think of David, Elena or Noah's parents being the guilty party, but there were too many ifs, ands or buts to risk Archie and Noah.

I sent Maxwell a message asking if the boys could roost in his hall again, but I got a negative; someone else was already booked in. I didn't have a whole lot of allies to call on. The boys didn't need a charge in Common and they didn't need the portal – they just needed a safe house. Or at least, somewhere no one would expect them to be.

I could call Emory and beg for some help from the dragons and the brethren, but Emory had bled money today to secure the mansion, and it felt like I was casting doubt on his measures. Besides, he'd done enough. I liked Emory, but we weren't friends – he was just shagging my best friend. I was sure we'd get to friendship eventually, because he seemed like a real nice dragon, but I was reluctant to add to the already sizeable tab.

Another possibility occurred to me. It was a long shot, but I'm always one to roll the dice so I sent another message. While I waited for a response, I tracked down Archie and Noah. As I'd expected, they were hanging out with Elena.

She looked up and met my eyes before looking away. She was nervous. Reluctantly I admitted to myself that I didn't have time to deal with her right now. She'd be first up on tomorrow's agenda.

Ace and Lauren were in the lounge, too, and they had David in their headlights. He was obviously uncomfortable. Ace flashed me a friendly smile but then turned back to his victim. I didn't have time to rescue David from the council's interrogation, so I shot him a sympathetic glance and left him to it.

I turned to Archie and Noah. 'Archie, Noah – with me,' I ordered. I was surprised and a little gratified when they both leapt to their feet, eager to help and prove themselves. I tugged them into the dormitory hallway. 'Pack a bag, both of you. Quickly.'

They disappeared into their rooms. Thankfully, Archie's room was once again secure now that Emory had arranged for the shattered balcony doors to be replaced. And not just with any old doors: oh no, he'd replaced them with bulletproof and shatter-resistant glass.

The boys didn't take long before they reappeared. I gestured for them to follow me and took them out to the rose garden. 'Archie, I'm pretty sure you were attacked because someone thinks you know something about the black tourneys that you might blab about. Is there anything you think you should tell me?'

He was scowling, really thinking about it, but eventually he shook his head. 'I'm sorry, I wish there were.' He looked down at his shoes. 'But I was high the entire time and everything is pretty blurry. I remember Mark parading me around, calling me the crown prince of the pack. He was laughing at my dad for not knowing where I was, what I was doing. It was that shit that finally woke me up. Mark wasn't my friend, he was being cruel and rude about Dad. At first I thought it was funny because *I* was often rude about Dad, but he's *my* dad to be rude about.' He looked up, searching my face for understanding.

I got it. We can all moan about our families because they're ours, but woe betide anyone else who dares to criticise them.

'I hated that Mark was Dad's number two,' Archie went on. 'I even raised it with Dad, but he said that his hands were tied for now. Council politics.'

'Council politics?' I queried.

'Yeah. I didn't get it then and I don't get it now.' He shrugged. 'Sorry. I must have seen something I shouldn't have, but I don't remember what.' He ran his hands through his blond hair in frustration.

'Never mind. Noah, same question. You must have seen something.'

'Maybe I did,' Noah agreed, 'but I don't know what. The whole thing was wrong to me. You can't unsee some of the stuff you see at the black tourneys. I seriously thought about paying a wizard to clear my mind but... My mum said that my memories inform who I am and what actions I take from here on out. That I shouldn't regret my experiences but learn from them.'

'She's a wise lady.'

'Yeah. I'm sorry.'

My phone beeped. I dug it out and smiled at the message. We were a-go. I took the boys to Manners' car, which was parked on the drive, and told them to get in and have a chat about going to Maxwell's, then to bitch and moan about the empty petrol tank and to decide to use one of their own cars instead. If anyone *was* foolish enough to be listening in, they might find themselves battling some fire elementals.

I texted Maxwell a heads-up that someone might have overheard me planning to send people to Rosie's, so he needed to be on his guard. He replied that he was always on his guard. He seemed unconcerned; he knew what he was doing.

Questioning the boys again had been bit of a long shot, but whatever they knew was buried deep in their memories or lost in a haze of drugs. Maybe Amber could dig it out for me. I sent her a text querying her thoughts on scrying the wolf and asking if she could do some potions to recover lost memories. She replied almost instantly with an affirmative for both; she'd be around the next morning at 10am sharp.

I blew out a relieved breath. I was sure that would lead to some progress, but it still meant that tonight I was going blind into the black tourney.

Chapter 26

I showered quickly and did my hair slowly. If I was going to be rubbing shoulders with the rich – albeit morally depraved – then I wanted to fit in. I dried my golden hair carefully so it fell in soft waves around my shoulders, then pulled on a form-fitting black fishtail dress. It was off-the-shoulder and it made me look rich and elegant. At least, I thought so. I did dramatic makeup, with contouring and red lipstick, and hauled on heels that looked like they should be impossible to walk in but had a secret platform sole.

I admired the results. I looked as glamorous as I could, which was to say pretty damn glam. I thought about taking some form of hidden weapon but, frankly, there was nowhere to hide it. And, as Esme had said, *we* were a weapon. With an instantaneous shift from two legs to four I'd lose the dress, but we could protect ourselves.

I grabbed a too-small clutch bag and slid in my phone, lipstick and some cash; there was no room for anything else. I'd even had time to paint my nails. I didn't bother with false eyelashes because they'd be a pain in the ass with a mask. I love taking the time to doll myself up nicely. I don't get to do it often, but when I do I go all out.

You look ready to mate, Esme said approvingly.

Er, thanks. Some things just didn't quite translate, but I guessed she meant I looked nice. That was what I took from it, anyway.

There was a knock on my door and I opened it cautiously. I could have done with a spyhole. Luckily, it was Manners. He was dressed in a black tuxedo, which he filled impressively. Muscles bulged and rippled and I wondered where his weapons were, because he was definitely carrying them.

I'd rarely seen him lost for words but his mouth dropped open slightly and he gawked at me. A note of interest flashed in his eyes that I hadn't seen there before; it had just occurred to him that I was a woman, as well as his boss.

He thinks you look ready to mate, too, Esme said smugly.

Yes, thank you, Esme. I got that as well.

I gave Manners a smile. 'Cat got your tongue?' I asked cheekily.

Why would a cat have his tongue? It is clearly in his mouth. You can see it while he is ogling you.

I struggled not to laugh aloud. *It's a traditional saying. It means he can't speak.*

You humans are so odd.

Manners' eyes ran down my body before he almost visibly shook himself. He cleared his throat. 'You clean up well,' he muttered. His usual suave charm was absent.

I grinned. 'You do too. Let's go mingle with some criminal elements.' I sashayed down the hallway, leading the way and putting a little extra sway into my walk for his benefit. It's nice to be appreciated now and again.

We approached a mirror and I noted with satisfaction that Manners' eyes were glued to my ass. Heh, heh, heh. I felt triumphant, though I refused to examine exactly why that was.

We didn't encounter anyone on our way to the front door. When I opened it, a black stretch limousine awaited us, together with a certain deadly assassin. Bastion was also dressed in a tuxedo, but he barely spared me a second glance. He opened the door. 'Get in,' he instructed laconically.

'Why, thank you, Bastion. You look wonderful, too,' I said, a tad sarcastically.

'This isn't a social function,' he reminded me tersely. 'This is business.'

'And why is it yours?' I asked cheekily.

'Because you're Jess's friend,' he said, 'and it would upset her if you died.'

I rolled my eyes. 'Gee, thanks. I'm overwhelmed by your concern for my well-being.'

He ignored me. I sighed dramatically and slid into the limo. Manners climbed in next to me and Bastion sat opposite. The car started to move off as soon as the door was shut.

'You've got a driver, Sam?' Manners teased Bastion.

'I've got everything,' Bastion responded. Then he turned pointedly to the window and ignored us both.

'Chatty guy,' I whispered.

Manners seemed to have recovered his aplomb. He flashed me a two-hundred-watt smile. 'You can't get him to shut up,' he agreed.

The drive to London wasn't long and Manners and I talked casually. 'What do you think of Ace?' I asked suddenly.

He paused. 'I think he has an agenda,' he answered finally.

'Don't we all?' I countered.

'No.'

'You have an agenda – you want to keep the pack safe.'

'I want to keep *you* safe,' he corrected.

'I don't need to be kept safe. I've got Esme.'

'You're not infallible and you're not immortal.'

'I know that, but in comparison to a human we're fast and strong. We're fighters,' I said proudly.

'I know you are, but that doesn't mean you don't need to be careful.'

'We're here,' Bastion interrupted. Next to him was a large container like a hat box. He opened it and passed me a mask. It was so pretty, black and sparkly that I wanted to coo over it, like a jackdaw. Reluctantly, I secured it around my eyes instead. It was ornate and covered my face from the nose up.

I reapplied a fresh coat of lipstick – I love that fresh-on sheen. I was ready to rock and roll. Manners pulled on his mask, plain black like Bastion's.

'If we encounter trouble, follow me. I have an exit strategy,' Bastion ordered.

I expected he had several, nevertheless I nodded my agreement. I hoped we wouldn't need an exit strategy; I was hoping for a glass of wine and a few horrible fights that I could try not to watch.

Manners got out of the car first and held the door open for me. As I slid out, he offered me his arm. We waited for Bastion – but when he left the limousine, it wasn't on two legs but on four. He was bigger than an ordinary lion and his four paws were huge.

My mouth dried instantly and every nerve in my body told me to run. Esme let out a sound like a hiss in my head and her fear terrified me because it was the first time I'd felt it. Bastion's yellow eagle eyes met mine and I knew he missed nothing. We'd never seen him in griffin form up close and personal. After our chat with Wokeshire, Bastion had walked away from us first before shifting. I'd seen Bastion fighting once in griffin form but he'd been an aerial fighter on our team, and we'd been too busy dealing with the rival werewolves to focus too much on him. Now there were no distractions and his predatory scent permeated the air. A primeval reaction had us filled with wariness.

'Lead the way,' I managed to say, pleased I didn't stutter.

Bastion's white-feathered head moved impossibly fast, snapping left and focusing on the doorway where presumably we were going to try and gain entrance. It was dark and cold. I told myself that was why I was suddenly shivering.

We were outside a huge, cavernous warehouse with blacked-out windows. I had no idea where we were, but I could hear the river Thames. I couldn't hear a single sound emanating from the building. Runes, I'd bet. I'm a fast learner.

Bastion reared back and hit the double doors with one decisive bang of his forepaw. They slid open to reveal a trio of troll bouncers dressed in black tabards. They had long flowing hair and large, pointy noses. They were also nearly seven feet tall and not so much well-muscled as bulky, like hulking rugby players. Suddenly I was less confident of our chances of fighting our way out if we needed to. Maybe Bastion knew what he was talking about when he mentioned an exit strategy.

Bastion didn't present an invitation, he just stared down the trolls with his icy golden eyes until one of them stepped aside. Trying not to move too quickly, I followed.

There was the hubbub of a full crowd and the room was hot and noisy. I was dismayed. Why were so many people eager to watch two living beings tear themselves apart? I tried to keep my face blank but I was grateful for the mask.

Everyone was in black, like they were at a funeral. No guesses as to why these events were called 'black' tourneys.

Some women were in full-on couture gowns with trains, as if it were a ball, only the hors d'oeuvres were fist fights between magical creatures. This was fight club meets *Pride and Prejudice*, and the prejudice part was alive and well.

The black tourney-goers were clumped in sects. There was a handful of fire elementals in one corner, ogres in another and dryads in a loose circle. It was harder to tell what the more human counterparts were, though I could see that some were vampyrs. I'd expected – hoped – that most of the bloodthirsty patrons would be vampyrs, a prejudice of my own left over from watching too many Dracula movies. Alas, they seemed to be in the minority. There was a bit of everything here, a cosmopolitan melting pot of the Other realm, all bound by a desire to see some violence.

Waiters were circulating the room offering Champagne flutes. I watched with disgust as the vampyrs were brought glasses of haemoglobin, though I guessed it was better than having someone attacked. I took a glass of Champagne. I was desperate to down it, but I held it instead; I wanted to fit in but I didn't want to risk drinking anything in this place.

In the centre of the warehouse was a large cage. It was empty and its floor was pristine, which reinforced the idea that the black tourneys moved around and didn't take place in one location twice.

Tall tables were dotted around and the candles on them created a soft, atmospheric light. My nostrils were filled with the scent of vanilla, cinnamon and sandalwood, something I'd smelled before. I sneezed rapidly, trying to clear my nose of the heady scent, but I couldn't; it was all I could smell.

Esme paced impatiently in our mind, angry that one of our senses was being dulled deliberately. Across the room, I watched as members of another small group started to sneeze. Wolves – I'd bet my favourite handbag on it. Manners sneezed. He tried to do it subtly but the urge was too strong. We'd been outed as werewolves.

Chapter 27

Luckily, Bastion hadn't been wrong about his reception. All over the room, people were pulling away and whispering, pointing at him. I didn't know whether they knew that he was Bastion, the deadliest griffin assassin ever to live, or just that they knew he was a griffin and that was enough. Next to him, we boring old werewolves weren't worthy of commentary, which was irksome because I was really rocking that dress.

As I looked around the room, I saw someone else sneeze: a woman, standing by herself, a lone wolf. I watched her move through the room. There was something achingly familiar about her – I knew her, I was sure of it – but with the mask covering her face it was difficult to place her. She turned to pick up a Champagne flute from one of the roving waiters. As she turned, I saw her bare shoulder and the vicious scar that ran down it. My heart stopped. Dammit – it was Elena.

I took a step towards her but at that moment the lights that shone down on the cage started to dim. The one sole light in the centre cast long shadows. When I looked back to where Elena had been, she had gone.

'Ladies and gentlemen, creatures, and Other, welcome to the black tourney!' the master of ceremonies announced in a long drawl. The crowd roared with excitement. I felt vaguely sick.

'For your delectation tonight … Ares has a new challenger!'

Another spotlight came on, illuminating a whole bloody orchestra. The conductor gestured and I recognised the sinister strains of 'Dance of the Knights' by Sergei Prokofiev. It fit, I guess.

The crowd parted and in stalked a unicorn, being led roughly by a halter collar. Three trolls marched alongside him, heavy axes in their hands. It was clear the unicorn was there against his will, albeit he wasn't recognised as a sentient being.

I dug my fingers into Manners' arm. He put an arm around me. 'Steady,' he murmured. 'We can't fight the whole room.'

I knew he was right, intellectually I really did, but emotionally I wanted to shift into my wolf form and let Esme loose to rip into troll and vampyr flesh. It was one thing for sentient beings to choose to fight in the cage – a crazy choice, but a choice nonetheless – but this was no choice.

The unicorn was being forced and I could see it wasn't the first time. His white coat was marred by rippling scars and puckered flesh. Poor Ares. His red eyes flashed with hopeless rage as he was shoved into the cage and the door slammed shut behind him. He screamed his wrath, rearing up and clawing down the metal bars with his reptilian feet. The cage sparked and clanged but remained depressingly intact.

'Requiem Dies Irae' by Verdi started and out of the shadows phased a vampyr.

'Young,' Manners murmured. 'This isn't a done deal.'

The vampyr was bold and smirking. He played to the crowd, bowing and blowing kisses. He was unconcerned about being in a cage with a rageful beast. Was it wrong that I suddenly hoped the unicorn would pulverise the vampyr into tiny pieces? Maybe I belonged here more than I thought I did.

The unicorn screamed again, an ear-splitting sound that cut through the fancy strains of the orchestral music with ease. The white beast lowered his head and his horn and charged at the vampyr.

Laughing, the vampyr backed into the shadows and phased away. He popped up to the unicorn's left and moved with shocking speed, slashing down Ares' neck with a dagger. Thankfully the dagger was small, but I guessed it was more to drag out the fight than from any sense of fairness.

The unicorn screamed again, but this time with pain. It whirled around. The vampyr phased away again, then popped out to the right. The unicorn danced away from his attack just in time.

The vampyr grimaced and put on some extra speed, moving so fast that it was hard to track him with the naked eye. I watched, gobsmacked, as he ran up and over the cage ceiling, his momentum keeping his feet glued there even while he was upside down. No wonder the Common thought vampyrs had a link with bats.

The vampyr cavorted around, playing to the crowd. He dashed in with his dagger, a little nip here, a little nip there. Fast though he was, he was also predictable. He phased left, then right, then ran around the cage – then rinse and repeat.

I watched the unicorn and for a split second it looked back at me across the space between us. Then it focused on the vampyr, so confident in his success.

This time, when the vampyr phased left, he moved directly into the lowered horn of the waiting unicorn. He staggered back off the horn but, before he could phase again, Ares reared up and smashed his clawed feet into his chest. It opened like a tin of beans, and blood and organs poured out.

But Ares wasn't done. He reared up again and again, slamming into the vampyr and pulverising him into so much ground meat. No amount of supernatural healing was rescuing this vampyr.

A few moments passed and the bloody mess shifted into ash. Ares was the victor. He threw back his head and whinnied his success. The crowd roared back in appreciation, stamping their feet and clapping their hands. I saw money exchange hands as bets were settled.

The main lights flickered on again and the orchestral music changed to an upbeat type tempo. Canapés were being offered to distract the guests whilst the trolls tried to secure Ares again. Three of them entered the cage, this time with cattle prods as well as axes. They weren't taking any chances with a unicorn in bloodlust. They gave Ares several jolts of electricity whilst they forced him into a halter, then led him away. The unicorn seemed to watch me accusingly.

He was a bold hunter, Esme said approvingly. **Canny. Let's free him.**

I love it when we're on the same wavelength. *Yes,* I agreed. I knew Ares wasn't the primary reason we were here, but priorities can change. Right is right and wrong is wrong, and leaving the unicorn there was just plain wrong.

I turned to Bastion. 'Go and speak to Ghost. See what you can find out about Mark and his attendances here.' My tone was a shade away from an order.

Bastion's eyes fixed on me and for a moment I thought he might refuse, but he turned and padded away. He walked over to some steps, above which was a mezzanine floor. There was a select gathering there with prime viewing stations. I tore my attention away.

I looked around once more. I couldn't spot Elena and clenched my jaw in frustration, then mentally let her go. I'd deal with her later; right now, my priority was freeing Ares and any other poor creatures being forced to fight.

I grabbed Manners' arm. 'Let's find a bathroom,' I suggested. As I crossed the vast warehouse, I scanned for Elena, but I didn't see her.

Manners and I stepped out of the main room into a corridor. To the left was a sign for the toilets, to the right a hulking troll standing guard. I flounced towards him, doing my best spoilt-girl impression. Always try the easy way first. 'Are the beasts back there?' I demanded imperiously, pointing behind the door.

He barely spared me a glance. 'No one goes there,' he rumbled.

I batted my eyelids. 'But do you know who my daddy is?' Black humour filled me for a moment; even *I* didn't know who my daddy was.

'He can be the bloody sultan, but you're still not getting in.'

'I'll make it worth your while,' I said in a sing-song voice.

'No,' he said flatly.

The hard way, then. I concentrated and gathered my piping powers, reached down into that well of power and drew it up. I kept a flirtatious smile on my face as I touched his gigantic hand and kept smiling as I released the full might of my power.

It slammed into him, not nicely, not to talk but to control. That was the reason pipers are so hated. Under the Connection's rule, they – *we* – are allowed to pipe and control non-sentient creatures like unicorns. Piping sentient creatures is strictly forbidden and could land me with a solid stint in the Connection jail. I'd never done it before – and frankly I didn't know what I was doing – but I had to do *something* to free Ares. It turns out that I'm an 'ends justify the means' girl. Who knew?

I threaded my fingers through the troll's bulky hand. I wasn't sure if I needed to maintain physical contact to keep the control hold in place, but now didn't seem like the best time to experiment. 'Is the unicorn Ares behind this door?' I asked.

'Yes,' he replied instantly.

'Unlock the door and take us to him.'

Behind me, Manners made a strangled noise but I ignored him. We could argue about it later.

The troll unlocked the padlock on the door and led us in. The lights flickered on; Ares had been kept in darkness. I tried to swallow my outrage and focus on the mission. The room was filled with cages and tanks but thankfully only a few were occupied. I guessed tonight's main show was going to have willing contenders. I thought of Noah; maybe not willing, just blackmailed.

A merman and what looked like a very large seal were in one of the water tanks. Since this was the Other, I guessed it was a selkie. Ares was in one cage and a gargoyle was in the one next to him.

'Get them out,' I said to Manners, pointing to the tank. Its lid was secured by a number of boulders that presumably trolls could lift on and off easily – troll security isn't particularly sophisticated.

I turned my attention to the caged gargoyle. 'Let him out,' I ordered the troll. We stepped forward together and he unlocked the cage.

'Thanking you, you beautiful wench,' the gargoyle said joyfully. 'I'll happily roger you in thanks.'

'Erm, that's kind of you but I'm okay. Just get home safely.'

'Right you are. Tally ho, maiden.' He bobbed me a strange little bow and headed for some roller doors. He flapped his little wings and rose high enough to man the controls. He jammed the button on 'up' and the double doors started to rise. 'Bit of a kerfuffle out here, my fine Jezebel,' he called back to me. 'Best exit sharpish.' With those words of advice, he flew out and left us.

Manners had managed to move the heavy boulders and was helping the merman out. As he set him on the ground, the watery creature's tail shimmered and separated into legs. And other things.

I averted my eyes. Manners gave the merman his tuxedo jacket; it fell to below the merman's hips so it covered everything important. The merman reached into the tank and the selkie leapt gratefully into his arms. I blinked.

Either mermen were strong, or the seal was lighter than it looked.

'A little help?' I called.

Manners strode towards me. 'What's up?'

'I need to talk to the unicorn so it doesn't kill us when I open the gate, but I can't do that and keep control of the troll. At least, I don't think I can.'

'No problem,' he said calmly. He hefted the smaller boulder that had been on top of the tank and slammed it into the back of the troll's head. The troll dropped like a sack of potatoes.

'Did you kill him?' I asked accusingly.

'Do you care?' he countered, raising that sexy eyebrow of his. He relented. 'No. It takes more than one little bash in the skull to kill a troll. He's down and out, but not dead.'

I focused on Ares and gathered my magic, but he was too far away to touch. I let out a soft sigh and felt my magic being expelled with the sound. That's right! The Pied Piper was called that because he played a pipe! I was such an idiot.

I gathered the magic again and this time I hummed 'Twinkle, Twinkle, Little Star', all the while willing Ares to talk to me. I could feel my magic reaching towards him, like floating fingers. When It touched him, I felt the connection between us, tenuous and weak but there all the same.

I want to free you, I said to him.

In response, an image exploded in my brain: a field, a wood, a carriage.

Yes. I agreed. *Free. Home.* Unbidden, an image of the mansion rose in my mind. Yes, for good or ill it *was* my home now. *If I free you, you can't hurt any of us.* I pictured Manners, the merman, the selkie and myself. *And no one in Common,* I added, picturing a commuting crowd in London.

I felt Ares' agreement and his impatience. He wanted to be free. *Now.* As I took the key from the fallen troll's fingers and unlocked the crate, he surged out. He met my blue eyes with his red ones. He held my gaze for so long that the moment hummed with *something,* but I couldn't say what. He threw his head back and whickered, stepping forward to nuzzle me gently before plunging though the open roller door and into the night.

I glanced around the room. It was empty, bar Manners and the unconscious troll. 'Where did the merman go?' I asked.

'Out.' He pointed to the exit.

I wanted to leave too, but we'd arrived with a mission to find out about Mark and I'd discovered diddly squat. I was also curious what the gargoyle had meant about a kerfuffle.

I eased closer to the door and looked out. Shit. The Connection had arrived, and it looked like they were readying themselves to carry out a full raid.

Chapter 28

'Time to go,' Manners advised.

'No shit, Sherlock,' I agreed. Hopefully Bastion had secured some intel from Ghost. 'This way?' I pointed though the roller doors.

'Yeah.' Manners reached up and untied his mask. I followed suit. Without his tuxedo, he didn't stand out so much in his trousers and shirt. He eyed my dress with regret. 'It's a crying shame,' he muttered. Before I could work out what he was going to do, he pulled a dagger from an ankle holster and attacked the fishtail of my dress, hacking away at it until I was left in an immodest LBD – little black dress. Without the fishtail and the mask, my outfit was far more hooker than ball.

I glared. 'You owe me a new dress.'

'Legs, I'll buy you three.'

I let the new nickname slide; besides, my legs were currently very much out. 'Three dresses, just as good as this one,' I bartered.

'Better,' he promised.

I was stalling because I was nervous. 'All right, what do we do here?' I gestured towards the Connection, who were gathering around the front. Any minute now, they'd spread out and find us.

'We walk out quickly and casually. If we get near the Connection detectives, we act drunk. Can you act drunk?'

I snorted. 'I invented drunk. Of course I can.'

'If we get separated, try and get the train back. If you get into any trouble, wolf up and let Esme out for a ride. Just make sure when you swap back to human there are some clothes nearby that you can steal.'

'It's a cold night. It's not like there are loads of clothes hanging on the washing line,' I pointed out.

'You'll figure out something. Let's move.' On the word 'move', he slipped his arm around my waist and we moseyed casually out of the warehouse. The scent of him filled my nostrils; it was a relief after having that damned candle invading my senses for so long.

Manners smelled delicious. Esme let out a contented noise, almost like a purr, in my head. Wearing next to nothing and being pulled against his taut body was just the tiniest bit distracting. I concentrated on putting one foot in front of the other.

'Hey!' someone called.

Manners' hand tightened on my hip but we didn't stop.

My pulse was racing. I didn't want to spend the night in the Connection jail, and I really didn't want to get any part of my mind wiped. I didn't even want to know what they'd do if they found out I'd controlled a troll with my piping powers. Panic raced in my veins, and flight or fight was kicking in big time. When you're in danger you can fight, take flight, freeze or frolic. It was lucky the latter wasn't the strongest impulse and I didn't break down into my best dance routine.

'Hey, you two!' someone shouted again. 'Stop and turn slowly.'

I could almost feel Manners running through the options. I wanted to run but he slowly turned us around as requested. I saw his hand move to the small of his back, where no doubt a weapon rested. I guess his reflex had settled on fight.

The detective approached us. Noting the triangles on our foreheads, he knew we were Other. 'What are you doing here?' he scowled.

Fighting would get messy very quickly. He was only one detective, but there were another ten a few feet behind him. Even Manners couldn't kick that many asses in one night. So because I looked like a hooker… 'Earning a living, honey,' I replied, giving him a wink. 'This one is real feisty, but maybe you could wait five minutes until we're done.'

Manners smacked me hard on my ass, making me gasp. 'It's going to take more than five minutes, love,' he promised with a leer.

I gave an inane giggle. 'Perfect,' I sassed back. 'I charge on a time-spent basis.'

He pulled me into his body. 'Then send me a damned big bill,' he breathed. 'I'm having you all night.'

His lips crashed down on mine and my brain fizzled and died. I could feel every hard line of his body. I opened my mouth to his assault and, unbidden, gave a loud moan. My pulse started to race as he kissed me harder, deeper, with a need and a passion I would never have expected to be lurking beneath his controlled, military façade.

'Bloody hell,' the Connection detective swore. 'Just not here. Move along.'

I pulled away reluctantly from Manners and looked up at him, eyes dazed and legs wobbly. I hoped he could tell he'd robbed me of speech and it was on him to answer.

'Sure thing, officer.' His voice was rough and gravelly. He looped his arm around me again and we strolled away.

It was a long time before we spoke. We walked to the nearest train station – it was late, but we'd make the last train out. Bastion would have to fend for himself. I guessed that in a worst-case scenario the guy would just fly.

Greg's arm was still around me and I wasn't in a hurry to remove it for a number of reasons, not least of which was because it was cold as a witch's tit and he was extraordinarily warm. And I suddenly realised that I was thinking of him as Greg, not Manners; a man, rather than my second. That was a complication I wasn't ready for. I'd been studiously trying to ignore how sexy he was for weeks, and now he'd kissed me, and all my pretence that he was just like family had gone out of the window.

We got our tickets and waited five minutes for the next tube. We stayed on the underground for half an hour before making our way to Marylebone station, where we could get a train overland to Beaconsfield. From there, we could get the pack to pick us up or we could wolf it and run together. Esme was in favour of the second option. Her preferred next action was mating with Greg.

He wants you too, she pointed out.

Now is not the time to get laid, I said firmly.

Why on earth would you want to get laid? she asked in genuine confusion. **You're not an egg.**

That made me laugh out loud. Greg looked at me questioningly but I shook my head. I was *not* going to explain that one.

Greg and I still hadn't spoken, but as we boarded the train I noticed a group of relatively young guys casting me leering looks. I glared back. I was entitled to have my legs out and not be pawed or molested. So my dress might be a bit slutty, but I wasn't sending out an invitation or any 'come and get me' vibes. The glare should have cemented that, but some men don't know how to take a hint

They sat on the train in the next set of seats to Greg and me. The feminist part of me wanted to ignore them or give them a firm lecture; the tired part of me just wanted a quiet journey. The tired part won. I turned my body into Greg's and slung my legs over his lap. He instantly placed a warm hand on my thigh and sent a possessive and quelling glare to the guys. They did some elbow shoving amongst themselves but turned their attention away from us. I relaxed; I wasn't in the mood to be harassed.

The adrenalin was going, leaving me cold and shocky. I'd watched an horrendous battle and I'd seen someone die, albeit a vampyr, but his undead life had certainly ended. He was now just dead. It had been messy and horrific, and

I'd probably have nightmares. Then I'd taken control of a troll against his will, which didn't fill me with the warm and fuzzies, and I'd released a raging unicorn on the world before neatly walking smack dab into a Connection raid, which could have seen us arrested or mind wiped. Not to mention that I was operating on a scant few hours' sleep. I'd felt rejuvenated when I woke up after my four hours, but now it was taking its toll.

I let my head drop on Greg's shoulder. I'd just rest my eyes for a moment.

'Sweetheart, wake up,' Greg murmured, giving my shoulder a gentle shake. 'We're at the station.'

I blinked, automatically checked my mouth for drool and was pleased when there was none. I rubbed at my gritty eyes and winced when my fingers came away black. 'Shit. Do I have panda eyes?' I asked plaintively.

He grinned. 'It's not so bad. I bet some women do it on purpose – smoky eyes.'

I caught sight of my reflection in the train's window and grimaced. I was a state, but there was little point in doing damage control now.

The train's brakes let out an ear-splitting screech as it slowed to a stop. Greg and I waited for the button on the door to light up then pushed it. Knowing we were leaving, the boys in the carriage threw out a few choice comments about my dress and potential profession.

Greg started back into the train but I grabbed his hand and pulled him back. 'Leave them. It was the look we were going for,' I pointed out.

'Doesn't make it right for them to speak to someone like that.'

'No,' I agreed, 'but let's go home. I'm too tired to deal with this now.'

Waiting at the top of the steps was a familiar stretch limousine. The passenger door opened and Bastion stepped out in human form. 'Get in,' he instructed. 'We have a problem.'

I sighed. When did we not?

Chapter 29

The warmth of the limo was a welcome relief, but I realised with some dismay that it meant I didn't have any excuse to keep Greg draped over me like my own personal blanket. He seemed to reach the same conclusion and removed his arm from my shoulders. Damn.

'What did you learn?' he asked Bastion.

Bastion levelled a quelling glare at me. 'Besides the fact that you two can't be trusted not to wreak havoc?'

'The Connection was coming for a raid anyway. Who knows where Ares would have ended up if we hadn't released him?'

'Perhaps in a unicorn sanctuary rather than roaming loose in London?' When he said it like that, it didn't sound so great. It had been the right decision at the time, and I stood by it. How was I to know that the Connection was coming and my rescue was largely otiose?

'If we hadn't been rescuing Ares, we'd have been stuck in the crowd like everyone else. We'd be in a Connection jail cell right now, like the rest of those rich tossers.'

Bastion shook his head. 'Don't be naïve, Lucy. Most of those tossers never saw a handcuff, let alone a cell. They never do.' He sounded a mite weary.

'They bribe their way out?' I surmised.

'Flash enough cash and you can get away with anything.'

I supposed that Bastion would know that better than anyone, because he got away with murder all the time. He read the thought on my face and his glare intensified.

'What did you get from Ghost?' I asked.

'A lead. The vampyr that was bothering you at Rosie's? He's part of the vampyrs' Red Guard.' He said it with a flourish, like I should gasp in shock.

Greg leaned back in his seat. 'Shit,' he swore.

'What?' I said impatiently. 'What's the Red Guard? And why do we care?'

'You've heard of the KGB and the SS?' Greg asked.

I nodded.

'The Red Guard are the vampyrs' equivalent, knights supposedly tasked with bringing order to the vampyrs and their interests. Their authority exists outside of the clan structure, and they have the ultimate say in any clan business. If you're a head of a clan and the Red Guard come visiting, you get nervous.'

'Wokeshire didn't seem nervous,' I pointed out. To be fair, Wokeshire hadn't seemed anything; he'd kept his emotions very much under wraps.

'Wokeshire didn't know the Red Guard were here until you showed him the photograph,' Greg pointed out. 'And the Red Guard vampyr was posing as a young vampyr, impetuous and unknowing in the ways of halls. The Red Guard are here and, for whatever reason, they're undercover.'

'The question is,' Bastion leaned back in his seat, 'what are they investigating?'

'Did Ghost have anything else to say? About Mark?'

'Mark was a regular, both as a fighter in fur and as a spectator. He earned decent cash from taking part and from laying down bets. That's as far as we got before we were interrupted by some rude Connection officials.'

'You made it back here in good time.'

'As I said, I have escape routes.'

'Did Ghost get away?' I asked.

Bastion gave me another look that said I was being naïve. I sighed. Of course the mysterious black-tourney dude got away.

The limousine crunched up the gravel to the mansion. 'Will you come by tomorrow?' I asked Bastion. 'We're going to get Amber DeLea to scry Archie's memories.'

'I'd best not,' he said after a pause.

'Why not?'

'I killed her lover.'

I blinked. At times it was so easy to forget that this taciturn man was a deadly assassin.

'Yeah, it may be best if you make yourself scarce.' Amber is as scary as Bastion in her own way. Besides, I wanted her to focus on the task at hand.

'I will run down other avenues.'

'Why? I mean why are you helping me so much?'

'Jessica Sharp sent me to assist you,' Bastion said finally. 'I will not fail her.'

'Well, that's nice.' I said faintly. Once again, my best friend was saving my bacon.

Bacon? I could have some bacon.

Not now! It's bedtime.

Okay, but let's groom ourselves first. She wanted a shower – she was obsessed with showers. I did have panda eyes and hair full of hairspray, so maybe it wasn't the worst idea.

Alright, I agreed.

'I'm turning in,' I said. 'It's late. We can talk more in the morning.'

Bastian gave a regal inclination of his head. Greg and I hauled ass out of the limo and watched it trundle away. The silence hung thicker than an elephant's wang. Well, this was awkward.

Greg cleared his throat. 'Goodnight.'

'Night,' I squeaked. *Awesome, just awesome*.

'I'll check the security here before I turn in.'

I nodded. 'Right you are.' *Right you are?* Ugh. Who even says that? Men usually eat out of my hands, and I let them. Greg, though... I liked Greg. And that kiss had been...

I blew out a breath that misted in the cool air as I watched him go inside. I was achingly tired but my head wasn't clear. Sleep would be a long time coming if I went to bed now.

Shall we go for a run? I asked Esme.

Always, she responded eagerly.

My dress was utterly ruined so I peeled it off – it could go in the bin. I kicked off my ridiculous heels and shifted into four legs. I let Esme take front and centre and relaxed into her capable paws.

She was happy and alert. She was scenting the air as we trotted round the grounds when she smelled something unusual. The breeze told her the direction it was coming from, and we ran into the rose garden and out the other side. There, chewing on the manicured lawns, was Ares.

I had no idea how he'd got there in the time it had taken us to take two trains and a limousine. I guessed he could just go as the crow flies.

There's a unicorn on our land, Esme remarked.

So it would seem.

We slunk up to Ares cautiously. He watched us approach with brimstone eyes then whickered a greeting. He didn't seem like he wanted to disembowel us, but what did I know?

Shift to human, Esme suggested.

I agreed and we blurred until we had two legs again. 'Hi,' I greeted the unicorn. His ears twitched in response. 'How are you doing?'

Nothing. With this realm, anything is possible and I'd half expected Ares to reply.

Slowly I gathered my piping skills and drew up the magic. I could have hummed a tune, but instead I stepped a little closer and laid my hand on his dazzlingly white fur. As I opened a connection between us, I felt gratitude and contentment. He was a little hungry, but he was happy not to be in a cage.

Home? I asked. I got back the firm image of the mansion grounds. It was the image I had inadvertently sent him. Oops.

I sent the image of many werewolves in the grounds and got a feeling of indifference in return. Okay, then. It looked like the pack now had its very own resident unicorn.

I gave Ares another pat and tried to convey a feeling of welcome. I had all sorts of misfits in my pack, so why not add a battle unicorn? I sent an image of going for a run as Esme and added him to the image – did he want to come for a trot with me?

He gave a distinct nod of his huge head. I shifted back onto four legs and let Esme take the reins again. She ran joyfully and Ares ran easily by our side, throwing back his head and whinnying his joy at his freedom. Esme gave him a wolfy grin in response, then threw back her head and howled. There is such simple, honest happiness in running together.

We ran the boundaries of our land half a dozen times then returned to the mansion. I shifted to human and my tummy let out a loud rumble. 'Wait here,' I said to Ares. 'I'll just be a moment.'

I ducked inside the mansion and found my dressing gown hanging neatly by the front door. How the hell had it got there? I blushed a little suddenly, realising Greg had gone to monitor the security cameras and I had promptly got naked in front of them. Mystery solved: he had kindly put out my robe for me. See, who says I can't do this detective shit?

I pulled on the robe and went to the kitchen to look for something for myself and for Ares. He'd like carrots, right?

Esme snorted. **Did you not see his teeth? He eats meat.** Her tone conveyed her approval.

He was eating the grass! I objected.

Acting like an equine is a last resort for them. Meat. He wants meat.

I had no doubt she knew best, so I pulled out a box of ham, some leftover cooked sausages and a few raw-beef patties and headed back out.

Ares was waiting patiently by the front door.

'I didn't know which you'd prefer,' I explained. I refused to feel stupid for talking to a unicorn; people speak to their pets all the time. Besides, he wasn't just a horse with a horn and I'd felt his mind on mine. I opened the huge box of ham and peeled back the plastic lid, placed the other meat on the ground for him and snagged a couple of sausages for myself. Ares went straight for the burger patties.

'You prefer it raw, huh?' I commented. 'I'll get more stuff in for you tomorrow.'

His ears twitched but he ignored me, happily munching away like the happy little carnivore he was. When the food had been devoured I said, 'I don't have a stable or anything.' I pictured a stable with a roof on it and sent the image to him while I touched his fur. I tinged the image with regret.

He snorted and sent back an image of trees, then he turned and moseyed away into our scant woods. I guess battle-hardened unicorns didn't need a roof over their heads. Good to know.

I yawned widely and slipped back inside the house. In the kitchen I ate a few rounds of toast before I went to my room to shower and collapse into bed.

No matter what Bastion said, I couldn't help but feel pretty good about rescuing Ares, and it was clear Ares felt the same. Esme and I were content as we tumbled into sleep.

The blare of the alarm on my phone woke me. Despite only catching a measly five hours and some change, I felt refreshed and ready to go. There were definite upsides to this werewolf business, besides having a friend on a constant mental ride-along.

Morning, Esme.

Esme sent the image of herself doing a luxurious stretch. **Good morning, Lucy Barrett.** Her voice was warm with affection.

I struggled to pull myself out of bed. The mansion was always a little chilly in the morning – the old central-heating system could really do with an overhaul. Another thing for another day. I cleansed, toned and moisturised. I didn't bother with much make up, just a quick swipe of mascara.

Putting mud on your eyelashes is odd, Esme pointed out, not for the first time.

It's not mud. Putting mascara on your eyes is tradition, I explained.

It seems odd to me. It is good that it doesn't affect your ability to hunt, she conceded.

I grinned to myself. *Sometimes it makes it easier to hunt.* I thought of Greg.

Humans are odd.

Without a doubt.

I headed to the kitchen to grab some breakfast. The other wolves were starting their day but for once the conversation didn't lull when I walked in.

'Who ate all the ham?' Mrs Dawes asked the room at large, her hands on hips, her tone accusatory. 'That was for sandwiches for lunch!'

I held my hand up. 'Sorry. I gave it to our unicorn.'

Silence fell. Mrs Dawes broke it. 'We have a unicorn?' She sounded excited.

I grinned. 'Yes, his name is Ares and he's decided to live in our grounds. He likes raw meat. I was improvising yesterday.'

'You named the unicorn after the God of War?'

I shook my head. 'He was already named that. I rescued him from a black tourney.' I said it casually and looked around the room. No Elena. Noah tensed at the mention of the black tourney and met my eyes. 'Later,' I mouthed to him. He deserved to know what had gone down.

Archie let out a low whistle. 'You rescued him from a black tourney? Aren't you worried about Ghost tracking you down in retribution?'

I considered it. 'Not really. I'm friends with Bastion, and he's scarier. I reckon Ghost will leave me alone.'

'You're friends with Bastion?' David said incredulously. 'The three-hundred-year-old murderous assassin?'

'He's got a great skincare regime,' I quipped. I dug into a massive bowl of cereal. 'Archie,' I said between mouthfuls, 'Amber DeLea is coming to see you. Make sure you're available around 10am. Has anyone seen Elena?' I asked loudly.

There were lots of headshakes then conversation around me resumed. Hmm.

'She's a late riser,' Archie commented. 'She often goes late to Black Park to run.'

'Alone?'

'Yeah, mostly.'

'We're supposed to go in pairs,' I pointed out.

'We all need alone time now and again. She'll show up later. She's a freelance journalist, so she can make her own hours.'

'I didn't know she was a journalist.'

'Yeah. She got into it when her brother died.'

'What happened to her brother?'

'He died.'

'Thanks,' I said drily. 'I'd gathered that.'

Archie shrugged. 'I don't know more than that.'

'You dated for how long?' I muttered. 'It's a wonder she didn't dump you first.'

He coloured slightly. 'I'm rich and adorable.'

I snorted. 'I don't think anyone has ever called you adorable.'

'You're right. I'm manly and fierce. Kittens are adorable.'

I meant it more because he could be a condescending asshole, but sure: manly and fierce. I finished my breakfast with a gulp of hot coffee and swung by Mrs Dawes again to apologise for the ham snafu. She waved me away cheerfully and said she'd add unicorn-suitable food to our shopping list. She seemed pleased to have a unicorn on the grounds; maybe she'd been yearning for a pet.

I wondered whether anyone else would have got away with snagging the ham without complaint, but I suspected there were other rules in place for the alpha. Which handy because I was about to break some.

Chapter 30

I skulked into the dormitory corridor and knocked loudly on Elena's door, but there was no response. I dug in my pocket for Greg's wolfy-master key and slid it into the lock. It turned easily and my heart started to pound. If Elena was having a gentle snooze, she was about to get a rude awakening.

I opened the door cautiously but there wasn't so much as a peep from inside. The room was dark and the curtains were still drawn. I slipped inside soundlessly. Elena's bed was empty. I shut the door behind me and opened her curtains.

I felt like I was going to have a heart attack. How Jess did this snooping thing as part of her job, I'd never know because I was about to keel over from panicking about being discovered. I managed to get my heart to slow by promising it Ben & Jerry's ice cream later.

With daylight pouring into the room, I grimaced. Archie had said Elena was messy but he'd been downplaying it – Elena was a slob. Dirty clothes were cast around the floor, and every surface was covered with stuff. I'm a tidy minimalist and this mess actually made my head hurt. I was itching to start tidying but I was here as a snoop, not a cleaner.

I stepped into her en suite, which had been hit by the same hurricane of mess. There were shampoo bottles and makeup and hairbrushes filled with clumps of hair; there was soap and flannels and towels and *clutter* on every surface. Nothing was tidy, let alone clean.

I gingerly opened the bathroom cabinet and found an array of things you'd expect: toothbrushes, toothpaste and face masks. Next to the facemasks was a prescription bottle. I pulled out my phone and googled the name. It was an anti-depressant and she had enough of it to make an elephant happy. I guess a wolfy metabolism makes it hard to get regular medicine. I put it back where I'd found it.

The room was in such disarray that I didn't have the first idea where to start looking for clues. I stepped over the discarded clothes and went to the drawers, but there was nothing in them except clothes. The wardrobe had boxes and boxes stacked up in it. I sat down on a patch of clear floor and went through them. Shoes. A drool-worthy amount of shoes.

I stood up and went to close the wardrobe door and there it was: a clue. A really fucking huge one that I'd been oblivious to for the last half an hour. When I told Greg this story, I would cut that bit out.

On the inside of the wardrobe were pinned news articles, some written by Elena but most by others. They had started about two years earlier and were clearly by someone in Common. They cited an underground fighting ring. One article was about the sad death of Jackson Malloy and next to it was a picture of him. I didn't need a genealogist to tell me that Jackson was Elena's brother. According to the articles, he'd been killed in one of these underground fighting rings.

Big fat bingo. I took a picture of the wardrobe door and backed away. I did a cursory search of Elena's bed but didn't find a big silver knife marked 'incriminating evidence'. Still, it wasn't looking good for her. Reading between the lines, her brother had been killed at a black tourney and I'd bet my bottom dollar Mark had been involved. If that was the case, why had Elena been at the tourney last night? Had the Connection arrived and foiled her nefarious plans for revenge?

I let out a low whistle. *Well, Bob's your uncle.*

I do not have an uncle named Bob, Esme said, making me snicker.

It just means 'there you go'.

Where do we go?

The guy in this article was Elena's brother. He got killed at a black tourney. I think Elena killed Mark to avenge her brother's death.

And Archie?

He broke her heart.

His attacker sliced Archie's stomach open, Esme pointed out. She was right, the attack had been brutal.

Hell hath no fury like a woman scorned. I cut Esme off before she could butcher that one. *Women with broken hearts do crazy shit,* I explained.

I checked the time and swore loudly: 10.40am. I'd been engrossed in Elena's room for far longer than I'd intended and I was late for Amber DeLea. I grimaced. Great. She wasn't the type to forgive tardiness.

I checked over the room.

The wardrobe door was shut, Esme pointed out. **A good hunter leaves no tracks.**

Thanks. I shut it and closed the curtains again before I tiptoed out of the pigsty. I locked the door behind me and headed off to meet Amber in my private living room.

The February light was pouring in but the room was still decidedly frosty. Now I understood why Lord Samuel always had a blazing fire. My grate was cold and empty, and I wished for some dancing flames to fill it.

Amber DeLea was sitting on one of my sofas, with Archie and Greg on another. Her green eyes were as chilly as the room.

'Sorry,' I said breezily. 'I was sleuthing.'

Her expression didn't change. 'My bills include travel and waiting time.'

Her bills made me wince, but I tried hard not to show it. 'Sure. Best get to it, then. Have you managed to find anything else about 3418?' I asked.

'No,' she said curtly. 'The books I have checked are all in order. Your supplier isn't a witch.'

'You're saying it's from the Connection?'

She shrugged. 'They're the only others who are licensed to hold it. Other than that, there's the black market.'

I bit my thumb. 'So, 3418 is a dead end.'

Amber gestured to Archie. 'We're here for him,' she reminded me. 'First he needs to transform, then he needs to give himself wholly over to the wolf.'

Archie spoke. 'And then Lucy will pipe him?'

Greg raised an eyebrow at me. 'I thought we were keeping your piping skills on the down low?'

'We were – are. I just told Archie and Liam. And Amber knows already – because of the thing with the ouroboros.'

'Sure,' he said evenly.

Archie stood. 'I'll get my kit off, shall I?'

'No time like the present,' I agreed.

He slithered out of his clothes and started to transform. It took him a good few minutes; watching the transformation made me thank my lucky stars once more that Esme and I were so far from ordinary by werewolf standards.

Whilst waiting for Archie, Amber had pulled out various jars of gloop from her ever-present tote bag, along with her paintbrushes and disposable gloves. Someone – I assumed Mrs Dawes – had already supplied her with a fancy-looking bowl of water. I'd never seen someone scry before, but Jess had told me it hurt like a bitch.

Archie was finally on four legs, but he was unnaturally still. 'Archie,' I called out. He swung to look at me. 'You're supposed to be letting Fred take control.'

He blinked again. We waited for a long minute before finally his eyes turned golden yellow.

'Hey, Fred,' I said, as I gathered my piping powers from within me. Fred was looking a little on the wild side, so I decided not to risk my hand by touching him and instead hummed out a little tune, 'The Grand Old Duke of York'. The strains of the music touched his ears and transported my magic with them. I felt a loose connection form between us.

Hey, Fred, I greeted him warmly.

Hello, alpha, he responded cautiously. **He has let me have control again.** His voice was bemused.

I winced a little. Fred probably wasn't going to be too impressed when I explained about the scrying thing. *I have brought the witch back.* I gestured to Amber.

She saved our lives. She has nothing to fear from me.

She wishes to scry an image from your head. Archie cannot remember his attacker. The drugs he was given have wiped his memory.

Yes, I understand. I have been present throughout the planning.

Then you get that this is going to hurt?

What is pain to a wolf? The hunt must succeed or we will become prey again. We are not prey. The last thought was growled out, both in my mind and out loud.

Amber swallowed hard at the vicious noise and I took perverse delight in her discomfort. She wasn't as cool as she made out. 'Fred is on board with the plan,' I told her. 'He understands that it will hurt, but he doesn't want to be attacked again. He is willing for you to try to scry from him.'

PROTECTION OF THE PACK

Amber nodded and snapped on purple disposable gloves. She opened one of the Kilner jars and dipped her paintbrush in some dark-blue stuff. Even to my human nose, it stank.

I'm sorry, it smells bad, I apologised to Fred.

Like the rancid corpse of a ferret, he agreed, his nose wrinkling in distaste. He let out an audible growl and Amber paused, her eyes wide.

Are you okay for her to put that on you? I double-checked.

As long as I can groom myself afterwards.

'Fred is okay to shower after we're done here, right? That stuff stinks.'

'Of course,' Amber agreed.

'Then go ahead. Do your thing.'

'I'm going to paint a few runes on your head,' she explained to the wolf. 'Then you will need to touch your nose to the water.' She gestured to the bowl. 'Please hold your nose there for a few moments while we get a picture of whoever attacked you. It will hurt at that point. I'm sorry.'

Fred gave a distinct nod, and Amber lifted her brush nervously. She dabbed on a little of the potion; when it became clear that Fred wasn't going to attack or devour her for covering him in rabbit-corpse juices, she continued.

A few moments later, he gave a low whine which alerted all of my alpha instincts. The urge to hit Amber, to get her away from him, was so strong that I had to battle with every inch of my will to stop myself lashing out.

'The bowl,' I said tightly to Fred. 'Can you touch your nose to the water? Then we can be done.' Unable to help myself, I laid my hand on his fur and stroked him reassuringly. He leaned into my touch, and I knew he needed the comfort. It was unnatural to let him be in pain and not to do all we could to stop it. It hurt Esme and me, too.

He stumbled a little as he made his way to the bowl. Greg had his phone out, ready to take a photo of the image. Fred lowered his snout to the water and I waited for the image of Elena to form. It took a moment before the image rose to the surface, as clear as day.

Well, hell.

Chapter 31

I had been fully prepared to see the image of Elena rise up, maybe even Noah's mum, Sally. But I hadn't been prepared for the image of Lauren Gallagher, sixth in the Devon pack and council member extraordinaire. Mark had been attacked before she'd officially arrived and I hadn't even included her on my suspect list. Why on earth would she kill Mark and attack Archie?

I touched Fred's shoulder lightly. *We're all done. You can stop now.*

It hurts, he panted, pulling his nose back from the water.

I'm sorry, I apologised with all of my heart. Guilt cut through me; I was supposed to protect the pack and I was causing Fred pain. I could feel how much it upset Esme. *I will hunt down the one that hurt you now,* I promised.

Then it is worth it, Fred whimpered. He loped back to Archie's pile of clothes and willingly transformed back into two legs.

Archie dressed with shaking hands, then crouched low. His hands were pressed to his head. 'Damn, my head hurts.' He tried to shake off the pain and stood up. 'Lauren?' he said, bemused. 'I haven't spoken two words to her. And I swear those two words were respectful. I don't understand.'

Greg frowned. 'Mark took you to the black tourneys. I think someone thought you saw something you shouldn't have done. We suspected that someone was pulling Mark's strings and making him hold back from challenging your father. We suspected Jimmy Rain, Mark's former alpha, but someone in the council arranged for Lord Samuel to travel to Liverpool to investigate Rain under the radar. With no pack back up, Lord Samuel was alone and vulnerable.'

'You think someone in the council lured my father there to be killed? But why?' Archie crouched down again. He looked young and lost.

The door swung open and in walked Elena. 'Because he was helping me bring down the black tourneys.' She turned accusing eyes on me. 'You were in my room – your scent is everywhere. You had no right to invade my privacy.'

'I'm your alpha,' I growled back. 'I have every right, especially when we saw you at the tourney last night.'

Elena sighed and sat down next to Archie. 'And what a clusterfuck that was. Months – years – of hard work and all the main players walked away. The Connection is a joke. Lord Samuel warned me, but I wanted to do it by the book. I wanted to see them rot in jail.'

She turned and raised tired eyes to meet Archie's. 'So now you know. It's my fault your dad is dead. If he hadn't been digging into the black tourneys, the council wouldn't have sent him up to Rain to be taken out.'

'What's the council got to do with it?' I asked.

'Everything. I've been investigating the tourneys since Jackson died. I've spoken to a lot of people, but most weren't willing to go on the record. A number of council members helped start the tourneys, though I still don't know who. The council has records of every lone wolf without a pack. Someone handed the list over to the black tourney organiser for the loners to be rounded up and slaughtered. The message soon got around: to be a lone wolf was to be a dead wolf walking. Jackson refused to be cowed, especially when he found out that our pack leader, Beckett Frost, was hip-deep in the tourneys. I applied to transfer here, and Jackson went lone. We all know how Jackson's story ends,' she spat out bitterly.

Beckett Frost was Ace's brother and alpha. Damn. I frowned. 'But why kill Mark? He was all for the tourneys.'

'He was,' she agreed, 'until he was told to throw his fights. Mark was an asshole and he wanted to win. He wanted to be alpha, but he was told to bide his time. He threw his aggression into the tourneys, then he was told to throw a few fights. He wasn't happy to lose, and he wasn't happy to remain number two.'

'How do you know all of this?' Greg demanded.

'Mark told me,' she admitted unhappily. 'He was blackmailing me. He'd found out what Lord Samuel and I were doing. He said that if I didn't pay him, he'd make sure I ended up just like Jackson. But while he was bragging about how neatly he'd trapped me, he told me about blackmailing the council members involved in the tourney. He had evidence of the fights being fixed. Not only that, he had evidence about each of the council members that he would give to the Connection if they didn't make him the alpha here. I didn't tell Lord Samuel because I *wanted* Mark to blackmail those shits responsible for Jackson's death. It seemed fitting.'

She looked at Archie again. 'I'm so sorry. If I'd known what they were going to do, I'd never have sat on the information.'

'And instead of capitulating to Mark's demands, they sent Ace and Lauren,' I interjected.

Elena nodded miserably. 'I'd do anything to change it,' she said miserably to Archie. 'I'm so sorry.'

Archie shook his head. 'I can't do this now. My head is splitting and I just – I can't.' He walked out of the room. Elena reached out a hand to him as he strode past then let it fall again. She was blinking rapidly, struggling to hold back tears.

I felt bad for Archie and I watched him go with regret. He'd finally come to accept that although I had killed his father, I wasn't wholly to blame. Now Elena had pulled the rug out from under him. The whole thing had been a set-up from the very start; Lord Samuel really hadn't stood much of a chance.

I wondered whether he'd known that. He'd been all too happy to throw his lot in with Jess and fight a werewolf pack against monumental odds. I understood now that he'd chosen to go out on his own terms.

'Come on,' I said to Greg. 'Let's check the cameras and find out the location of our esteemed council guests.'

We left Amber packing up her jars and went to my office. Greg slid behind the desk, logged onto the computer and brought up the security cameras. We checked the communal areas first, then we reviewed the footage from the dormitory corridors. I cursed myself for not including cameras in the rooms. Who needs privacy?

There was no movement in the guest wing, and no way of knowing if Ace and Lauren were in their rooms. 'We could go back through the guest-wing footage,' Greg suggested.

'Or we could just knock,' I countered.

'Yeah, that'd work too.'

The computer screen flicked to my living room. Amber had packed up and left without another parting shot about the bill. That wasn't like her. The screen flickered and changed to the corridor outside of my office. 'Change it back to the living room,' I ordered sharply.

Greg obliged and I swore loudly. I pointed to the bottom right of the screen, where we could see a jar open on the floor. There was no chance that Amber would have left that willingly; she never let a potion jar out of her sight.

'Check the driveway!' I barked.

Greg flicked to the camera on the drive. Lauren was driving their car and in the back seat next to Ace, eyes filled with fury and fear, was Amber.

'Fuck!' I swore. I tore out of the room and pelted down the stairs, throwing off clothes as I ran, and transformed as I burst out of the door. Esme and I felt steady on our four legs, and we were desperate to catch them. They'd grabbed Amber as a hostage, and it was my fault that she'd been there to be grabbed.

Their car was already speeding away. We fixed our sights on it and ran after it. Greg was ahead of the game, and I saw that he was closing the wrought-iron gates as Ace's car approached. The car didn't slow. It hit the half-open gates at speed, wrenching one of them clean off its enormous hinges. The car took significant damage but not enough to stop it. It careened out of the driveway and onto the main road.

The car drew away from us effortlessly. We followed, but we knew in our hearts that it was hopeless. The fastest we could go was maybe 30mph.

They're gone, Esme admitted bitterly.

For now.

Esme turned and trotted us back to the mansion. Time to call in the big guns.

I shifted outside, then slipped into the mansion where Greg and Liam were waiting. Greg held out a robe and my phone. 'I'm sorry,' he said tightly. 'I let you down. When Bastion told us our car was bugged, I should have thought to sweep the mansion for bugs, too. The living room was tapped. I've found four so far.'

'Not your fault.'

'I'm head of security. There's no one else to blame.'

'How about the fuckers that took advantage of our hospitality to kill and attack our packmates?' I all-but yelled back. 'We will hold *them* accountable. The blame game helps no one, and I need you focused. We need to get Amber back.'

Greg straightened and nodded. I could see his hand twitching, barely resisting giving me a military salute.

'Search their rooms. They left in a hurry – see if they left any clues about where they would go.' I handed Greg the master key and he left with Liam.

I pulled out my phone from the pocket of my robe to call Bastion. As usual, he answered with silence.

'I need your help,' I said firmly. 'Ace and Lauren are the ones who killed Mark and attacked Archie. The wolf council has been involved in the black tourneys, providing lone wolves to slaughter. Mark was trying to blackmail the council. The members killed him and were trying to kill anyone else who might have been involved in his little scheme. Ace and Lauren have kidnapped Amber DeLea. I need you to lean on Ghost and find out where they are.'

'That's a tall order,' Bastion said finally. 'She's a griffin.'

She? 'You're Bastion.'

'There are lines I won't cross.'

'So any other species is fair game but another griffin isn't?'

'There's barely thirty of us left in the world. So ... yes.'

'I don't care if you're as endangered as a dodo,' I snarled. 'Ghost is responsible for the deaths of hundreds.'

Bastion sighed. 'We all battle with our curse, one way or another. *All* griffins are responsible for the deaths of hundreds – to kill is in our nature and we have no choice in the matter. Jessica Sharp saw first-hand what Shirdal did when he hadn't killed for seven years.'

Jess had told me about the horrific slaughter Shirdal had committed. She hadn't blamed him for it – after all, he'd saved her life – but she'd had nightmares about it.

'I don't accept that,' I argued. 'We all of us have free will. You *choose* to kill.'

'If we didn't control the urge one way or another, we'd slaughter the world,' he admitted tightly. 'I'll speak to Ghost and see if I can get her to help us willingly. The black tourneys are a means to an end for her. I doubt she cares a whit for her fellow council members. I'll do what I can.' He hung up without a goodbye.

That wasn't the promise I'd been hoping for, but it would have to do for now. I didn't have much choice but to wait.

I contemplated calling Steve Marley and updating him, but if I wanted to retain my authority as alpha then I needed to deal with this in-house. If I didn't, I'd lose what little respect I'd already gained from the pack.

Greg and Liam returned from Ace and Lauren's rooms. 'They didn't leave anything behind,' Greg reported unhappily. 'Both of their rooms are spotless.'

We were back at square one and I had no allies and no leads left to tug on. We brainstormed for half an hour but moved along no further.

Finally, Bastion returned my call. 'Ghost says the Red Guard are also here to shut down the black tourneys. They've been dogging her organisation for months. They don't want vampyrs involved in the tourneys, they think it is beneath them and tarnishes their reputation. Ghost thinks the Red Guard were working with Lord Samuel. Lord Samuel wasn't as naïve as Elena about the Connection plan. Though he hoped the Connection would bring down the black tourneys, he had a backup plan too. Plan B was passing information along to the Red Guard. They might have acted less scrupulously than the Connection.

Lord Samuel didn't care about the means, he just wanted the tourneys shut down, one way or another.'

'Ghost told you all of this willingly?'

'She's been enjoying toying with Lord Samuel and the Red Guard, but what's the point in one-upmanship if no one knows about it?' he commented drily.

'Does she know where Ace and Lauren are?'

'No, but the Red Guard might. The leader of the team is called Voltaire. Ghost has been keeping them busy by throwing out lots of red herrings around the mansion.'

'Wonderful,' I said flatly. So it was Ghost's fault I'd got pinned down in the kids' play area waiting for five vampyrs to move on.

I turned to Greg. 'Can you get me Wokeshire's number?'

'On it.' He stepped out of the room.

Liam cleared his throat. 'If we're going in hot and heavy to rescue Amber, can I suggest calling in the top thirteen? It will help show that you trust us.'

I hadn't even thought of that. I opened my mouth then closed it. Had I been putting up barriers between myself and the pack?

We'd have to go in forcefully and I needed to know I could trust the wolves at our heels. No, I didn't trust all the pack yet, nor did they trust me. It was a two-way street and we hadn't walked far enough along it yet.

'Have we got a phone tree?' I asked Greg as he came back in.

He grinned. 'Nothing so antiquated. We've got a WhatsApp group.'

'What would happen if we called them in? I guess they come when they finish their work shifts?'

He snorted. 'No. If there's an emergency call, we all duck out, call in sickies, whatever is needed. Pack comes first. If you need us, we're there.'

I swallowed against the sudden lump in my throat. I'm a social girl, I have lots of friends, but this was something else. 'Summon the thirteen.'

It is nice to belong, Esme said astutely.

Yes, it is.

Chapter 32

I'd summoned the top thirteen members of the pack and Greg had called Wokeshire. We had a telephone number for the Red Guard so I called it and left a succinct message, but so far there'd been no response. I guess we weren't playing ball. I had kind of figured that the enemy of my enemy was my friend, or at least my ally, but I guessed vampyr–werewolf prejudices died hard. Maybe they'd played ball with Lord Samuel, an alpha of some repute, but I was a low-down nobody alpha. It looked like they weren't going to give me the time of day.

Of the thirteen, Mark was dead and still hadn't been replaced, and Archie was out because of the pain from the scrying. That left us with eleven, and we couldn't take them all. Ace and Lauren had already proved to be deadly and deceptive; they'd struck at us in the heart of the mansion not once, but twice. I wasn't willing to leave us undefended in case of strike three. This was our *home*. Our stronghold.

Elena showed up looking pale but determined. She had something to prove. David looked equally determined. As the others trickled in, there was an energy and tension in the mansion I hadn't felt before.

My phone rang with an unknown number. I answered it, hoping it was a ransom demand from Ace or a lead from the Red Guard. It was neither of those: it was Joyce, the dryad. 'Hi, Lucy.'

'Joyce? This isn't the best time.'

'The elders asked me to ring you because some were-wolves are sniffing around the elder tree. They are very disappointed – they thought this issue had been resolved. I'm sorry, but they're really quite upset.' She was shooting for an even tone, but I could tell she was upset too. She'd put her neck on the line to help me and Jess, and I guess it reflected badly on her.

'Do you know the wolves?'

'No, but they must be local. They're with Amber De-Lea.'

Oh shit! 'They're not local. I'm on my way. Don't approach them,' I cautioned. 'They're dangerous.'

'This is the Other. Everyone's dangerous,' she said drily before ringing off. She wasn't wrong.

'We've got a location,' I confirmed. 'The dryads' elder tree. Ace and Lauren have attacked us twice here in our home, and I won't risk a third attack. This could all be an elaborate ruse to draw us away and attack here again. I'm taking Greg, Elena, Liam and David with me, the rest of you stay here and secure the mansion. When we leave, roll the metal shutters down, shift and stand ready for attack. I won't be blindsided again. Let's move!'

I was gratified that no one argued, though I saw some raised eyebrows particularly when I called David's name. This was his opportunity to prove himself, to carve a place in my pack, and I hoped I wouldn't regret giving him the opportunity. As for the others? It was simple: I trusted them. I hoped it was enough to keep us all alive.

Greg gave those that were staying a quick overview of the security system. When he was satisfied that they'd grasped the basics, we piled into Elena's car and peeled off to Black Park. On the way I left another message for the Red Guard. They were my solution; if I killed Ace and Lauren, I was going to suffer consequences from the council, but if I didn't kill them, I'd suffer consequences from my pack. I was between a rock and a hard place, but the Red Guard might be the solution I needed. I was happy to use anything to get the result I wanted, even the werewolves' sworn enemies.

However, they seemed determined to ignore me, which frankly pissed me off. I wasn't used to being ignored. If they weren't playing ball, I was leaning towards option one: kill Ace and Lauren and rescue Amber. I'd deal with the council later. That was a problem for future me – poor, dumb bitch.

I texted Bastion because it seemed rude to have had his help this whole time and not give him the chance to be a part of the final takedown. Also, if the Red Guard let me down, maybe he'd be willing to slaughter Ace and Lauren for me. He could kill someone and satisfy his urges, and I got my enemies dead. It was win-win.

I could feel Esme growling in my head. She wanted the blood on *her* claws; Ace and Lauren had hurt *her* pack and she would bring retribution down on them.

We parked up and decamped from the car, heading the rest of the way by foot. It was a weekday so the park wasn't too busy, but I was still aware that there were Common civilians out and about, vulnerable and unaware of the dangers lurking amongst them.

Half of us shifted and half of us remained on two legs – Greg shifted and I stayed on two legs, for now. I called a halt four hundred yards away from the elder tree, closed my eyes and reached towards my piping magic. I brought it to the surface and held it there, bubbling and impatient. I touched the nearest tree, reached out to it and the tree network it was a part of.

I needed to see the elder tree. I rustled through the trees' consciousness until I came to the clearing. Sure enough, there were Ace, Lauren and Amber. Lauren was on four legs, determinedly sniffing and digging as she walked about, clearly searching for something. Ace was still in human form.

'If you don't locate Mark's little stash,' Ace growled to Amber, 'I'll happily rip your throat out.'

'I'm trying,' she protested, 'but I need more time to prepare the proper runes.'

'You're supposed to be the most powerful witch in the area, touted to become the next Symposium member, and you can't even do a proper locator rune?'

'Firstly, I'm the most powerful *healer*; secondly, if you knew exactly what object I was locating then I could do it easily. How am I supposed to locate something without knowing what it is? Magic can only do so much.'

'It's Oates' blackmail material. It'll be photos, or a USB drive, or a bloody floppy disc, for all I care. Whatever it is, however it's stored, you have half an hour to find it or I'll spill your blood here and find a new witch who can.'

'There's no need to be rude,' Amber glared back. 'Didn't your mother teach you any manners?' As she said 'manners', I swear she looked right at me, in the trees. Somehow, she sensed me. I knew next to nothing about a witch's powers; I'd thought they were all runes and potions.

'My mother taught me to win at any cost,' Ace snapped. 'Manners are for weaklings. I don't need to say please, I take what I want.'

'And how is that working out for you so far?' Amber asked facetiously.

'It would have been fine if Mark hadn't died so suddenly. I thought we had hours left to torture him and find the evidence, but the fucker died. He was as inconvenient in death as he was in life.'

'And you attacked Archie, hoping he'd know where the blackmail material was.'

'He came with Mark a few times to the tourney, him and young Noah. Noah was next up, but that frigid bitch Lucy squirreled him away somewhere. I've got you now so I don't need them. Mark said he hid it here, and he was in too much pain to be lying. If only he hadn't died so damn quickly, he could have been more bloody specific then we wouldn't have needed to attack Archie or spend so long with this pathetic little pack.'

'Pack rumours say you seemed quite enamoured of the alpha of the pathetic little pack,' Amber pointed out.

He snorted. 'What do you know of pack life? She's weak. I could woo her, mate her and become alpha. Or I could simply kill her and take her place, but she has such a nice body I thought I'd fuck her first. Even that idea has lost its shine. This place is backward. She wants to be everyone's friend. It's pitiful.'

His gaze sharpened on Amber. 'I know what you're doing, but playing for time won't help. No one is coming for you – they don't know where we are. And if you don't find me my bloody evidence, you'll be dead in half an hour.'

'I'll be dead in half an hour anyway,' Amber said calmly. 'You won't let me walk away from here.'

'There are two ways to die.' Ace smiled unpleasantly. 'Trust me, you want option one.'

'Only two?' Amber replied faintly.

'The rest are variations on the same theme,' he promised darkly.

I started to pull myself back from the tree's awareness but the elder tree reached out and grabbed me, hauling me back deeper into the clearing. It pushed me forward and showed me my apology birch tree. The dryad elders had buried it where the ground had already been disturbed. Beneath the roots of the apology tree lay blackmail.

Having shown me what it wanted, the elder tree released its hold and I lurched back to my body with a gasp. I felt like an idiot. The elder tree had shown me the disturbed ground before. How much easier would life have been if I'd understood what it was trying to say to me days ago?

My small pack circled protectively around me. Five trees over, Bastion stood on four legs in full griffin form, lounging against the tree in languid arrogance.

I ignored him for a moment. 'Ace and Lauren are up ahead. Mark buried his blackmail material by the elder tree. He told them that much, but they haven't been able to find it so they've kidnapped Amber to get her to do a locating rune. She's stalling for time in the hope of being rescued. Let's not disappoint her.'

David and Elena exchanged confused glances, wondering how I'd got my information. Now was not the time to get into my piping.

'I'll swoop in and lift DeLea out of danger,' Bastion offered. 'The rest of you can deal with the two wolves – that's pack business.'

He made it seem easy, but I was nervous. I didn't want anyone else in my pack to die. And Ace was second to his alpha brother, whilst Lauren had already demonstrated her total ruthlessness and lack of hesitation to get her hands – or claws – dirty. Bastion was right, though: getting

Amber to safety was our top priority. She'd been dragged into wolf business by me, and she didn't deserve to die for it.

On the surface, I had good odds; I had numbers on my side. We had five to their two. But the truth was that I had David, whom I knew struggled with the violent side of pack life. Liam was capable and smart but still a little on the young side. And Elena? She had a lot of emotions flying about that might cloud her judgement.

Other than that, it was me and Greg. I trusted him and Esme to kick ass, but those odds still didn't fill me with the warm and fuzzies. But we had little choice; if I wanted to be alpha of this pack, I had to protect it – even the dead members who turned out to be complete little shits.

'Everyone shift,' I ordered. I waited until we were all on four legs before I stripped and transformed myself. We were downwind of the breeze that was carrying the scents of Ace and Lauren.

I let Esme take front and centre and surrendered control to her. She gave a small yip and we all charged forward. Bastion leapt up, his great white wings lifting him easily above the tree canopy. We gathered speed and momentum and raced towards the clearing, hearts pounding and blood singing. The hunt had begun.

As we burst into the clearing, Ace swore. 'Protect me,' he barked at Lauren as he started his own shift. I knew from experience we had no more than two minutes before he'd be in wolf form.

Esme didn't give a shit about chivalry. He would be easier to kill on two legs and she wouldn't hesitate to rip his throat out *if* we could get to him. The five of us ranged out, circling our enemies. Esme threw her head back and howled her intentions. The pack echoed her eerie call.

Greg and Esme charged toward Lauren who ran to meet us, teeth bared. With our tail high with confidence, we pounded forward. Lauren's tail was flicked down because she knew the odds weren't with her, but she ploughed towards us just the same. Esme felt a flicker of approval; Lauren would go down fighting to protect Ace, as she should.

Esme increased her speed and lowered her head, butting firmly into Lauren. Braced as Lauren was, our speed and bulk were such that we tossed her to the floor. Esme showed no hesitation and no mercy as she ripped into Lauren's side with her teeth.

Lauren let out a yowl, but although she was down she wasn't out. She found her feet again and surged back up, swiping at us with her claws to force us back before she leapt, teeth ready to rend our flesh. Before she could make contact, Greg slammed into her, echoing Esme's charge. He ripped into Lauren's leg and Esme aimed for her throat.

Lauren's coat was thick and she turned at the last minute, leaving us with a mouthful of fur and the faint tang of blood. It was not the killing blow that we need-ed. Esme spat out the coarse hair and yipped to Elena, Liam and David. They were still hesitating to attack Ace whilst he was human. The humans were in control of their wolves, and centuries of human manners had bred in that it was wrong to attack an opponent when they were vulnerable.

Esme called to their wolves to attack but it was already too late. Ace's shift was almost complete, and he would not afford them the same courtesy.

We focused again on Lauren. She was bleeding badly from our first attack and she broke away, heading into the woods to escape. If it had been up to me, I'd have let her go. Maybe she'd learnt her lesson. But Esme was in charge and she had no mercy. She called for Elena and Greg to give chase. Lauren had killed Mark and she was accountable, no matter who had given the orders.

Greg and Elena harried Lauren, nipping and ripping at her, as we turned our attention to Ace. He was growling low in his throat, threatening, hoping to scare us off, but

Esme crowed in delight and mockery. She wasn't so easily scared; Ace had sought to use us and her outrage was riding high.

We ran the few paces to Ace and collided with him. Esme hadn't managed to gain as much momentum this time and he stayed on his feet. He ripped into our foreleg and pain flared, but we danced back easily and ripped into him in turn.

Liam and David were here now, by our side and ready to attack Ace because he was in wolf form. David lunged forward and tore into Ace at the same time as Esme; they were as co-ordinated as synchronised swimmers, albeit significantly more deadly. Liam joined the fray, pummelling Ace, throwing him to the ground, and Esme went in for the kill. She bit into Ace's neck and held on with her strong jaws as he struggled to regain his footing. As she bit deeper, blood poured out. David and Liam kept Ace on the ground, and slowly his struggles ceased.

Esme released her deadly hold, threw back her head and howled her triumph. Greg's echoing howl bounced off the woods. Moments later, he and Elena joined us, dragging the prone corpse of Lauren behind them.

'Isn't this nice?' a condescending voice drawled from the shadows. 'The dogs have already been fighting amongst themselves. It would be rude of us not to help finish them off.'

The Red Guards stepped forward out of the shadows. The vampyrs were dressed not in the classic black, but in maroon cloaks; to me they looked just a little too much like the *Monty Python* sketch and I was tempted to say 'Nobody expects the Spanish Inquisition!', but I doubted they would appreciate the comparison.

There were at least five of them phasing in and out of the shadows in harmony, constantly moving, keeping us looking this way and that. Esme bared our teeth and let out a ferocious growl and their leader, Voltaire, stilled long enough to smirk at us. 'I'll take that one,' he called to his companions, drawing a dagger and tossing it lightly between his hands.

There was an ominous thud as Bastion landed between the vampyrs and the pack. 'Enough,' he said coldly to the vampyrs. 'You've got what you want.' He gestured to the ravaged bodies of Ace and Lauren. 'These two were sent by the council to bury secrets about the black tourneys. The rest of the wolves have nothing to do with the black tourneys.'

'And we have to accept your word for that do we, griffin?' Voltaire, sneered.

'I am Bastion. Are you questioning my word and honour?' Bastion's voice had dropped menacingly. Even Esme shivered a little. We hoped that tone was never directed at us.

'No,' the vampyr said finally and sheathed his dagger. 'Of course not.' He inclined his head in unspoken apology, keeping Bastion in his eyeline at all times.

I changed, and tried to be blasé about my nudity. I walked forward as if I walked naked in the woods every day.

Voltaire totally ignored me. 'I'm not questioning your honour, but this is none of your business.'

'I will determine what is my business. Lucy Barrett is my business.' Bastion gestured to me. 'Two of the ringleaders of the black tourneys are dead. Your hunt has been a success.'

'These two were nothing but sheep in wolves' clothing.' The surrounding vampyrs snickered at their leader's joke. 'They weren't ringleaders. My hunt is not over. I'm not done here.'

He was giving me an opportunity. With the pack still not quite united, I didn't have a chance of tackling the corrupt council members – but maybe the Red Guard did. If I gave them the blackmail material, maybe they could clean house for me.

I moved forward a little, finally attracting Voltaire's attention. 'Order that no vampyrs will attack me or my pack for so long as I live, and I will get you the evidence you need to bring down the black tourneys.'

I was hoping to get a full year hassle-free from the vampyrs, a nice little victory to bring home to my pack. I expected him to bargain, to say he didn't have the authority to grant that, but his gaze sharpened on my face as I struggled not to give the game away. Finally he nodded. 'Agreed, wolf bitch. It hardly matters because your weakling wolves are not the threat they once were. Give me the evidence.'

'Witnessed,' Bastion said sharply.

'Witnessed,' called another voice, as the female dryad elder stepped out from a tree at the edge of the clearing.

The vampyr's jaw clenched but he nodded. 'So mote it be. Where is the damned evidence?'

'Buried under that sapling,' I pointed to my apology tree.

One of the vampyrs nearest to the sapling pivoted towards it. 'Don't you dare,' the dryad's voice cracked out. 'I will retrieve it.' She stepped up to the sapling and crooned to it softly. When she gave a gentle tug, it relinquished its hold on the earth and its roots were drawn effortlessly out of the soil. 'Now you may dig,' the dryad intoned.

The vampyr grimaced; they had no shovels with them. 'Manners,' I called, 'dig a little, will you?'

He trotted forward and obligingly started digging in the hole. In moments, it was significantly larger in size. He stopped as his claws came upon a plastic bag. He drew back with a bark.

The vampyr pulled out the bag from the earth. He opened it up. 'USBs,' he called to his leader. 'Lots of them.'

Voltaire met my eyes one last time. 'We're done here,' he said flatly.

'Do you want their bodies?' I gestured to Ace and Lauren. It would be one less thing for me to deal with.

'Their blood is spilt upon the ground. We have no need of their deceased flesh.' With that final sneer, the vampyrs phased into the shadows and left without so much as a ta-ta. And I thought we were getting along so well.

Chapter 33

With the danger dealt with – for now – I turned to the dryad elder. 'Do you have something we can put their bodies in?' Lauren's body had already begun the shift back into human form.

The dryad elder nodded. 'One moment.' She disappeared into the tree.

She took a good five minutes to return; when she did, she was carrying two body bags and an armful of jeans and T-shirts for the pack. I desperately wanted to ask why she had body bags lying around. Apparently even the dryads were more dangerous than I'd thought.

'Thank you,' I said to the elder with a little bow.

'Thank you for attending to the matter promptly,' she responded warmly.

'They weren't my wolves.'

'No, so I gathered. You are not in breach of our treaty. Be well, Lucy Barrett of the Home Counties pack.' She nodded and disappeared into the tree again. This time, she didn't reappear.

'Get me down from here!' Amber screeched from high above me. She was still perched precariously on a branch at the top of the tree's canopy, and her shriek lacked her usual poise. Was the scariest witch of the south afraid of heights?

With the tiniest huff of laughter, the griffin rose with a huge gust of air as he flapped his pale wings. He reached Amber, carefully gathered her in his forepaws and gently carried her back down to earth. He set her down and shimmered back into human, complete with his ever-present clothing. Lucky sod.

Amber glared at him. 'This changes nothing between us,' she spat at him.

He raised an elegant eyebrow. 'There *is* nothing between us.'

'You killed Jake.'

'I have killed many.' He shrugged, like Jake's death was inconsequential.

Amber leapt towards him with a cry, but froze abruptly as she felt cold steel at her throat. 'Do not forget what I am,' Bastion said, his voice laced with threat.

'A monster.'

'An assassin,' Bastion corrected. 'Next time you attack me, it will be your last action.' He spoke evenly, factually; if Jess had been there, she would have said his words rang with truth. I swallowed hard and I saw Amber do the same.

Bastion sheathed the knife back to wherever the hell he'd got it from. 'It's been fun,' he said to me.

'Your definition of fun needs looking at.'

His lips tipped up minutely. 'So Jessica tells me.' He inclined his head, shifted into griffin form and flew away. Amber watched him with hard eyes until he disappeared from view.

The pack shifted and dressed in the clothing we'd been gifted. The dryad had forgotten to bring us shoes, which wasn't ideal, but at least we hadn't been left buck-naked carrying dead bodies through the woods. Black Park backs onto Pinewood Studios, and there are a lot of film sets in and around the woods. The locals are well used to odd sights by now. If anyone had seen us, I'd have shouted 'Action!' and hoped they were fooled.

Luckily we didn't encounter anyone. Liam went ahead and pulled the car to the side of the road so we didn't need to trail the dead bodies through the car park. When they were loaded in the car, I cleared my throat.

'I know the last few days have been less than ideal, but we've avenged the pack and we retain its honour. We've also dealt a severe blow to the black tourneys, albeit they will never know it was us.'

I held Elena's eyes; she couldn't go bragging because this was one of our pack's secrets. No one could suspect the role we had played lest it get back to the council. Ace and Lauren had diplomatic immunity; technically we should have reported them to the council and let them deal with it. However, with corruption rampant that really hadn't been an option.

Elena nodded her agreement. She was grinning, pride shining in her eyes. Something had been restored in her.

'Back to the mansion,' I ordered. 'We'll shower and grab some pizzas. I think it's time we had a movie night.'

My announcement was met with grins; the whole team was relieved that the confrontation had played out the way it had. Liam sent out a pack-wide WhatsApp inviting them all to the mansion for pizza and action movies. I texted Mrs Dawes and asked her to get in some beer and wine.

We piled into the car and headed home. When we drew into the drive, I asked the team to carry the bodies out beyond the rose garden, then dismissed them.

I waited until they were all inside before I called Ares. 'Ares, dinner!' He came quickly, looking quizzical. 'I don't know how much of this you fancy, but here.' I unzipped the body bags. I needed to dispose of some bodies, and Ares needed some dinner. It was Esme's idea; she is nothing if not practical.

Ares whinnied in delight, grabbed Ace's hand in his mouth and started to drag the body into the trees. He trotted back a moment later, red eyes looking suspiciously happy as he did the same to Lauren.

'Okay,' I called out to him. 'Good talking to you. *Bon appetit*.' I gathered up the empty body bags and carried them inside the house. They would need disposing of, too.

I walked into my office and, as I'd half-expected, Greg was there. 'Any ideas about how to dispose of these body bags?'

He grinned. 'Our unicorn didn't fancy those too?'

'Ah, you saw that.'

'Yes. I've wiped the footage from our systems before it was backed up to the cloud.'

'Good thinking.'

'I'll deal with the body bags.' The smile dropped from his face and he cleared his throat, looking awkward. 'There's a personal fax for you.'

I laughed a little. 'A fax? What is this, the nineties? Why do we even have a fax machine?'

'It can be handy,' he said defensively. 'The dragons still use them.'

'The dragons are allergic to innovation and technology,' I pointed out. 'Bar Emory, of course. Who faxed me?'

'Jinx.'

I raised my eyebrows in surprise. 'What on earth is she faxing me for?'

Greg cleared his throat. 'Um, I saw it come in so I looked, I'm sorry if that's an invasion of your privacy.'

I waved it away. I had no deep dark secrets that I needed to keep hidden from him; I had no deep dark secrets, period.

'It's your adoption papers,' he confirmed quietly.

My breath caught in my throat and I tried to calm the pounding of my heart. Suddenly feeling hot and sweaty, I wiped my palms on my trousers. *Play it cool, Lucy.*

'Oh, good.' I picked up the pile of faxes, excitement and nervousness thrumming through me. Finally, some answers about my parentage.

Dry mouthed, I scanned the papers then sighed when I realised the papers were the same ones my mum had sent me, riddled with holes and blank spaces. 'Dammit,' I muttered. 'You'd think the agency would have managed to keep a complete record.' Despite my best efforts, disappointment tinged my tone. Jess is a private detective extraordinaire and I'd really thought she would pull off a miracle.

Greg cleared his throat again. 'I've seen papers like those before. Many times.' He was hesitant, nervous.

'What are you doing filling out adoption papers?' I asked, frowning.

'Not all Others breed true. Sometimes, if the baby is shown to be Common, they get sent for adoption.'

'That's horrible. Parents in the Other get rid of their own child because they're not magical?'

'Most couples consult with the witches or seers to make sure they'll breed true *before* marriage or mating. It's another reason why there are so few inter-species marriages. There's less chance that mixed marriages will breed magical progeny.'

'That's insane.'

'Is it? Imagine how hard it would be to always have to lie to your children. The Verdict forbids us to speak of the Other to anyone from the Common. You'd need an excuse every time you needed to go to the portal to re-charge, every time you were needed by the pack. If you had a Common child, you'd have to live off the mansion site because there would be too many odd things happening that you couldn't explain.'

I opened my mouth to argue and closed it again. It seemed closed minded to me, not to mention horrifically cold. I could never, ever send a child of mine for adoption, not after I knew what it felt like to be unwanted by my birth parents. It had dictated every move of my life and filled me with a desperate need to be liked, to belong.

I focused back on the papers because this topic was too raw for me. 'So, you've seen adoption pages riddled with blanks like this? Is it normal for agencies to be wholly incompetent and fill out barely half the paperwork?'

He shook his head. 'The agency will have filled out the paperwork properly. The blank spaces are where the answers have been covered by privacy runes.'

I sat down heavily. 'Runes?'

'It's another one of the jobs witches do, securing sensitive information from Common and Other alike. If you got a hold of the original papers, you'd be able to get a witch to undo the runes.'

'What does that mean?' I asked, but I already knew the answer. Dread was curling in my gut. I needed him to say it.

Greg met my eyes with sympathy. 'It means one or both of your parents were from the Other.'

They were Other and they'd given me away because I was not.

Grim determination filled me. I was going to find them and, one way or another, I was going to teach them what a mistake they'd made.

What's Next?

Don't panic! More tales are heading your way shortly. Continue Lucy's Adventure in Guardians of the Pack.

Available to pre-order on Amazon now, Guardians of the Pack is out on 6th October 2022.

Heather G. Harris' Other works:-

The Other Realm Series

0.5. Glimmer of Dragons, a prequel novella.

    1. Glimmer of The Other

    2. Glimmer of Hope

    3. Glimmer of Death

    4. Glimmer of Deception

The Other Wolf Series

    1. Protection of The Pack

2. Guardians of The Pack

3. Saviour of The Pack, coming 4th November 2022

About Heather

Heather is an urban fantasy writer and mum. She was born and raised near Windsor, which gave her the misguided impression that she was close to royalty in some way. She is not, though she once got a letter from the Queen's lady-in-waiting.

Heather went to university in Liverpool, where she took up skydiving and met her future husband. When she's not running around after her three children, she's plotting her next book and daydreaming about vampires, dragons and kick-ass heroines.

Heather is a book lover who grew up reading the Brian Jacques and Anne McCaffrey. She loves to travel and once spent a month in Thailand. She vows to return.

Want to learn more about Heather? Subscribe to her newsletter for behind-the-scenes scoops, free bonus material and a cheeky peek into her world. Her subscribers will always get the heads up about the best deals on her books.

Subscribe to her Newsletter at her website www.heatherg harris.com/subscribe.

Contact Info: www.heathergharris.com
Email: HeatherGHarrisAuthor@gmail.com

Social Media

Heather can also be found on a host of social medias:

Facebook Page

Facebook Reader Group

Goodreads

Bookbub

Instagram

Tiktok

Reviews

Reviews feed Heather's soul. She'd really appreciate it if you could take a few moments to review her books on Amazon,
Bookbub, or Goodreads and say hello.

Made in the USA
Columbia, SC
13 June 2024

37035604R00228